Sweet SWAGGER

A NOVEL BY

Mike Warren

Author of *A Private Affair*

Life Changing Books in conjunction with Power Play Media
Published by Life Changing Books
P.O. Box 423 Brandywine, MD 20613

Library of Congress Cataloging-in-Publication Data;

www.lifechangingbooks.net

ISBN- (10) 1-934230707 (13) 978-1934230701
Copyright ® 2009

Dedication

I would like to dedicate this book to all the brothas and sistas who struggle with their sexuality every day. This one's for you!

Acknowledgements

First, as in all things, I would like to thank my Lord and Savior Jesus Christ, from whom all my blessings flow. And without Him, I am nothing but because of Him, I am everything!

To Debra, I know that when the world turns its back on me, I know that I can count on you to always be there. And for that, I thank you!

To my children, Tony, Kesheia, Mike, Marlonn and Marlowe, I love you all for your acceptance, patience and understanding.

To my family... My oldest brother Robert, thank you for your acceptance and being one of my biggest fans.

To my other brothers and sisters, Rosa, Deborah, Reese, Gary, Tonya, Demetrious, and Anthony, thank you for your support and spreading the word about my books. The best advertising in the world can not beat "Word of Mouth".

To my step-mom, Josie...what can I say. Thank you so much for your support and just being there!

To my oldest (no pun intended) LOL, and dearest friend, Ronnie, I thank you for always being there and having my back. Whenever the chips are down, I know that I can always depend on you, no matter what. You've been a true friend for a long time. I thank you and love you for that!

To all of my friends (too many to list) and they know who they are, thank you guys for just putting up with me. I know I can be a handful... Take that whatever way you like. LOL.

To all the major book stores, Borders, Barnes & Nobles, Urban Knowledge, Black & Noble, and African American book stores, thank you for the book signings and your support. I look forward to visiting you guys with my new book.

To all the blog talk radio shows who have invited me on their show for an interview, **it's been real**. The conversations about my book at times have been heated and intense, but I've loved every minute of it. Thank you for allowing me to talk about my sometimes controversial book on your shows. And all I can say is, **Prepare for round 2!!!**

To all of the reporters who were bold enough (LOL) to interview me for their magazines, (on and off line), thank you for your support and getting my story out there.

To all the book clubs (gay and straight), thank you for welcoming me with open arms. I specifically have to thank Nick from GBM Book Club in New York. I seriously have to give you your props in helping not just me, but all our African American writers get to the fore front of our craft. I thank you, thank you, thank you! Now, if only I can get you to return my damn calls in a timely manner!!!!!!!!!! LOL. I also want to give a special shout out to the First Saturday book club here in Baltimore. You guys are amazing. Thank you for having me as a special guest. I look forward to being roasted in your next meeting.

To all the other writers out there who are on their grind every day, hang in there. Our time is NOW. A special shout out goes to my boy, Dwayne Vernon, author of "My Man, My Boyz" and his sequel, "Deception, Lies and Truth". Thank you for being my friend because only you really know what we go through! (Read between the lines).

Last but not least, my LCB family. My publisher, Tressa, you are truly amazing! Every time I speak with you, I learn something new about this thing we call writing. To my editor, Leslie, you're still a "firecracker," but that's a good thing because that makes you as good as you are. Thanks to my test reader, Aschundria Fisher and a special shout out to all the other writers on the LCB roster. We are the shit!

Mike Warren

Becool031@yahoo.com

www.myspace.com/mikewarrentheblack1

http://twitter.com/becool031

www.lifechangingbooks.net

www.facebook.com (search Mike Warren)

Isaiah: 43:25 I, even I, am he that blotteth out thy transgressions for mine own sake, and will not remember thy sins.

The Holy Bible

In
The King James Version

Chapter 1

"Cameron, did you hear me? I love you and want to be with you. Please don't make the same mistake I made."

Cameron just stood there like a deer caught in head lights. I wasn't sure what was going through his mind. Although I'm sure it didn't help the situation any as I heard "oooohs" and "aaaahs" coming from the guest that were invited to Cameron's wedding. I knew this wasn't the time or place for the best man to admit his un-dying love for the groom. But what choice did I have? I couldn't let Cameron go through with this marriage, besides; I knew he loved me more than he loved Chauntel.

Everyone in the church sat in their seats with their mouths hung open with shock and disbelief on their faces and waited patiently for Cameron's response. I dared not turn to see the reaction from my mom or Cameron's mom. I knew they both would be hurt that I'd ruined Cameron's wedding. I looked at Chauntel and saw the hurt and anger in her eyes as they started to well up.

"What's the meaning of this? Is this some kind of sick joke?" I heard Chauntel's father stutter.

Again, I knew I was wrong for what I'd just done but it was too late. There was nothing I could do about it now. However, the guests were now agreeing with Chauntel's father as I heard some of them mumbling. I even heard someone in the audience crying, which I knew was either my mom or Cameron's mom.

"I knew they were gay!" I heard coming from one of the female guest as some started to laugh.

"Okay people simmer down. We're still in the house of the Lord." Reverend Johnson leaned over and whispered in my ear. "Sean, what are you doing?"

"I'm trying to stop Cameron from making the biggest mistake

of his life," I whispered in reutrn.

In the midst of all the confusion, Cameron just stood there shaking and trembling as though he didn't know what to say. I saw him look at Chauntel then back at me like he was watching a tennis match. Then suddenly, Reverend Johnson leaned over and whispered something in Cameron's ear, and I saw him nod his head.

Reverend Johnson cleared his throat. "Before we continue with this marriage, I think it would be best if we take a few minutes so that the groom and all those concerned can discuss this situation in private."

"Discuss what in private!" Chauntel yelled, as the tears began to roll down her face.

"I just think that we shouldn't discuss this here and that you two should go into my office and talk," Reverend Johnston replied, in a soft voice. He pointed at Chauntel and Cameron.

Chauntel grabbed Cameron's hand. "Do you love me?"

"Yes," Cameron replied softly staring into her eyes, "But…"

"But what?" Chauntel asked, before he could finish his sentence.

"I need to talk to Sean in private," Cameron said, while lowering his head.

"What's there to talk to Sean about?" Chauntel questioned, while holding on to her bouquet of flowers with one hand and clutching the pearls around her neck with the other.

"Please Chauntel, let me talk to Sean for five minutes, okay?" Cameron seemed to plead.

Chauntel stared fiercely into my eyes as if she wanted to kill me. Suddenly, she grabbed the bottom of her gown and ran down the aisle of the church with tears streaming down her face. I waited to see if Cameron would run after her, but he didn't.

Instead, her father decided to run after her, but before he left, he looked at me and Cameron. "Do you realize how much you two have embarrassed and hurt my daughter? I will deal with both of you when I come back."

I don't know about Cameron, but I knew not to be there when he came back because Chauntel's father was known to not take bullshit from anyone. I wasn't afraid of him, but I didn't want to go to jail for fucking up an old man. The wedding guests were still in shock and continued to whisper amongst themselves. Seconds later, Reverend

Johnson asked Cameron and I to go down to his office and wait for him, so we all could talk.

"Sure," I responded.

Once inside of the Reverend's office, I locked the door behind us, grabbed Cameron and held him in my arms.

He looked up at me teary eyed. "Why Sean, why now?"

"Because, I love you Cam," I replied, holding his chin up with my hand. I loved to call him by that nick name.

"Look, Sean, this is my life you're fooling with. Don't say something you don't mean!"

"But I do mean it. Don't you understand that?"

Cameron pulled away from me and sat down on Reverend Johnson's couch with a confused look in his eyes. His eyes were still watery as he lowered his head. I kneeled down in front of him, then took his hands inside of mine.

"Cam, look at me."

He quickly raised his head.

"Cameron, I love you with all my heart. You've taught me so much about myself and what it truly means to love someone. I know that when we first met, I couldn't understand men being with each other and loving each other but now, I know what that feels like."

"Sean, how do you know for sure?" Cameron asked, placing his hand on my face.

"I know because I just confessed my love for you in this church, in front of God, our family and friends. I know because I think about you all the time. I know because you make my heart smile. I know because I would put your needs and wants before my own."

Cameron smiled then leaned in and kissed me softly on the lips. Our kiss seemed to last a lifetime, until someone knocked on the door. It startled us both as I rose up from the floor and asked, "Who is it?"

"Sean, Cameron can I speak to the both of you?" my mom asked.

I wasn't sure what my mom wanted to say, but I knew she wasn't happy by the tone in her voice. I looked at Cameron and he just shrugged his shoulders. Not wanting to keep her waiting, I opened the door as my mom walked in and sat in Reverend Johnson's chair. Both Cameron and I waited patiently and nervously like we were going to be scolded.

"Sean, you know that I love you and no matter what, I'm still your mother and I will continue to love you," my mom said while staring me straight in the eyes. She continued, "And Cameron, I know I'm not your mother, but I have loved you as though you were one of my own. So, even though I'm not too thrilled with this display of affection, I want you two to know, I'll still be there for both of you. Whatever you decide I'll have to deal with it. Now that I have said my peace, I will leave so you guys can continue talking."

When my mother got up to leave, she gave me and Cameron a hug and kiss on the cheek.

"See, we have to be together now. That's what my mom wants."

Cameron smiled. "I don't think that's exactly what she said."

"So, let me ask you a question. Do you still love me?" I asked staring into his eyes.

"Yes, but what are we supposed to do now?"

"We can do what you once suggested that we do."

"And what's that?" he asked, lowering his head.

"Run away."

"Run away and do what?"

"Run away and fuck all day, everyday," I said, softly. I smiled, showing my dimples that I knew he couldn't resist.

"Sean," Cameron began to say, "you sure picked a hell of a time to tell me all this."

"I've been trying to tell you how I felt since the first time we made love but you've been so busy with the wedding, you didn't give me a chance."

Suddenly, we heard a lot of commotion out in the hall way. It sounded like people arguing and headed in our direction. I stood up and walked to the door to make sure it was locked. Then there was a loud knock at the door.

"Private Mathews, can I see you for a moment," a familiar voice asked.

I froze. I couldn't believe loud mouth Jamaal had followed me here to the church. I stood quietly and tried to listen to the conversation he was having with someone else outside the door. Cameron looked at me as if to ask, what was going on. I put my finger to my mouth to let him know to be quiet.

"Private Mathews, I know you're in there. Now open the door or we will be forced to break it down," Jamaal demanded.

Dayum...he must have brought the whole battalion of Military Police with him, I thought.

I was caught. There wasn't anywhere I could run. I looked over at Reverend Johnson's window and thought Cameron and I could climb out and run for our lives, but I didn't want to put Cameron in the middle of this mess that I was now facing. I'd already done enough to him for one day. With all the excitement of what was going on, I hadn't even told Cameron that before coming to the church, I'd stopped at Thomas' house and found him dead, lying in a puddle of his own blood. I knew Jamaal was here to lock me up for the murder, which I did not commit. Before opening the door, I walked over to Cameron and held him in my arms.

"Sean, what's wrong?" he whispered in my ear.

"I just want you to know that whatever they said I did, I didn't do and I need you to believe me," I whispered back.

Cameron pulled away from me. "What do they think you did?"

"Private Mathews, this is your last chance. Are you going to open this door?" Jamaal yelled.

I walked over to the door and opened it slowly. Suddenly, about seven or eight Military Police rushed in and tackled me down to the floor like a fugitive on the run. They didn't waste anytime hand-cuffing me.

"What the hell is going on?" Cameron shouted then stepped up to Jamaal.

As strange as it was, I began smiling because Cameron had never taken up for anybody, not even himself. But now he was all up in Jamaal's face trying to defend me.

"Private Jenkins, I would advise you to stay out of an official government investigation," Jamaal warned.

"Fuck you and your official government investigation! Why are you putting handcuffs on him? What the hell did he do?" Cameron continued to yell.

Jamaal looked over at me lying on the floor, pinned up by his Military Police force and began to read me my Miranda rights for the murder of Specialist Dule Thomas. The look on Cameron's face was completely shocked as the MP's pulled me up and began to escort me out of the church. The wedding guests looked on with horror as well. Once outside, one of the MP's opened the door for me to get in the back seat of their jeep. I was hoping to get out of there before my mother had a chance to see me in handcuffs. But just before we pulled off, I saw her running toward the truck. She looked at me with despair written all over her face. At that moment, I couldn't hold back the tear that seemed to fall from my left eye.

Chapter 2

I was taken to the MP station were I was stripped nude and searched for any weapons on my body. I knew the MP who'd searched me or at least knew of him. He too was a Down Low brotha who Cameron had informed me about. His name was SFC Roberts. He was a dark skin brotha that talked with a lisp and had this medical condition of blinking his eyes rapidly. I stood in a room with just him, naked as the day I came into this world. SFC Roberts placed a pair of rubber gloves on and begin touching my body, searching the crack of my ass. He then kneeled down in front of me and began to grab hold of my dick. As he held onto the head, no more than an inch from his mouth, he looked up at me with a smile on his face.

"Man, do what you gotta do and get off my dick!" I yelled, with an attitude.

SFC Roberts' smile disappeared into a smirk as he opened my pee hole to examine it. He then instructed me to put on an army-green colored jumpsuit that was hanging on the door. I was then finger printed and my mug shot taken. I was number 0936377843.

After all the paper work had been signed and completed, I was taken to the Stock Aide; a military prison for soldiers who'd gone Absent Without Leave, better known as AWOL or committed some unlawful crime. I was placed in a jail cell all to myself. Fortunately, there weren't very many soldiers who'd done any crimes that required them to be locked up. I entered my new home that was only 10x10 in diameter and looked at the old beaten down cot to my left side and a filthy sink and toilet to the right side.

I was tired and laid down on the cot to collect my thoughts. All I could think of was Cameron, and the look on my mom's face as I was pulling off in the jeep. My thoughts were interrupted as I heard Jamaal's voice.

"Well, well, well, so you thought I wouldn't catch you huh, Private Mathews?"

Suddenly, I sprung up from the cot and stood eye to eye with Jamaal as he stood outside of my cell. "Catch me do what, asshole?" I asked with flared nostrils. A reaction that always occurred whenever I got angry.

"I might not have been able to prove you're a damn homo Mathews, but now I got something better. How's murder in the first degree sound?" he asked with a silly smirk on his face.

"I didn't kill anybody!" I spat angrily.

Jamaal had hate and contempt in his eyes. "Well, Private Mathews, we have a witness who actually said they saw you and your car at Thomas' house earlier this afternoon."

I stared at him, but didn't say a word.

"That's right at Thomas' house. You know...the house where I found my damn cousin, lying in a pool of his own blood."

"And who is this witness?"

Jamaal started laughing as he began pacing up and down the hard cement floor. I knew he was getting a big kick out of having me behind bars, even if it was for a crime that I didn't commit. I really didn't understand why Jamaal was so gun-ho about fucking up my life. What had I ever done to him to cause such revenge?

"So, who is this fucking witness you're referring to?" I asked, becoming more impatient.

"Me," Jamaal replied smugly.

"You?"

"Yes, me. You didn't think that I would follow you when you left your room this morning like a bat outta hell? I saw you go into Thomas' house. I also saw when you ran outta there with blood on your hands." Jamaal then got close to my face. "You think I'm going to stand around and let you get away with killing my cousin and not do anything about it?"

I knew there was nothing I could say. I'd definitely gone to Thomas' house earlier that morning just so I could talk to him and apologize for all I'd put him through. However, I had no reason to kill Thomas. Besides, I was only in lust with him. He was my first enjoyable sexual experience with another dude, and that's all. Why would I kill him?

"What's wrong Mathews, cat got your tongue?"

"No, the cat don't have my tongue asshole. But as God is my witness, I DID NOT KILL THOMAS!" I yelled at him.

"I just have one question faggot, how did you do it?"

"Look muthafucka, I said I didn't kill him."

"Just so you know, it's just a matter of time. The coroner is performing an autopsy as we speak. So get used to being behind these bars faggot, this is gonna be your new home," Jamaal said, laughing to himself as he walked away.

"What about my one phone call asshole? Don't I get at least one phone call?" I yelled, banging on the steel bars.

I tossed and turned for most of the night. I kept having nightmares about Thomas. Every time I would close my eyes, I saw myself entering into Thomas' house. The front door was cracked and as I peeked in and called out his name. There was no response. I walked in and the place was empty, no furniture, no stereo…nothing. I crept through the living room and out to the kitchen. Kitchen cabinets were open but nothing in them. I opened the basement door and yelled downstairs but again, no response. I crept back through the living room and up the stairs to Thomas' bedroom but this time I didn't smell a foul odor as I had when I found his dead lifeless body.

This time I smelled sex and heard moans and groans coming from Thomas' bedroom. When I peeked inside, I saw Thomas fucking this little boy who couldn't have been no older than thirteen. I couldn't believe what I was seeing. Thomas had the little boy in the doggy style position with a letter opener to the back of his neck.

At that moment, I approached the top of the stairs to get a better look as to who the little boy was and all I could see was the tears running down his face from the pain Thomas was causing him. The little boy noticed me and with sadness in his eyes, he seemed to be begging me for help. I put my finger up to my mouth as to signal the little boy to be quiet. Thomas hadn't noticed me so I slowly entered the room and pounced on Thomas to get him off the little boy. As I grabbed Thomas, the little boy jumped off the bed and balled up in the corner, shaking and shivering. As I was about to swing on

Thomas, he suddenly disappeared. I looked around the room but Thomas was no where to be found. As I got closer to the little boy, he began to grow older. I thought my eyes were playing tricks on me. I stood there as he suddenly became a man. I tried to get a good look as to who he was but he had his hands up to his face. I kept asking whether or not he was okay but he wouldn't respond.

That next morning I was awakened by my favorite MP, SFC Roberts clinking on the steel bars with my morning grub. "How did you sleep Mathews?" he asked.

"How do you think I slept?"

"Look, don't take your shit out on me. I can be your best friend or your worst fucking enemy, you decide?" he said handing me my tray of sorry military food.

"Whateva dude," I responded, while grabbing the tray. Even though the food wasn't the best, it didn't matter this time because I was starving.

"Yo, Sean, your boy Jamaal really got it in for you, huh?" he asked, looking me up and down.

Dayum I thought to myself, he wasn't even trying to be subtle with his shit.

But it also dawned on me that he could help me. He could let me have my one phone call. I looked at him out of the corner of my eye and saw that he was still standing there, staring at me while licking his lips. Cameron had taught me that there were some DL Top brothas who didn't get fucked, but loved to suck dick and SFC Roberts was one of them. Right then and there, I'd decided that if he let me make a phone call, I would let him suck my dick as a trade off. So I thought I would test the waters so to speak.

"So, Roberts, I need to make a phone call. Can you help a brotha out?" I smiled devilishly, showing my dimples.

"Hmmm, well Sean, if I do that, what's in it for me?" he replied, licking his tongue at me.

I tried to play it cool. I didn't want him to think it was my idea. I quickly placed a small piece of bread in my mouth, then stood up and zipped my jumpsuit down to the beginning of my pubic hair.

"What do you want?" I asked, walking slowly toward him. I was showing off my well defined six pack.

"What are you offering?" he asked, being cute and coy.

"Yo, Roberts man, I'm gonna be straight up with you. I need to call my peoples to let them know I'm a'ight. And that would make me terribly grateful if you let me do that," I replied in my sexiest voice. I placed my hands in my jumpsuit then began playing with myself.

I thought it was funny how Roberts began to salivate as he watched me bring my manhood to a full erection. Since Roberts and I were the only ones in the entire place, I decided to unzip my jumpsuit as far as it could go, and then let it fall off my shoulders to the floor, leaving me standing there totally nude. With my dick pointed right at Roberts, I watched as he squirmed and looked to his left and to the right hoping no one was watching.

"You like this, Roberts?" I said, pointing to my dick.

He smiled and gestured with his finger for me to come closer so that my dick would hang out between the cell bars. I knew he wanted to wrap his mouth around it. I walked up to the steel bars as he instructed while playing with my nipples. Moments later, he kneeled down to take me in his mouth and I watched him slowly engulf all of my manhood. Roberts's throat was hot and it felt good.

It had been a minute since I had some good head. I wanted Roberts to get in the groove of things before I would stop him. I wanted to make my phone call and I wanted to make sure he was going to be a man of his word. Roberts started stroking himself as he continued to slobber on my dick. Suddenly, I pulled away from him and stepped back. The expression on his face was priceless; it was like taking a pacifier from a baby. His bottom lip began to quiver as though he was about to cry.

"Mathews, why did you do that?" he asked, looking up at me with disappointment on his face.

"You do understand that I need to make a phone call, right?"

"Yeah, I got you. Just let me finish and I'll let you make two."

"You know that if I don't make my phone calls, I will come looking for you once I'm out!" I warned, pointing my finger at him.

"Mathews, I got you, a'ight?"

As soon as I walked back up to the steel bars, he grabbed my dick so fast and rammed it down his throat, that he began choking. However, Roberts didn't stop; he continued to hose me down like a true champ. Within minutes, I was cummin' in his mouth and he swallowed every last drop of my juices as he too began to climax while jerking himself off. Once we were done, I backed away from the bars, turned around and put my prison jumpsuit back on. I just stood there and watched Roberts trying to get himself together too.

"So, when can I make my call?" I asked impatiently.

"Is now too soon?" he replied, pulling out his cell phone from his pocket and throwing it to me.

I had to give Roberts credit. He wasn't an attractive brotha to say the least, but he was a man of his word and could suck a mean dick. I knew if I didn't get out of here soon, I would have to keep him around. Roberts stepped outside the door to give me some privacy and to stand guard. I called my mom first to let her know that I was okay. She was hysterical and began crying on the phone. I tried to assure her that I was fine and that they locked me up because they said I'd killed Thomas. But I immediately told her I didn't do it. It warmed my heart to know that my mom truly without hesitation believed me.

"How's Cameron? Where is he?" I asked.

There was a long pause as though my mother didn't want to answer the question. "Ma, you there, where's Cameron?"

After taking a few deep breaths my mom began to say, "Sean, Cameron and Chauntel got married yesterday."

I suddenly felt a headache coming on. *Did she just say what I thought she said? Cameron wouldn't have married Chauntel after I confessed my love for him.*

"Ma, tell me he didn't."

"Yeah, Sean he did. I'm so sorry."

I felt the tears rolling down my face as though they were water falls. I couldn't believe Cameron would've done that to me. Not after I confessed my love for him and to the whole damn world.

"Hello...Sean, are you there?"

"Yeah Ma, I'm still here. Look, I gotta go. I'll call you tomorrow. I love you."

I hung up the phone, laid down on my cot and began crying like a baby. After a few minutes, I heard Roberts opening the door to the dungeon, letting me know someone was coming. I quickly hid the cell phone under my mattress and waited for who ever was coming to visit me.

"Private Mathews, I'm 2nd Lieutenant Glover and I've been assigned to your case."

I looked up and saw this white dude standing in front of my cell. He looked as young as I did and fine as shit, for a white boy anyway. He stood about 5'10, 160 lbs., black wavy hair and had the sexiest green colored eyes I'd ever seen. And with my gaydar in tack, I knew he was gay. I stood up and walked over to the steel bars. He immediately took a step back.

"What's wrong with you man. I was just going to shake your hand. I know you can't be scared of me behind these bars, are you?" I asked.

"No, Private Mathews, I'm not afraid of you. I'm just here to get your side of the story," he replied, taking out a pad and began writing something on it.

I started to explain to Lieutenant Glover the whole story. I even told him about the relationship that Thomas and I had. I noticed that he began to smile as I told him how much in love I was with Cameron and tried to confess my love to him at his wedding and that's were Jamaal and the MP's picked me up. I didn't worry about telling Lieutenant Glover that I was gay for two reasons, one: I knew he was gay as well and two: whatever I said to my lawyer would be in confidence.

"Hmmm, I see, but isn't it true Private Mathews that you attacked Private Thomas while he was on duty at the guard house on May 1st of last year?" he asked, still writing on his pad.

How the fuck did he know about that? White boy must have seriously done his homework, I thought to myself. "Well, Lieutenant, why don't you just call me Sean?"

"Okay, Sean it is," he replied with a smile.

Dayum, I liked the way he said my name. He made it sound so damn sexy. "And what is your first name Lieutenant, if you don't mind me asking?"

"My first name is Justin."

"Nice to meet you, Justin," I replied, extending my hand.

Justin's handshake was soft and warm. I turned around to lie back down on the cot while explaining to him what caused the altercation between Thomas and I. Fortunately he seemed to understand what I did because he made some kind of joke about me being a knight in shining armor. He continued asking other questions and I answered them all. I periodically caught him smiling at me and looking down at my crotch as he continued to write something down on his pad. I knew he wanted me and as a result wanted to help me all he could.

He told me that he'd gotten a copy of the coroner's autopsy report and that Thomas' death was a result of a gun shot wound to the left side of his skull and several punctures in the chest with a sharp object. He continued to say that the murder had taken place late Friday night or early Saturday morning between the hours of 11 p.m. Friday to 2:00 a.m. Saturday morning.

There is truly a God somewhere. That was my alibi. I was with Reverend Gabriel Jones during that time. I had gone to see him at his hotel room promptly that Friday evening at midnight. He could vouch for me, Hell even my wife Venus was there, she could vouch for me as well. Although, I didn't want to get too happy, not knowing how reliable those autopsy reports were anyway? I thought.

"Justin, how reliable are those autopsy reports?" I asked, excitedly while getting up from the cot, smiling from ear to ear.

"They will definitely stand up in court, why?" he asked curiously.

"During that time, I was with a friend of mine," I answered excitedly.

"Who's this friend?" he asked with his right eyebrow raised.

"His name is Reverend Gabriel Jones," I said, thinking about the position that it might put him in if we had to go to court.

I knew Gabriel was very serious about his religion and didn't want anybody to know that he too messed around with other guys on the DL, but would he risk his position in society to help clear my name?

"Do you have this Reverend Jones' phone number so that I may call him and would he testify on your behalf if need be?"

I wasn't sure if Gabriel would testify on my behalf but I did know that being a man of the cloth, he first and foremost would have to tell the truth. I gave Justin Gabriel's phone number and Justin said he would return later that evening after he had spoken to Gabriel. I laid back down on the cot to take a nap and began having the same nightmare. I always got to the point of where the little boy turns into a man huddled up in the corner crying with his face in his hands and I

14

wake up.

However, this time was different; as I reached down to help him up from the floor, he stood up completely naked with a bloody letter opener in one hand and a gun in the other. His face was exposed and I saw who he was, then he began shooting me and before I could feel the first shot enter my body, I woke up in a cold sweat shaking and shivering.

Chapter 3

After spending another night in that dungeon, I was finally set free the following morning. Gabriel had come through for me and pleaded my case vouching that I was indeed with him during that time. My wife, Venus had even come forth and given a sworn, written affidavit vouching that I'd been with the both of them. As I walked out unto the sun light, I saw my mom and my son standing there waiting for me. I ran up to both of them.

"Sean, are you okay?" my mom asked with tears in her eyes.

"I am now, Ma," I replied while hugging her.

"Hi Daddy."

"Hey, Lil Man. I love you," I said, while picking him up in my arms. I gave him a big kiss on the cheek. My son's name was Khalil, but I'd been calling him, Lil Man since the day he was born.

He giggled. "I love you too, Daddy."

It was Monday morning and because of what I had been through, I was given a few days of leave so that I could get myself together. My mom wanted me to come home with her but since Venus and I lived downstairs from her, I really wasn't in the mood to see Venus at the moment. My mom informed me that Venus had moved out and back home with her parents, so I would have the place to myself. I had no idea she'd done that, so I was actually looking forward to going home.

Why Venus decided to leave me was understandable. However, the fact that she left me to be with Gabriel is beyond me, considering that he too was gay. I honestly believed that growing up in a Christian home, Venus just wanted to be married to a minister and become a First Lady, regardless of the minister's sexual orientation. Although I wondered how and why she could just up and leave her son? But, whatever her reasons were, I'm glad she did.

After a few days being at home, playing with my son and having my moms waiting on me hand and foot, I was beginning to feel like my old self again. I still had that same nightmare that I had while in lock up and I wasn't sure what to do or who to tell. I hadn't spoken to Cameron since I'd been home but I had heard that he and Chauntel had moved into their new apartment in Northeast Baltimore. I knew he was going to be leaving soon to go overseas to Korea and finish up his military time there.

I was tempted on so many occasions to call him on his cell phone, but decided not to. I was no longer hurt by what he did. He didn't really know what happened. He wanted to get away from all the drama and start life fresh with a wife and a new baby. I couldn't blame him for that. However, I was missing him terribly and each time I thought about him, it brought a smile to my heart and a stiff dick to my pants. It was Thursday evening and my mom had Lil Man. I wanted to find somebody's son to fuck for the rest of the night, so I decided to pull out my cell phone and make a call.

"Hello," someone answered.

"Hello, can I speak to Justin?" I asked unassumingly.

"Speaking."

"Oh, good evening Justin, this is Private Mathews, Sean Mathews."

I tried to sound like Sean Connery as James Bond. I could hear Justin laughing on the other end of the phone. He'd obviously gotten the joke.

"How are you, Sean?" he asked, like he was happy to hear from me.

"I'm good, Justin thanks for asking. Ah, the reason why I'm calling is because I was hoping that I could take you out to dinner or something to celebrate our victory. That is if you aren't busy this evening?"

"Hmmm, sounds like a plan to me. Where you wanna meet?" Justin replied.

"How about Mamma Lucia's, you know the Italian Restaurant up on route 197?"

"Yeah, I'm familiar with it."

"Okay, cool. How about I meet you there in an hour? It's six thirty now, so I'll meet you there by seven thirty."

"A'ight bet. See you there."

I pulled into Mamma Lucia's Restaurant exactly at seven thirty and they were packed. Cars were everywhere in the parking lot. I wasn't sure what Justin was driving so I didn't know whether he was there or not. As I got out of the car, I noticed a white dude that looked like Justin but I wasn't sure. I was so used to seeing him in his officer uniform that it surprised me as I approached him wearing pretty much the same outfit that I had on. Justin was standing at the entrance of the restaurant, smiling with his hands in his oversized jean pockets that hung off his ass, a white wife beater, a huge silver chain with a lock hanging from it and a brand new pair of white Air Force Ones. He greeted me with the brotherly hug, while giving me a pound.

"I'm glad to see you."

"Likewise," I replied, with a wide smile. "It seems like it's gonna be a nice little wait with all the people standing around," I continued while looking around at all the people standing in line.

"Don't worry about that, I have a table already, follow me."

I followed Justin checking out his ass the whole time. Much to my surprise, for a white boy, Justin had a nice little plump back on him. I couldn't wait to see it up close and personal. Justin led me to a cozy little booth for two next to a window. The place was jumping with customers; you would have thought they were giving food away for free. People were eating, talking, laughing and appeared to be having a good time.

We sat down at our booth and just looked at each other. Justin was a good looking white dude. I'd never been with a white dude before, but if I did, Justin would definitely fit the bill. While staring at him, I began to wonder if the myth was true about white guys. I wondered if they could in fact give a hell of a blow job. Also, why he was wearing that over-sized dog chain with the lock. My thoughts were suddenly interrupted when the waitress came over to take our order. I ordered my usual spaghetti with meatballs and Justin decided to get the same.

I tried to start a conversation. "So, how were you able to get a table so fast, did you tip somebody?"

"Naw, I didn't have to. My uncle owns this restaurant," Justin replied. He smiled, showing his straight pretty white teeth.

"Oh, really, so you're Italian?"

"Naw, my aunt happened to marry an Italian."

"Oh, I see, cool," I responded, looking around the restaurant and remembering the times when Cameron and I used to come here.

"So, Sean, tell me more about you?"

"There's really not much to tell. I do wanna thank you for taking on my case and getting it to the judge so quickly."

"No need to thank me, Sean. Fortunately, you did have an air tight alibi and Adjutant Judge Barber believed your friend Reverend Gabriel Jones. He's the one you should be thanking."

"Yeah well, I'll call it even, considering good ole Reverend Gabriel Jones impregnated my wife," I replied sarcastically.

Justin's eyes widened.

"Yeah, that shit is a long story, so don't even ask."

Justin and I sat there for over two hours eating and laughing as though we were old friends. He told me almost everything about himself. He was twenty nine, and had just joined the army less than a year ago. He'd grown up in a middle class neighborhood and always wanted to be a lawyer. His dad was a lawyer and so was his brother. He also told me that he was somewhat in a relationship with another man.

"What do you mean somewhat. Either you are or you aren't?" I asked curiously.

He began telling me that he had met this black dude that lived out in Jessup, Maryland about a year ago and that they would kick it from time to time. But this dude had a SIR.

"What the hell is a SIR?" I asked looking dumbfounded.

"A SIR is someone who takes care of you. A SIR is like a Master. He can have a lover, but he can also have his main BOY's on the side. For example, the guy I met in Jessup is BOY number one and there's BOY number two and now I'm BOY number three."

"What the fuck are you talking about?" I asked shaking my

head. I tried to understand the lifestyle he was into.

Justin continued to explain how he got involved in this four-some. His SIR had a lover and three BOY's and that he was BOY number three. He explained that SIR had control over his lover and his BOY's and that SIR would take care of them all emotionally, physically and financially. And that SIR lived with his lover while BOY number one lived in Columbia, boy number two lived in DC and he was boy number three and lived up the street from SIR and his lover.

This was sounding like some "Color Purple" bullshit. The idea of calling someone SIR was like being a slave. There was no way in hell I could see myself calling someone SIR, other than being po-lite. However, the more I listened to Justin, the more I realized that he obviously was happy with that kind of arrangement. Needless to say, I had a ton of questions.

"So, does that mean you have to ask SIR permission about everything you do, including sleeping with other people?"

"No, I don't have to ask his permission to do anything or sleep with anybody. But, I do have to let him know where I'm going and what I plan to do. That is if I do decide to sleep with someone else. I can also have a lover if I choose to," he stated proudly.

This was some fucked up shit. I had never heard such bull shit in all my life. Although I must admit, being a SIR was definitely something that appealed to me. Justin also told me that as a SIR you can decide who you want to be with for the evening and that as a BOY, you can also sleep with SIR's other BOY's, in which he'd done at some point and time.

"You white boys are definitely off the fuckin' chain," I said, cracking up.

"For your information Private Mathews, this has nothing to do with being white. SIR is black; as well as BOY number one and BOY number two. SIR's lover and I are the only ones that are white." He sounded offended.

"Yo, Justin, I'm sorry man. I didn't mean to offend you. If that's what you like, go for it. I'm not here to criticize you one way or another," I replied, throwing my hands up in the air. I then leaned closer to the table and whispered, "So, when can I have some?"

"When do you want some?" he asked, acting coy.

I gave him my sexiest look. "Now."

❦

We'd decided to go to his place since it wasn't that far away from the restaurant. He told me he lived in Laurel right off route 198. As I followed Justin to his place, I started thinking that an enlisted man in the Army was not allowed to have a romantic relationship with an officer. However, this excited me; this was going to be my first officer and my first white boy all in one. Ten minutes later, we pulled into Justin's driveway. I didn't know whether he was buying or renting but it was a beautiful town house.

The lawn was perfectly manicured, there were bushes that lined the walkway and potted plants that hung outside each of his four windows, two on the first floor and two on the second floor. As we entered his home, I couldn't help but think that his place definitely had a woman's touch to it. He had a lot of little what-nots placed everywhere. I turned and white doilies were on his coffee and end tables.

Justin offered me a seat on his Queen Anne, plush, light blue sofa as he went to get us something to drink. I looked around the room and his taste of style seemed to be that of antique. I thought how odd this was considering he was so young. Then I started thinking whether or not he lived alone. Maybe this was his parents' house and they were away on vacation or some shit. Or worst yet, this might have been SIR's house.

Justin came back with two glasses of wine. "So, what do you think of my house?"

"It's nice, do you live alone?" I asked, taking the glass.

He sat next to me on the sofa. "Yes."

"Cool," I responded, feeling a little better about being here alone with him.

After being caught by Thomas' wife twice, the last thing I wanted to do was get caught doing something I had no business doing. I'd truly learned my lesson the hard way.

Justin continued making chit chat, but my mind starting drifting off as I began thinking about Thomas. Thomas was dead and the MP's still didn't have a suspect in connection to his murder. My mom had told me that Thomas' funeral was being held tomorrow at the chapel on base at 11:00 a.m., but I couldn't decide as to whether to go or not. I didn't know whether I could handle seeing Thomas lying in a coffin because I had never been with someone sexually who had died. I wasn't being no punk, but I think deep down inside, I was afraid to go.

"Sean, are you okay?" Justin asked. He waved his hand in front of me.

I focused my attention back on him. "Yeah, I'm sorry. What did you ask me?"

"I asked if you were ready to hit this ass."

"I was ready the first time I saw you, white boy," I replied, with a sexy smile.

Justin led me upstairs to his master bedroom and it was definitely on from there. He threw me down on his king size bed then kneeled in front of me. I watched as he began taking off my boots and jeans. I don't wear underwear, so after taking off my jeans, Justin looked at my semi erect ten inch dick like he'd just won the lottery.

I had to be a little conceited. "It's nice, huh?"

All Justin could do was smile right before he started sucking me off like there was no tomorrow. I laid back on the bed enjoying the way he slobbered on the head of my dick while stroking my shaft with his right hand and massaging my balls with his left. My breathing became heavier as I began to moan and groan in delight. I wasn't a three minute brotha, but the way Justin was sucking on my tool, it was becoming hard for me to control my urges of exploding. I guess the myth was true.

"Dayum white boy, hold up," I managed to say through my panting and heavy breathing.

Justin stopped, looked at up me. "What's wrong am I hurting you?"

"Hell naw, the shit feels good, but you betta slow this shit down, not unless you want a mouth full of nut?"

Justin smiled, stood up and slowly began to undress himself. My eyes were glued to him as he stood before me naked. He looked like a Greek God with his hard, smooth, silky muscular body waiting for me to touch. He had a ring on each nipple as well as a ring on his navel which I found to be sexy as shit.

But for the life of me I still couldn't understand why he wore that big ass dog chain around his neck. He saw me staring at him as though I could eat him up and began turning around so that I could see all of him. He had the prettiest plump muscular little ass I'd ever seen for a white boy. I knew he had to have some black in him somewhere in his family tree.

"Do you like?" he asked, smiling.

"Yeah, I like a lot," I said, taking off my t-shirt and throwing it on the floor.

For over an hour, Justin and I made love as though we were the only people in the world. It was weird because even though I wasn't in love with him and he wasn't in love with me, our passion and lust for one another made us sensitive to each other's touch. It's strange how the lightest touch could bring about the most sensuous feeling. Justin's body was smooth to my touch; his body scent was pure and sweet. He laid on top of me sucking my throbbing tool as I ate out his plump muscular ass. Beads of sweat poured off his body onto mine and contrary to popular belief, white folks don't smell like a wet dog when they perspire.

At this point, I couldn't take it any longer. I wanted to enter him and I wanted it doggy style. So, I pulled him off of me and put him in the doggy style position. As I was about to enter him he stopped me.

"Hold up," he said.

Justin reached over to his night stand and pulled out some lube and a condom. "Here, put this on," he said, handing me the condom while lubing him self up.

He'd caught me off guard. I didn't know whether to be upset or thankful that he actually wanted me to use protection but now was not the time for debate. I wanted him and I wanted him now, so I placed the condom on and slowly began to enter Justin's beautiful ass. Both he and I moaned as I tried pushing my dick up into him as far as it could go.

"Sean, take it easy, this is not a real pussy, bruh."

I had to laugh to myself thinking that obviously his SIR wasn't packing like me. Therefore, I was going to stretch his asshole so that his SIR would know that someone bigger then he had been there. Justin began biting on the pillow to decrease his sounds of discomfort.

After a minute or two, Justin was backing his ass up on my

dick like a pro and the more I pounded into him, the wetter his ass became. I don't know whether it was the little bit of wine I had or the fact that he was white, or that he had perfect ass to fuck or a combination of all the above, but I was definitely losing control. At that point, Justin backed his ass up on me and pulled my nut out even though I wasn't ready to cum yet.

"DAYUUUUUUM!" I yelled, as my nut squirted out of my body. I continued to jerk and twitch.

Just as I came, Justin began jerking himself off and within seconds exploded his semen onto the spread that covered his bed. I then pulled myself out of him while trying to catch my breath and composure. *This white boy got some good ass*, I thought to myself looking down at him.

Justin had gotten up and went into the master bathroom to clean himself and had brought me a wet soapy wash cloth to clean myself as well. It didn't take long for us to start up round two and afterwards we collapsed in each others arms. For the next hour or so, we laid there talking and caressing each others body. Once again, I was still curious about the big ass chain and lock around his neck.

He told me that having a SIR meant that he had to wear it at all times, other than of course being at work and having his military uniform on. This allowed other people who were in this lifestyle to know that he had been somewhat ordained as a BOY and that he belonged to someone else. I didn't know that there were so many others involved in this type of life style whereby you had to let them know by wearing a dog chain. Hell, I didn't know that this lifestyle even existed until I met Justin. He never once used SIR's real name and I didn't want to know, but I knew it would be a matter of time before SIR and I would bump heads.

Chapter 4

I couldn't remember what time I'd gotten home the night before, but I was awakened by the aroma of my moms good ole home cooking. I laid there trying to get myself together and realized that since my last night in the Stock Aide, I hadn't had that nightmare of Thomas and that little boy. I felt like Thomas was trying to send me a message by letting me know who killed him. Now that I knew who the little boy was, who could I talk to? Who would listen and what proof did I have other than a dream?

The smell of my moms good ole home cooking was making my stomach growl so loud; I could barely keep a thought in my head. I jumped out of bed, threw on some sweatpants and climbed upstairs to her apartment taking two steps at a time. I could hear Lil Man laughing as I was about to knock on the door.

"Hold on Sean, I'll be there in a minute," I heard my mom say.

Dayum, how did she know it was me? I thought to myself. My moms finally opened the door and the aroma from her food almost knocked me down the steps.

"Well, good morning sleepy head," my mom said, giving me a hug.

"Morning Ma, how did you know it was me?"

"You think after being your mother for twenty-four years, I don't know you'd come running every time I cook?" she replied, laughing.

She had a point. My mother could do some serious burning when she wanted to. I walked into her kitchen to find, Lil Man already sitting at the kitchen table throwing down on grandmas' famous egg, ham and cheese omelet, fried potatoes with onions and a big stack of pancakes.

"Hold up Lil Man. Save some for me," I said, smiling and

kissing him on the forehead.

"Good morning Daddy," he replied, while still stuffing his face.

"Sit down Sean and I'll fix you a plate," my mom stated.

I did what I was instructed and took a seat right across from my son so that I could watch him while he ate. It amazed me how Lil Man had turned three this year and was the spitting image of myself. All I could think was, where was the time going? Time was moving so fast. I didn't want to wake up one day and wonder why I hadn't spent enough time with my son. My thoughts were interrupted by my mom as she asked me the dreaded question.

My mother handed me a plate of food. "So, Sean, are you going to your friend Thomas' funeral?"

"I don't know," was all I could say.

"What do you mean you don't know? What if it was you, wouldn't you want him to come and pay his last respects to you?" she asked, standing in front of me with her hands on her hips and waiting for a reply.

I filled my face with her food. "Yeah Ma, I guess."

"What's wrong, Sean?" she asked, as she sat down in the chair next to me.

"Dag Ma, why does something have to be wrong?" I didn't look her in the eye.

"Khalil, take your food in the living room for Grandma and watch T.V. while I talk to your father. And don't spill any food on my floor."

"Yes, Grandma," he said, smiling from ear to ear.

Normally my mom wouldn't allow Lil Man to eat in the living room and watch T.V. at the same time, so this was a treat for him.

"So, I'm only going to ask you this question one more time Sean, what's wrong?"

As I looked at my moms, I knew she meant business like most urban city moms who didn't take shit off of anybody. So, I began to tell her the short version of my relationship with Thomas and the nightmare, about Thomas and this little boy. I told my mom how the little boy who had become a man had stood up and aimed a gun at me, but before he started shooting, I had a chance to see who he was and after telling my mom who it was, she just looked at me with her mouth hanging open.

She immediately stood up. "You're going to that funeral and I'm going with you."

∾⊱⊰∾

Within forty five minutes, we dropped Lil Man off at Venus' mother's house and sped down 295 South heading toward Ft. Meade to attend Thomas' funeral. I looked at my watch and it read 10:45 a.m. giving us just enough time to give our respects. I had a queasy feeling in my stomach as we entered the front gate. Everything reminded me of Thomas including coming through the front gate where he would always be standing guard. We pulled up in front of the Chapel and parked. I looked around and it didn't seem to be many cars parked out front. There were a total of ten or twelve cars, a black stretch limousine and the hearse. I began to feel a little sad that not many people showed up and if it hadn't been for my mom, I probably would not have come either.

We walked through the doors of the Chapel and I stopped. As I stood there, I could see the bronze colored coffin that lay before me. My heart started pounding a mile a minute and my hands became wet and clammy.

"Come on Sean, you can do this," my mom said, taking me by the hand as we walked down the aisle approaching Thomas' coffin.

As I stood there looking down at Thomas, I became angry. I was angry because they had buried him in his uniform and I knew for a fact that Thomas wasn't that gun-ho about being in the military.

Why in the fuck did somebody bury him in his uniform? I thought to myself.

The next thing I felt were the tears that started rolling down my face. I'm not sure why I began to cry but for some reason, I couldn't stop. My watery eyes were glued to Thomas. He looked as though he was just sleeping and could wake up at any moment.

I leaned down and whispered, "I got your message and he will pay."

I kissed Thomas on the forehead and held onto my mother's hand while we took a seat in the back of the chapel.

The service had begun for the home going service of my friend and I just sat there numb, looking around the chapel to see who had come to pay their last respects. There were about fifty or so people that had come out. I tried to get a good look at Thomas' mother and someone who appeared to be his brother sitting up front in the first pew. Sitting next to them was loud mouth Jamaal who had become a serious thorn in my side. I didn't see Cindy or Thomas' daughters and I guess that was a good thing because I didn't want to have to bitch slap her ass. Fat-ass, Harrison was also in attendance with some dude that he was obviously involved with just by the way Harrison was looking at him. I instantly felt like throwing up.

Most of the attendees were other MPS, Thomas' co-workers. I also noticed SFC Roberts, the dude who gave me a blow job in exchange for letting me use his phone. He nodded in my direction and I nodded back. As I looked past Roberts, sitting there on the right side, my heart began to race again but this was a good thing. Cameron had been staring at me the whole time and I hadn't even noticed him until now.

I still loved Cameron and I wanted to hold him, smell him, kiss him, feel him, and taste him. But unfortunately, that wasn't going to happen because he was there with his wife, Chauntel. I nodded my head at Cameron and gave him one of my sexiest smiles. He too, gestured with the same. I could still see the love in his eyes as we stared at each other, until Chauntel happened to notice us looking at one another and she rolled her eyes at me and punched Cameron in the side to get him to stop.

Bitch, stop hating I thought to myself.

Suddenly, a bucket of tears started running down my face. I lowered my head so no one could see but my mom grabbed me by my hand and whispered, "Its okay, he's in a better place."

I tried wiping the tears away with my hand but it was no use. My nose began to run and my head began to pound.

My mom reached in her purse to hand me a handkerchief. "Are you okay?"

I wasn't sure whether I was crying because of the death of a friend who turned me out or the lost of a true friend who I was in love with but would never have.

"Sean, are you okay?" I heard my mom ask again.

"Yeah, I'm fine," I replied while blowing my nose with the

handkerchief.

With my head hung low, I felt someone's arm around me, I looked up and obviously Cameron had seen me crying and came over to console me.

"You cool, Sean?" he whispered in my ear.

I looked dead in his eyes with tears in my own and I wanted to kiss him right then and there. For the first time, I noticed just how fine Cameron was and his lips seemed to be begging to be kissed.

"Yeah, I'm cool."

Cameron sat there with me and my mom for the entire service. There were no words spoken between us, there was no need. We both knew how each other felt. Chauntel on the other hand, looked like she had a lot to say as I noticed her getting up out of her seat and wobbling over in our direction.

As big as she was I thought, *dayum she must be due any day.*

I whispered in Cameron's ear, "Here comes your ball and chain."

We both shared a smile.

"Cameron, what are you doing coming over here and leaving me all alone?" I heard Chauntel ask while sitting down on the other side of him.

When Cameron leaned over and whispered something in her ear, Chauntel got up and walked out of the church. I had to smile to myself, thinking *at least he got her ass in check.*

Minutes later, the service had finally come to a close and the Funeral Director took charge and asked if they could get some of the guys to act as pallbearers. I thought this would be the last time that I could do anything for Thomas and therefore, I volunteered. Much to my surprise, so did Cameron. I stood in front of the coffin on the left side and Cameron stood in front on the right side.

We loaded the coffin into the hearse and because I volunteered to be a pallbearer, I knew I would also have to go out to the cemetery but so did Cameron. Strangely enough, I just enjoyed being in his presence. It seemed like forever since that first night we made love. My mom and I followed behind in formation with the other cars heading toward Thomas' final resting place. In a way, I was glad that it was going to be here in Maryland so that if I wanted to, I could go and visit him.

Within thirty minutes or so, we pulled into Angel Heart Cemetery located in Greenbelt. All the cars followed in formation going through a small winding brick road until it stopped in front of a vacant plot with a green awning overhead with chairs in place for the immediate family.

We all got out of our cars and I walked over to the hearse to resume my duties as a pallbearer. Cameron stood on the opposite side of me and without anyone else noticing, blew me a kiss. Life is funny, I was holding Thomas' dead body in a coffin and my dick was becoming rock hard. We carried the coffin and placed it on top of the harness that stood over the empty plot. We stood at attention as the immediate family approached their seats.

As I looked out the corner of my eye, I was shocked to see Thomas' wife or ex-wife, Cindy. She was there dressed in all black pretending to be in mourning. I also got a closer look at Thomas' brother who looked just like him.

Dayum, they could have been identical twins. I thought as a smile crept upon my face.

Everyone took their seats except for Thomas' mother; her blood shot eyes were full of tears as she approached me and stared me up and down. I wasn't sure what she wanted to say but I could tell that her heart was heavy and that she wasn't in her right frame of mind.

She pulled her black veil from over her face. "My son would be alive today if it wasn't for you!"

By the time I had a chance to digest what she had just said; she hauled off and slapped the shit out of me. She slapped me so hard that I fell over onto Thomas' coffin and almost into his grave. Before I could bat an eye, my mom had come to my rescue and punched Thomas' mother dead in the face. My mom had a serious right hook. Before I could pick myself up off of Thomas' coffin, I saw Thomas's brother coming in my direction with his fist balled up. Cameron jumped in front of me and starting swinging at Thomas' brother while big mouth Jamaal leaped at me. Jamaal and I began fighting like cats and dogs.

The minister and the few attendees were standing there with shocked expressions and didn't know what the Hell was going on. Cameron and Thomas' brother went at it head and toe. Of course, poor Cameron wasn't much of a fighter but I saw him scratch and claw at Thomas's brother like nobody's business. My mom and

Thomas' mom rolled around on the ground trying to pull each others hair out.

The beautiful flowers that stood on easels were thrown around as the Priest, Funeral Director, Graveyard keeper and the MP's looked on in disbelief. The guests that came to the cemetery were in shock, and I heard a few of them shouting to the graveyard keeper to call the police, even though the MP's were standing right there.

Big mouth Jamaal started bleeding from the mouth with all the blows I was throwing at him. Jamaal did get a few good punches in as well but with the anger and frustration that was going on in my life, at that moment; I could have beaten Mike Tyson.

After fifteen minutes or so throwing down it came to a halt after we started hearing police sirens. Most of the guests, including me, my mom and Cameron got in our cars and drove off. To this day, I'm sorry for what had happened and that I didn't pay Thomas more respect by just leaving after his mom slapped me. But something tells me, Thomas got a big kick out of it. Looking down on us and laughing his ass off. I really wish I knew what he was trying to tell me in these dayum dreams. Hopefully, I will figure them out but in the meantime, I was going to seriously miss my friend, the first man who literally turned me on to other men.

Chapter 5

Two weeks had gone by since that crazy incident out at the cemetery and I still could feel the sting of Thomas' mother slap. Cameron and I had only spoken once since then via the phone. He seemed to be happy being married and was hoping that Chauntel gave birth to their son before he left to go overseas to Korea. I had gone back to work at my same job as a Sidpers Analyst and my days crept along like there was no tomorrow. It was Thursday, late afternoon and I still lived in the barracks on base. I couldn't wait to get back to my room just to chill and take a nap. I had a new room mate; his name was Tyree Marshall, a brotha from the hood of Chicago, Illinois. Ty as he preferred to be called, had just graduated from Advance Individual Training or A.I.T, as it was called and his Military Operational Specialty, MOS for short, was the same as mine 75DW5 Sidpers Analyst. He was a cool little dude that stood about 5'7, black as tar, had a nice little muscular body and could dance his ass off.

After getting off from work late, I headed to my room and all I could hear blasting on the stereo was the old song *Pop, Lock & Drop It* by Huey. I entered the room and Ty was in the room staring at himself doing some kind of dance that I had never seen and to be quite honest, it looked as though he was having some type of seizure. I stood there watching him as he gyrated and jerked his body. He looked angry as though all of his frustrations were coming out through his dance. He turned and happened to notice me looking at him and stopped.

"Oh fuck yo, I didn't know you were standing there," Ty said, wiping the sweat off his body with a towel. He turned the stereo down.

"Don't stop on my account," I replied, with a huge laugh. I sat on my bed and taking off my boots. "What the hell were you doing anyway?"

"I was crunking. Haven't you ever seen a nigga crunk before?"

"Hell no," I replied, lying across my bed.

"It's easy. C'mon let me show you how it's done," he suggested while trying to pull me up from the bed.

"Naw man, you go right ahead. That dance takes way too much energy. Energy that I do not have at the moment."

I laid there and watched as Ty worked up a sweat as he performed his crunking routine in front of me. Now that I knew what it was, I must admit, he was definitely turning me on by gyrating and jerking his shirtless small muscular frame in front of me. Ty and I had never discussed homosexuality and therefore, I didn't know where he was coming from. I personally didn't discuss my life style to anyone, not that I was ashamed of it. I only discussed it with those on a need to know basis. Simply put, if I was interested in having sex with a brotha, I was bold enough to let him know.

I then started thinking back to when I first met Cameron. He too stood in front of this same mirror singing and dancing to Patti Labelle's *Lady Marmalade*. Suddenly, my thoughts were interrupted as I heard my cell phone go off. I looked at the caller I.D. and saw that it was Cameron's cell phone number.

"Hey you," I replied in my sexiest voice.

"Yo Poppi, guess what?" he asked excitedly.

"What's up?" I asked, getting up and sitting along side the bed.

"I have just become a father. Chauntel just had the baby!" Cameron screamed into the phone.

"Yo, Cam, congratulations man. What did she have?" I was happy for my friend.

"A boy and thanks," he replied sounding a little sad.

"Cam, what's wrong? You a'ight?"

"I'm great, it's just…I have to leave out tomorrow morning for Korea."

"Oh shit that's fucked up. Did you inform Commander Randalls about becoming a new father? Maybe he can change your arrival date for your new duty station in Korea?

"Yeah, I just got off the phone with him before I called you and he said there was nothing he could do to change it."

"You know that's bullshit, right?"

"Yeah, I know. But I didn't expect him to do anything anyway because he had it in for us every since Jamaal began this whole investigation about us being gay," he replied sadly.

"Yeah, well that's true, but at least you were here for the birth of your son," I said, trying to make him feel better.

"I know but it's like now that my son is here, I don't wanna go."

I understood exactly how Cameron felt because Venus had just had Khalil before I went into boot camp and I remember not wanting to leave either.

"Hey Cam, you'll be a'ight. Remember, you're doing it for them."

"Yeah you're right. Hey look, I need you to do me a favor."

"Just name it."

"Chauntel was supposed to be taking me to the airport tomorrow but now since she won't be able to, I was wondering if you could take me?"

"Sure, no problem man, what time you have to be there?" I asked, anxiously looking forward to spending some time with him.

"I have to be at the airport by 9:00 a.m., so can you pick me up from my place around 6:30?"

"Okay cool, I'll see you then, DAD," I said jokingly before hanging up the phone.

❧

I pulled up at Cameron's apartment at exactly 6:25a.m. I looked up at his apartment and saw his living room light was on, so I knew he was probably sitting there ready to go. I contemplated about ringing his door bell and going inside but I knew if I did, I would want to make love to him one last time, which would cause him to be late for his plane and besides, I didn't know if he would reject my advances or not. So instead, I honked the horn. Sure enough, I saw him looking out his window and within minutes he came out of his apartment building carrying two large suitcases. I popped the trunk of my car and got out to help him.

"Hey, you," I said, giving him a hug.

"Morning, Poppi," he replied, hugging me back. It seemed like he didn't want to let go.

"You okay?" I asked holding his chin up.

"No, but there's not much I can do about it now, can I?" he replied softly.

We jumped in the car and headed down highway 295 headed toward the BWI Airport. It felt funny this time because Cameron and I had drove up and down this parkway so many times, laughing and joking around that now we both sat quietly as though we were going to a funeral.

"So, what you guys name the baby?" I asked, trying to break the ice.

"What else, Junior," he responded with a smile. However, Cameron's smile soon disappeared as he faced me and asked, "When you came to the church that Saturday, why didn't you tell me about Thomas?"

For some reason, his question had angered me. My temples began to pulsate and my nostrils began to flare. I pulled the car over to the side of the road and put it park and yelled, "Why the fuck did you get married?"

"I got married because I didn't know what the fuck was gonna happen to you and I was trying to do the right thing!" Cameron shot back.

"So, why didn't you come to the MP station and find out. You knew that's where they would be taking me," I responded trying to calm down.

"Look Sean, I don't wanna argue wit you," he said, grabbing for my hand. "There was a church full of people including my mother who came and were expecting a wedding to take place, my wedding. After the MP's had taken you and the commotion had calm down, Chauntel and I had talked, really talked, you know?" Cameron then held my face with the palm of his right hand and asked while looking at me teary eyed. "Have you ever been in love wit two people at the same time?"

"Yes," was the only reply I could give at the moment.

"So, you understand what I'm going through?"

"But what about us," I heard myself say as my eyes began to water.

"You know Sean, your timing is not the best," he said looking down at his flight ticket and trying to laugh.

I wiped the water from my eyes, placed the car in drive and continued heading to our destination. I started telling Cam what had happened to me once I had gotten to the MP station and how his boy Roberts sucked my dick so I could use his cell phone. I told him about Justin who had represented my case and because I had an air tight alibi, all the charges against me were dismissed. I also told him about my dream and how I thought Thomas was trying to send me a message by revealing to me who the little boy was that killed him.

Once I told Cameron who the little boy turned out to be, Cameron couldn't stop laughing, which in a sadistic way, was kind of funny. And for the first time, I too began laughing about it.

I pulled up to the unloading zone of BWI Airport minutes later, and doubled parked. I didn't want to go in and watch Cameron board the plane for some reason. So, I popped open the trunk of my car and helped Cameron with his bags.

"I still love you," he whispered in my ear while giving me a hug.

"I love you too and more than a brother."

"I'll write you and give you my new address and you betta write me back!" he said, punching me on the shoulder while forcing a smile.

I got in my car and watched as Cameron shuffled his way through the revolving doors. I had to laugh out loud as I watched him having a hard time getting through the revolving doors with his big ass suitcases and almost getting stuck. I knew most of what he was carrying with him was his cucumber facial mask kits and his large collection of Speedos. I continued to watch as he disappeared in the midst of other travelers. I sat in the car for a few minutes as the tears started to run down my face. On one hand I was still laughing at Cameron trying to make it through the revolving doors and on the other hand, I was deeply hurt to see him go. I said a special prayer so that my friend, no….my love, would come back safe and unharmed soon.

Chapter 6

It had been a month since Cameron left and I was missing the Hell out of him. My new roommate, Ty and I had been hanging out most of the time. I took him to the club called "Choices" a few times just to show him some Baltimorean flavor. Ty was cool as shit. One night while chillin' in the room, I decided that I would tell him about myself, just to see what he would say. Like I said, Ty was cool as shit and I believed that we had become close enough that he wouldn't change his attitude towards me and that I would still be his boy. Hell, truth of the matter, I was bored and so was he. We'd talked about everything under the sun except my lifestyle, so I said fuck it!

" Ty, you ever fucked around with another dude before?" I boldly asked.

"Hell no. I don't get down like that. The honeys like this too much," he said, lying on the bed. He grabbed his dick and started moving it in a circular motion.

I had to admit, Ty had his share of honeys. I remember one time when we were at the club and Ty started Crunking and afterwards the honeys were all over him.

He looked in my direction. "Where the fuck did that come from anyway?"

"Well, what would you say if I had?" I asked testing him.

"Yo, Sean, get the fuck outta here," he replied, falling out on his bed and cracking up as though I had just told him the funniest joke.

I had a serious tone. "Would that make a difference to you?"

I knew I had to be careful telling him that side of me because I knew how some brothas felt about homosexuality. After all, I used to be one of them a little over a year or so ago.

"Sean, you can't be serious. I've seen you with the honeys at the club man," he said, raising up and sitting on the edge of his bed.

"But what if I had, you're still not answering my question."

"Yo, dawg, that's some fucked up shit you talkin' bout!" he said sounding a bit angry.

At this point, I thought I would leave well enough alone. I had put myself out there to Ty just to get his reaction and things weren't going as I thought they would. I'm not sure what I had expected but I thought we had formed a close enough relationship that he would at least be respectful and understanding. Tomorrow was Friday, and I couldn't wait to go home and spend some time with Lil Man and my mom. I turned off the lamp next to my nightstand and began to doze off to sleep.

Friday morning formation for roll call was like any other formation except today was pay day. Normally our battalion wore fatigues Monday through Thursday but on every other Friday we wore our dress greens. While standing at ease, the captain introduced four new soldiers who were a part of our squad. One of them happened to be Specialist Dobber, who'd just finished a two year tour at Fort Shafter, Hawaii. All the guys eyes were glued to Specialist Dobber as she took her place in formation. She by far was the best looking white female I'd ever seen and wore the hell out of her Army issued uniform. From the looks of the females that were in our battalion they weren't as pleased to welcome her as the men were. They were all drooling like dogs. I looked over at Ty and he too seemed to be watering at the mouth. There was definitely something special about her and I too found myself getting aroused just looking at her.

We broke formation and all headed to our assigned work place. Moments later, I sat in my office thinking about Specialist Dobber. Needless to say, I was confused. How could this be? Since the time I had confessed to myself that I was indeed gay, I had not met any other female that I wanted to fuck. However, Specialist Dobber was indeed an exception. Even wearing that ugly ass military uniform, you could see that she had a banging body and I wanted to fuck the shit out of her. I guess in the long run, I was no different then the other fellas in my squad that I'm sure, wanted to do the same thing.

I started thinking, *was it just me or were white people now growing a phat ass?*

It's funny how some myths were true and how others began to fade away, especially the one about white people having a flat ass. Justin had definitely proved that to be wrong.

Half of the day had already gone by and I hadn't done shit. But, it was Friday and the one myth that still held true was that government workers don't do a damn thing on Fridays and I was living proof. I then felt a presence and looked up and standing before me was big mouth Jamaal. I hadn't seen much of him since our altercation at the cemetery and that for me was a good thing.

"Working hard Mathews or hardly working!" he stated with a stupid smirk on his face.

"Who wants to know?" I asked with attitude.

Jamaal leaned in closer to my desk and was within an inch from my face. "You think your ass is slick but you're not. I'm gonna get your ass thrown outta here if it's the last thing I do, FAGGOT!"

I leaned back in my chair, smiled at him. "Bitch, you making my dick hard so get the fuck outta my office before I have your ass locked up."

Jamaal looked at me with a confused expression on his face as though I knew something that I wasn't supposed to know. He then clenched his fist as though he was about to hit me and I stood up thinking that we were going to go at it once again until he realized where he was as he looked around the room and decided to turn and walk out of my office.

❦

It was lunch time, so I got in my car and decided to go to KFC. Ty usually called me and asked where we were going, but he hadn't called this morning. I guess he was still trying to ascertain the fact that I was gay. As I placed my order, I noticed Specialist Dobber sitting alone at one of the tables. After a few minutes of waiting for my order, I took my tray and approached Specialist. Dobber.

"Good afternoon Ms. Dobber, I am Sean Mathews. Do you mind if I sit here?" I asked, as polite as I could.

She smiled. "Be my guest."

I sat across from her as I tried to eat my three piece meal but the harder I stared at her the harder my dick got. It's funny; I didn't realize how difficult it was to eat with a beautiful woman in front of me and having a boner.

Her green eyes seem to accentuate her red shoulder length hair and her tan white skin. I guess that was from lying out on the beach in Hawaii, I thought to myself.

"Is something wrong Private Mathews?" she asked obviously becoming annoyed.

"No, I'm sorry. I'm just in awe of your beauty. Please forgive me."

"You're forgiven and thank you for the compliment, Mr. Sean Mathews," she responded with a smile.

"You're quite welcome and now that you know my first name, what is yours?"

"Catherine, but my friends call me Cat for short," she said, extending her hand.

"Well, Cat, it's a pleasure meeting you," I said, shaking her hand.

Cat continued eating her lunch as I sat there and watched as mine had become cold.

"Aren't you going to eat the rest of your food?" she asked. pointing at my plate.

"Naw, I don't think so."

"Why not?" she asked curiously.

"You've ruined my appetite."

"Well, thanks a lot. Maybe I should be going since I've caused you to lose your appetite," she replied sarcastically before getting up to leave.

"No, please don't go. I didn't mean that the way it sounded," I said, grabbing for her hand.

"Is that so? How did you mean it?" she asked, taking her seat.

"What I meant was, although I thought I was hungry, I'm not now. Sitting here looking at you, takes my breath away. You are a fine woman, but of course I'm sure you've been told that many times."

"I believe I've been told that once or twice but not quite the way you said it," she said as she began to blush. "And for the record Private Mathews, I think you're an attractive man."

"Is that right?"

I didn't finish eating the rest of my food but I did learn a little bit more about Cat, where she was from and how she grew up. She was a beautiful young lady. Her red hair and green eyes just sent chills through me. I've never been with a white honey before, Hell, after the last few months, I didn't even think I would be with a female again, but there was something about Cat that aroused me. I couldn't help but start laughing to myself, considering all that I had been through and here I was sitting here getting a hard on just looking into her eyes.

Cat startled me. "Sean, are you okay?"

"Yes, I'm fine. Now, what were you saying?"

She began to tell me that she was twenty four years old and had been in the military for almost five years. She also told me that she had a boyfriend who was black and that they lived together but had an open type of relationship. I couldn't help but think what brotha in his right mind would let this beautiful woman sleep around with other dudes?

Luckily for me, Cat seemed to be taken with me even though I told her I was gay, that didn't seem to faze her in the least. I knew I was taking a risk, considering she was in my battalion and she could rat me out. But lately, I had been wondering why is it that brothas couldn't be honest with the honeys and tell them up front where they were coming from? I mean after all, what did I have to lose? Either she could deal with it or not.

There would be no love lost, right? Besides, I really wanted to put this myth to the test. Females always claim that if brothas were upfront and honest at the very beginning, that they would give them a chance. I guess that is true because Cat didn't even blink an eye, instead she smiled and gave me her number and asked me to give her a call later.

⊙⊗⊗

As soon as I returned back at work, I saw that there were several messages on my desk. One from my mom and the other three from Reverend Gabriel Jones, one was marked **URGENT**. I noticed that the number he left was his cell phone number, so I picked up my desk phone and dialed.

"Hello." I heard Gabriel say in a soft tone.

"Hi Gabriel, this is Sean. I got your message, what's going on?" I asked nonchalantly.

"Sean, I'm here at Mercy Hospital with Venus. She been in labor since early this morning and things aren't looking too good," he replied sadly.

"And so, what do you want me to do?" I didn't mean for it to sound as cold hearted as it did, but I was at work, which was at least twenty miles away. Seemed to me the good Reverend needed to be calling on God, not me. After all, even though Venus was still my wife, she was having the good minister's baby, not mine.

"Well, Sean, I thought you would've wanted to know what was going on, that's why I called you. Besides, she's been asking to see you."

After thinking about it for a moment or two, I thought maybe that's the least I could do since they both helped me get out of prison.

"Sean, are you there?" I heard Gabriel ask.

"Yeah, I'm still here but look, I'm not gonna be able to get there until this evening because I don't have anymore leave time to take off."

"Okay, come as soon as you can," he replied then hung up.

I sat at my desk ruffling through paperwork most of the afternoon and thought about Venus and the baby she was about to deliver, Gabriel's baby. I was so busy thinking about Venus, I'd forgotten to call my mom back. I picked up the phone to give her a call but she wasn't home. I called her on her cell phone and she picked up on the first ring.

"Hello," she answered sounding out of breath.

I was concerned. "Hi Ma, where are you, you okay?"

"Yeah, Sean, I'm fine. I'm here at the hospital checking on Venus and running around after your son. Boy, bring your little ass over here and sit down," I heard my mom telling Khalil.

I laughed to myself remembering the time when my mom used to tell me and my brother the same thing. "So, what's going on, Ma?"

"Well, Venus is about to give birth to your daughter. Why aren't you here?"

I really couldn't answer her question. How could I tell her that Venus wasn't having my daughter? Since that night I met Gabriel in the hotel room a few months ago, I hadn't mentioned to anyone that my wife was not having my child and that she was having an affair with Gabriel, the same man I was having an affair with.

"Sean, why aren't you here?" my mom repeated interrupting my thoughts again.

"Ma, I got a lot of work to do here. I just can't up and leave. You know I don't have any leave left to take and Uncle Sam is not gonna allow me to leave out just like that," I said, hoping that my mother would buy my excuse.

I guess deep down, I really didn't want to be there, besides, what's the point. She was having another man's baby. A man of the "Cloth" a preacher man, a man I thought cared about me.

"Boy, get your ass up from there and come down here to this hospital and be with your wife. How does it look to have Reverend Gabriel here to give support and you're not here? You tell your Commander it's an emergency." My mom then became quiet for a second and softly said, "Sean, Venus is having complications, she might lose the baby, you need to be here with her."

Yeah, Reverend Gabriel was there to give his support alright. But contrary as to how angry I was that Venus was carrying his baby, I didn't want her to suffer losing her child. I wouldn't wish that on anybody. "Okay Ma, I'll be there in a few."

"Sean hurry, it doesn't look good." I heard my mom say before hanging up the phone.

⁂

Almost an hour later, I pulled up in front of Mercy Hospital and fortunately I found a parking spot close by and as I rushed to make it inside, I couldn't help but remember the night I brought Venus to this same hospital a few years ago and held her hand tightly while she gave birth to our son. A smile crept upon my face as I thought of the good times that Venus and I shared. Then of course, the realization kicked in and I was only there mainly because my mom expected me to be there. My mom thought she was about to become another grandmother and now wasn't the time to tell her anything different. I was gonna have to pretend as though I was becoming a father for the second time around.

I found the emergency door entrance and once inside, I walked up to the information counter and stood there patiently as the receptionist conversed on her cell phone. I began clearing my throat, hoping that it would get her attention. However, it didn't and she continued to run off at the mouth to whomever she was speaking to. I was becoming annoyed standing there waiting for her to finish her call. I tried to remember what floor the labor area was on. And it dawned on me, the ninth floor. I located the elevators and pressed the ninth floor button. As the elevator began it's decent, my heart began beating fast and my palms began to sweat.

After exiting the elevator, standing before me was Gabriel, my mom, Lil Man and some white dude in scrubs, who seemed to be having a serious conversation with my mother. As I began approaching them, I noticed my mom crying and so was Gabriel.

"Here he is now. Dr. Bittar, this is my son, Sean, Sean this is Dr. Bittar."

"Nice meeting you, Doc. What's going on here, why are you crying, Ma?" I asked looking at my mother.

"Follow me, son," Dr. Bittar said, with a concerned expression. He tried to lead me by the arm.

"Hell no, I'm not going anywhere until someone tells me what's going on?" I shouted while pulling away from him. "How is Venus and the baby doing?" I asked looking around to see if any of them would respond.

My mom just looked at me with pity in her eyes and really started balling.

"Sean, lets not cause a scene out here in this waiting area, follow me over in this office so that we all can sit down and talk," Dr. Bittar whispered, while pointing to a closed door.

My jaws began to tighten up and my heartbeat continued to race. I tried following the doctor to his office and with each step I took; I felt my legs trying to give out on me. I knew something bad had happened. With my mother, Gabriel and Lil' Man following close behind, we all entered the office and sat down.

Dr. Bittar sat his big mahogany desk. "Sean, I hate to be the one to tell you this, but Venus didn't make it and your daughter has lost a lot of blood and won't make it either if we don't find her blood type. We need to give her a transfusion immediately."

"What the fuck are you talking about, what happened?" I shouted as I stood up from my seat.

"Sean…please," my mother said.

Even Lil' Man looked up at me.

The emotions I felt by hearing that Venus was gone, seriously threw me for a loop. When I walked over to where Dr. Bittar sat, he rose from his chair. I stood in front of him, face to face with my fist balled up and my nostrils flaring. I was going to punch him in his damn mouth if he lied and told me that Venus was gone again. "Where's my wife, muthafucka?" I yelled as my spit hit his cheek.

"Sean, don't do this. It's not his fault that Venus died son," my mom said. She tried to pull me away.

My mom led me back over to the chair and I sat there in shock hearing Dr. Bittar's words over and over in my head. As I sat there, I looked over at Gabriel. He was deep into his praying mood. At that point, I became angrier at God. It was Him who'd taken Venus away.

"Why are you praying?" I yelled in Gabriel's direction. "It's God's fault that's she's dead!" I shouted with as much hatred and sarcasm as I could muster.

"Sean baby, please don't say that. You don't really mean that," my mom said, while trying to console me.

"Yes I do. Why is it that when everything goes right, people wanna give God the glory but when something goes wrong, they don't wanna blame him? God needs to take some responsibility!"

I felt the tears welling up in my eyes but I refused to cry. I'd been crying more in the last past two months than I'd ever done throughout my entire life. I was not gonna give God the satisfaction.

"Look Sean, I know you're hurt and confused right now but we don't have much time. We need to give your daughter a blood transfusion," Dr. Bittar replied with sympathy.

"Well, you don't need me for that," I spat, while looking in Gabriel's direction.

Both Dr. Bittar and my mother sat there looking at me as though they didn't understand what I was saying. At the same time, Lil Man came over and climbed on my lap.

"Sean, what are you talking about?" my mom asked.

I stood with Lil Man in my arms. "Ask the good Reverend. He's the one who fucked her."

After that, I walked out of the office and never looked back.

Chapter 7

I took Lil Man home and we both just sat in the living room in the dark, staring at the walls and each other. He was barely three and I knew he didn't understand what had just happened. I tried to explain to him the best I could that his mom was now in Heaven and that he would never see her again. I knew he would miss his mom and I wished there was some kinda way Venus could come back and I could give my life instead.

Eventually, we started to doze off to sleep but then suddenly, my cell phone began ringing. I saw that it was my mom and decided not to answer. I really didn't feel like talking to anybody. Just as I began nodding off again, the phone rang again and I noticed that it was Gabriel's number appearing on the screen. Again, I did not answer and let it go through to my voice mail. This time I decided to shut my phone off. I picked Lil Man up and carried him to his bed. I went into the bedroom that Venus and I shared then looked around. I hadn't been in here in quite some time. Everything still seemed to be in place. I lay across the bed and tried to get some sleep.

I awoke the next morning with Lil Man climbing up on the bed, nudging me to wake up. "Morning Daddy."

As I tried to rise up off the bed, I noticed that my clothes were drench and the sweat was still pouring off my body as though someone threw me in a pool of water. My dream, that dream… that nightmare, I had it again.

"Daddy, I'm hungry."

"Okay, go in the living room and watch T.V. for a minute so that I can get dressed and I'll get you dressed and we'll go to McDonalds for breakfast, how's that sound?"

"Yeah!" he yelled and he got off the bed running into the living room.

Within the hour, we were sitting in McDonalds eating our break-fast. I wasn't very hungry, but Lil Man ate not only his food but half of mine.

He must've really been hungry, I thought smiling.

As I sat there and watched him eat, out of the blue he asked, "Daddy, can we go to the hospital today to see Mommy?"

I just sat there and stared at him, I didn't know what to say. I thought he somewhat understood what had happened yesterday. My heart went out to him as the tears escaped from my eyes. "What's wrong Daddy, did I say something bad?" he asked.

"No son, you didn't say anything bad."

"Then why are you crying?"

"Because I love you so much." I tried to force a smile.

"I love you too, Daddy," he said, smiling from ear to ear.

How could I possibly get him to understand the death of his mother, when in fact, I didn't understand it myself? As I sat there and watched him eat and all the loud talking from customers, coming and going, I knew this wasn't the place or time. I pulled out my cell phone to call my mother when I noticed that I had not turned it back on from last night. I turned it on and saw that I had ten messages. One was from Gabriel and the rest were from my mother.

I called my voicemail and heard my mom's first message, *"Sean, where are you? You need to get back down here at the hospital so that they can check your blood type to see if it matches the baby's. I know you are going through a lot at the moment but you need to stop thinking about yourself and save your daughter's life."*

Didn't my mom understand that the baby was not mine, I thought to myself while deleting her message.

The second message was from Gabriel, *"Hey Sean, this is Gabriel, I don't know how to put this but according to the blood test, I am not the father. So, you need to come down here and let them take some blood to check to see if you are."* With that, I didn't even listen to the rest of the messages. I immediately called my mom.

"Sean, where are you?"

"Hi Ma, I just got your message, what's going on?"

"Sean, when you left, Gabriel tried to explain what you meant. I'm sorry to hear that Venus had an affair with him, but right now, you need to get to the hospital. Your daughter is in the Intensive Care Unit and she won't make it unless they can find her blood type."

Being in the military, I knew my blood type was B negative. Uncle Sam actually lists a soldier's blood type on your dog tags just in case of an emergency. I wondered if it was actually possible that the baby was mine and in some twisted way, Venus said the baby wasn't mine just to hurt me because I had hurt her by cheating on her.

"Sean, are you there?" my mom asked, interrupting my thoughts.

"Ah, yeah Ma, I'm here. Ah, by chance, did they say what the baby's blood type was?"

"Yeah, I believe they said B negative or B positive, it was B something. You just need to get down there."

"Okay Ma, are you home?"

"Yeah."

"Okay, can I drop Lil Man off with you so I can get down there?"

"Sure, just honk the horn and I'll come out and get him."

"A'ight. I'm on my way."

After dropping Lil Man off at my mother's place, I made it down to the hospital in thirty minutes. I caught the elevator back up to the ninth floor and approached the nurses' station. "Yes, can I help you?" One of the nurses asked.

"Yes, my name is Sean Mathews; can I speak to Dr. Bittar?"

"Dr. Bittar is making his rounds, was he expecting you?"

"Naw, he wasn't but if you tell him I'm here, I'm sure he'll see me," I replied, while becoming a little impatient.

"What is your name again, sir?"

"Sean Mathews."

Once I told her my name again, she made an announcement

on the loud speaker informing Dr. Bittar he was needed at the nurses' station. "You may have a seat in the waiting room Mr. Mathews," the nurse stated, while pointing in the direction of the waiting room.

As I entered the waiting room and took a seat, my mind was running a mile a minute. I couldn't seem to concentrate on anything for too long. I kept thinking whether are not Venus' baby was indeed mine and then I would become angry at Venus for lying to me and telling me that the baby wasn't mine. Then, I would feel bad at the fact that she was gone. Then it dawned on me that Venus and I were still legally married and that as her husband. I was still responsible for her funeral arrangements. FUCK! Venus had actually died and for some reason, I felt all alone.

It seemed as though, all the people in my life was leaving me. First Thomas, then Cameron was shipped overseas, and now Venus' death. At that moment, I felt as though God was punishing me for being gay! But I still refused to cry. If that's the way God was, I didn't want any part of Him or His fucked up religion.

"Oh shit, I got to call my Commander and let him know what was going on," I said to myself as the doctor entered the room.

"Yes, Mr. Mathews, I'm glad to see you," Dr. Bittar stated while walking toward me.

"So, how's my daughter, Doc?" I asked, standing up.

"She's holding her own but we need to check your blood to see if it's a match because B negative blood is a very rare blood type and we don't have much of it." When Dr. Bittar stated that my baby daughters' blood type was B negative, I knew then that she must have been mine and it instantly brought a smile to my face. "Doc, are you sure she's B negative?

"Absolutely, I tested her blood myself!"

"Well Doc, in that case, you can have all the blood you need," I replied, rolling up my sleeves and smiling from ear to ear.

After the initial blood test that confirmed that I was indeed the father, I gave several pints of blood to save my daughters' life. Dr. Bittar allowed me to stay in one of the rooms after giving so much blood so that I wouldn't past out. The nurses were instructed to give me as much orange juice and cookies that I could possibly eat and drink, to avoid fainting.

Awaiting my one hour observation, I called my mother on the phone to let her know that the baby was mine. She answered on the first ring.

"Hi Sean, is everything alright? I've been waiting here on your call," my mom stated excitedly.

"Yeah, Ma, everything is fine. They tested my blood and I am the father. So, how does it feel being another Grandmother?" I asked, smiling through the phone.

"Oh, thank God. I'm so happy for you baby. I knew she was yours!"

"Thanks Ma," I replied sadly.

"What's wrong Sean? I thought you would be happy."

"I am, but Venus is gone and now I have to plan for her funeral. I've never planned for someone's funeral before. I wouldn't even know where to start!"

"Have you talked with Venus' parents? Do they know?"

"Oh shoot, I hadn't even called them yet. I don't know if they know or not."

"Well baby, you need to call them, better yet, you need to talk to them in person, just in case they don't know."

"Ma, I'm on my way over there now, kiss my son for me and I'll call you back later."

Without waiting for a response, I hung up the phone and rushed out of the hospital making my way over to my In-Laws house.

In what seemed like eternity and with so many thoughts running through my head, I stood in front of their door and nervously rang their doorbell. I didn't know whether they knew Venus had died in child birth or not and if they hadn't, how was I gonna break the news to them. Would I still be treated like the loving son-in-law and the son they never had or would they shun me and treat me like I personally killed their daughter?

"Hold on," I heard Venus' mother yell through the door.

"Hey, Sean, how are you?" Venus' mother asked as she opened up the door

"Hi Mom, is Dad home too?" I asked while walking through the door.

"He's down stairs watching the game on T.V. Oh my goodness; Venus had the baby didn't she? What did she have? I hope it was a little girl. How much did the baby weigh? What did she name the baby?"

Venus' mom kept hitting me with all these questions, I knew they had no idea that their little girl had died in giving childbirth. I began to sweat and my throat felt as dry as a desert.

"I stopped by to talk to you and dad about something. Can you ask Dad to come up stairs for a minute?" I asked, taking a seat on their plastic covered sofa.

"Is everything alright, Sean? You don't look well," she stated sounding concern.

"Can you just go get Dad so I can talk to you both?"

I watched her as she walked to the dining room and down the stairs to the basement were Dad stayed most of the time since he had retired two years ago. Dad had the basement remodeled from Venus' and her sister's playroom to his sanctuary. He had a fifty inch flat screen digital T.V. installed so that he could watch the Baltimore Ravens play; he brought a brand new pool table, and a bar stocked with the best liquor. Dad didn't drink anything other than a beer every now and then, but his buddies, Mr. Drummond and old Mr. Samuels who both lived down the street, came over from time to time to watch a good game and drink until they would pass out.

"Hey Son," I heard Venus' father say as he and her mother walked into the living room and sat across from me in the two matching wingback chairs. "What's going on? Is something wrong?"

"Dad…Mom, I don't know how to say this but," before I could complete my sentence, tears began to run down my face. I was choking up and my voice began to crack.

"What's wrong? Are you okay?" Mom asked, as she came over to where I sat. She placed her arms around me for comfort.

I'd promised myself that I wasn't going to cry but for some reason, the guilt I had and the pain that I'd caused Venus came rushing through me. All the lies and cheating I'd done to her felt like a ton of bricks crashing down on me. Dad got up from his seat and came and sat on the other side of me while I buried my head on Venus' mothers' chest and cried like a baby.

"Son, pull your self together. Did something happen to Venus or the baby?" he asked as I tried to get myself together.

"Dad, Mom, Venus went into la…lab….labor last night and didn't make it," my cracking voice replied.

"What do you mean, Sean?" Mom asked nervously.

"Venus die..died last night while giving birth and I don't know what I'm gonna do. Khalil keeps asking me about wanting to see his mother at the hospital and even though I talked to him last night, I thought he understood but it doesn't seem like he does. I've never planned someone's' funeral before and…."

"Calm down Sean, just breathe," I heard my father-in-law say while rubbing my shoulder.

"Dad, I don't think I can take this," I replied as I began to hyperventilate. "I…I… I can't handle this," my heart felt like it was going to pop out of my chest.

My mother-in-law sat there like she was frozen, like she was put into a trance.

"Mom, are you okay?" I asked, while holding onto my chest.

Venus' mother then stood up and let out a sound or wail of some kind that I'd never heard before.

"NOT MY BABY!" Venus' mother cried while stretching her arms up toward the ceiling. "No…NOT MY BABY!"

I suddenly realized how selfish I was being. I was so caught up into my own feelings and guilt that I didn't think how hard this would be on Venus' parents.

"Valerie, it's gonna be okay, remember God doesn't give us no more than we can handle," my father-in-law said. He stood up and put his arms around his wife to console her.

"No…no…no!" my mother-in-law continued to scream. She wept inside her husband's arms.

"Sean, how's the baby?" Dad asked as tears formed in his eyes.

I wiped my own tears. "It was hit or miss for a minute but she's fine."

"Thank God she's alright," he replied.

The three of us sat there silently as I watched my father-in-law cradle his wife in his arms as she continued to weep. It seemed as though neither of us knew what to say. I guess we all were in shock. After a few minutes of watching Dad comfort his wife, who continued to cry, he leaned over and grabbed the family Bible that sat on the coffee table and began reading, ***John 14:1-4*** *Let not your heart be* troubled: *ye believe in God, believe also in me.*

I sat there and listened to my father-in-law go on and on read-ing the word of God. I was surprised that he was as calm as he was even though he was a Christian and a deacon of the church and used to people dying, this was his daughter. But for me, I was so upset with God and his teachings that all I wanted to do was get the Hell out of there as fast as I could. Unfortunately, I couldn't. My in-laws would take that as a sign of disrespect, so I sat there twiddling my thumbs and thinking about how I was gonna pay for this funeral. Then I re-membered that when I first enlisted, I had signed up for family life in-surance policy with the government. I knew once I left my in-laws house, I needed to get down to the hospital to get Venus' death certifi-cate so I could fill out the necessary paperwork in order to pay for the funeral and check on my daughter.

"Amen," I heard my in-laws say, disrupting me from my thoughts.

"Amen," I said, following suit.

"Son, would you like something to drink, some water or some lemonade?" My father-in-law asked while getting up and heading to-wards the kitchen.

"No, that's okay. I'm about to leave, I have to go down to the hospital and check on my baby girl," I stated while getting up.

At that moment, Venus' mom ran up stairs, crying hysterically as I heard her slam what I believe to be their bedroom door.

"Sean, before you go," my father-in-law began, "I know you might not have thought about this, but since you're in the military and the war is still going on, you never know when you might have to up and leave. Are you going to be able to raise two children by yourself? I don't mean to be insensitive or anything but having just lost my own child, you do have to think about yours as well now. If you don't mind, Valerie and I would be honored to raise our grandchildren for you. You know, until you were ready to do it yourself."

"Well, can I think about it and get back with you?"

"Sure, take your time. We all are family here and we stick to-gether by helping each other. Remember, that's love and that's what families do."

"Thanks Dad, I really appreciate that," I said, heading toward the front door. "Now, before I go, could you do me a really big favor?"

"Sure, what is it?"

"I know it's a lot to ask, but could you and Mom plan Venus' funeral and I'll pay whatever the cost is? I know it's not easy to make plans for your own child's funeral and I wouldn't ask if I knew what to do but…"

"Sean, don't worry about it. Valerie and I have been a deacon and deaconess down at First Tabernacle Church for over twenty five years. We know what to do. Besides, in a way it would help bring us a small amount of closure to our loss. It would be our honor."

"Thanks Dad. I really do appreciate that," I said, choking up once again.

Chapter 8

It was close to visiting hours being over before I left the hospital spending time with my newborn baby girl. Dr. Bittar was nice enough to find an empty room so that I could get to know my daughter as I held her in my arms and fed her for the very first time. There really is something about the smell of a newborn that can be captivating. As I smelled my daughter from head to toe, I had to laugh at myself thinking how funny it was that I was doing like most animal species do with their young.

Not only was I able to get to know her but in the four or so hours I was there, I was able to contact my Commander and inform him as to what happened. And much to my surprise, he was very helpful in advising me of the necessary paperwork I had to complete in order to redeem my family Service Group Life Insurance policy. I damn near fell out of my seat when he checked my file and informed me that for the death of a spouse, I would get close to sixty thousand dollars in a forty-eight hour period once the paperwork had been completed and submitted.

I know sixty thousand dollars may not be a lot for some, but as a Private First Class in Uncle Sam's Army, it's a hell of a lot of money to me. I've never in my life, ever had that kinda money and the thoughts of a new car, possibly a down payment for a new house or maybe taking a long over due trip to Hawaii kept swimming in and out of my head. Besides, I've always wanted to go to Hawaii but never really thought I would have enough money to do so. I remember when I first enlisted in the army; we soldiers are given a dream sheet. And on this dream sheet, you could choose whatever overseas duty station you would like.

That's why it's called a dream sheet because 95% of the time, you didn't get to go where you wanted to go anyway. So being a smart ass, I chose Africa, thinking that that's where they probably would wanna send my black ass anyway. And I noticed on the same sheet that Hawaii was listed as an overseas duty tour, so I thought why not, send me to Africa or send me to Hawaii.

Of course after I had done that, I hoped and prayed that it would be the latter. Hawaii is where I always wanted to take Venus for our honeymoon. Life could be so ironic at times. Based on Venus' death, now I was financially able to go if I wanted. As I looked down at my baby girl in my arms fast asleep, I knew right then and there what I wanted to name her.

"Venus Anne Mathews," I said, whispering in my baby girl's ear.

A smile crept upon my face as she began to fidget in my arms trying to wake up. And in a small way, I took that to mean that she understood and accepted her name.

On my way home driving through downtown Baltimore, my phone began ringing, which kinda caught me off guard because I thought I had turned it off. I looked at caller ID, and couldn't make out whose number it was, so I answered on the third ring,

"Yeah," I stated into the phone.

"Ah, can I speak to Sean Mathews?" the caller asked.

"Speaking, who's this."

"Hey, Sean, this is Justin. I see you forgot all about me, huh?" he inquired, as I heard him smiling into the phone.

"Hey Justin, my bad. I've been going through so much these last few days. I can't even begin to start telling you all the shit that's been going on."

"Well, sir, why not meet me somewhere for dinner and tell me all about it," he said with a hint of flirtation.

"Oh, wow, as much as I would like to, I'm really not up for it this evening. Can I get a rain check?"

"Sure, are you okay?"

"You know, that's a hard question, yes, no, maybe, I really don't know."

"You sure you don't wanna stop by my place and just talk?"

To be honest, I really did need someone to talk to but Justin's call sounded to be more of a booty call than anything else. And for the first time in a long time, sex was the last thing on my mind.

"Naw man, I'm sure. Again, maybe I can get a rain check?"

"Okay, Sean, no problem. I had you on my mind and thought I would give you a call. So if you need someone to talk to or to play with, give me a call, alright?"

"Will do Justin and thanks for calling, peace!"

Once I made it home and entered my apartment complex, I thought about checking in on Lil Man at my mom's, but I was really tired and decided to just take a hot shower and crash for the night. After getting out of the shower, I lay across my bed and turned the T.V. on.

But as tired as I was, I couldn't go to sleep. I tossed and turned thinking about everything that had been going on. In the past when I couldn't go to sleep, I would just jerk off and it was good night. It's hard to explain what I was feeling, the more I thought about the money that I would get from Venus' insurance made me feel good but on the other hand, I was feeling bad about Venus being gone.

I really wanted to talk to somebody but as I thought about my options, I didn't have anyone to talk to. I seriously thought about going upstairs and talking with my mom but I knew all she would do is just give me some motherly advice and I really didn't want that. I just wanted someone to listen. Just as I was about to doze off to sleep, my home phone rang. I looked at my clock again to check out the time and this time it read, 12:31a.m.

I thought, *who in their right mind would be calling me here at home this time of night.* Again, I didn't recognize the number and picked up the phone, "Who is this?" I asked with irritation in my voice.

"Hey you, you miss me?" the caller asked.

"Wow, Cameron, how you doing?" I asked excitedly.

"I'm doing good, Poppi. How you doing?"

I laughed in the phone after he said Poppi because he used to always call me that and even though I hated it. It felt good just to hear his voice.

"Cameron, I can't believe it, it's really you," I said, sitting up on the side of the bed. "I guess you heard, huh?"

"Heard what? I haven't heard anything niggah, I'm still in Korea. I had you on my mind and I wanted to hear your voice, is that okay?"

"Oh." I'm sure he could tell that I wasn't myself.

"What's going on Sean, talk to me."

"Venus went into labor yesterday and didn't make it."

"What do you mean, didn't make it?" Cameron asked excitedly.

"She didn't make it Cam, she died."

"Sean, are you serious?" he asked in disbelief.

"Yeah unfortunately I am," I replied, while heading to the kitchen to get something to drink.

"Damn. I'm so so sorry to hear that. How's the baby, is the baby okay?"

"That's the only good news about this whole situation."

"What do you mean?"

Cameron and I stayed on the phone for hours. He was still in Korea and they were six hours ahead of us in the states. I knew his phone bill was gonna be high as hell. I explained to him all of what had happened as well as the discovery of Venus' baby being mine and not Gabriel's. I also told him about the insurance policy and that I would be getting close to sixty thousand dollars as a result of Venus' death.

He made a joke about possibly bumping off Chauntel and us running away together. We both shared a light hearted laugh. After all, I knew he was just joking, or was he? Cameron also wanted to come home to be with me in my time of need, which I thought was nice but I declined his offer. I knew if he came back to Baltimore, Chauntel and his new born son, Cameron Jr., would take up most of his time and therefore, it would piss me off to know that he was so close but I still couldn't spend the time I wanted to with him.

Cameron and I talked until the sun came up. It felt good talking with him about old times, and how he was adjusting to being over in Korea. My friend had me laughing so much that my jaws were hurting. And it was just what I needed, someone to make me laugh and get my mind off my troubles. Before hanging up, I got Cameron's address and told him that I would mail him the money to pay for his phone bill. After all, he stayed on the phone for as long as I needed him and that was definitely the medicine I needed. I looked over at the clock for a third time and it read, 3:45 a.m.

⚜

It was around noon when my cell phone began ringing again. As I sat up to wipe the sleep out of my eyes, I answered on the fourth ring, "Yeah."

"Hey, Sean, this is dad. Your mother-in-law and I were going down to Marches Funeral home to pick out a coffin and we wanted to know if you wanted to come along to help pick something out."

"I can't do that. If you and mom can do that, I would appreciate it. I mean, anything you guys choose will be fine with me. That is if y'all don't mind?"

"No, Son, we don't mind. You just take the time you need and get yourself together, remember you have my grandson and grand daughter to take care of."

"Thanks, Dad. By the way, I'm going down to the hospital to bring your grand daughter home today."

"That's great," he then became quiet for a second and then asked, "Ah, had you thought about what mom suggested to you about raising our grandchildren for you?"

"Actually, I had. What time will you guys be home?"

"Hopefully, no later than four this afternoon, why?"

"I thought I would stop by and bring your grand daughter, Venus with me."

"Venus, is that what you named her?"

I could tell he was smiling through the phone.

"Yeah, it is. I thought that was the least I could do to honor Venus' name."

"That's good, Sean, I'm glad to hear that. So, let us get going and I'll see you later?"

"Sure thing."

Before heading out to the hospital and dropping off the paperwork to my Commander. I took a quick shower, threw on some jeans and a V-neck sweater, with my fairly new black and red Air Force Ones and headed upstairs to talk to my mom and check on lil man. As she opened the door, I noticed lil man sitting on the floor in the living room watching cartoons.

"Hey Ma," I replied walking through the door and over to where Lil Man sat on the floor.

"Well, good afternoon to you, too," my mother replied sarcastically while closing the door.

"I'm sorry Ma, how's my favorite girl doing?" I said, as I went over to give her a hug.

"I'm fine, but your son is a handful!"

"You know you love it. Hey Lil Man, gimme some love," I said scooping him up in my arms.

"Hi Daddy, I missed you. Granny spanked me," Khalil said, snitching on my mom.

"I sure did and if you have another tantrum, I'll spank that bottom again. And that goes for your father as well," my mom responded. Her hands were on her hips and her head swung from side to side.

I couldn't help but laugh as he laid his head on my chest as though he was using me to protect and hide him from his grandma. "A'ight Lil Man, you know granny loves you. Sit here and finish watching your cartoons while daddy and grandma talk, okay?"

"Okay. Oh Daddy, can I have some Kool-Aid?" he asked, whispering in my ear.

"Sure." I placed him back on the floor and headed to the refrigerator where my mom always kept a pitcher of cherry Kool-Aid.

"What are you doing?" My mom asked as she followed behind me.

"Getting my son some Kool-Aid."

"Oh no you don't, I told him he couldn't have any. It's almost time for his nap and he's not going to be pissing in my bed."

"Oh okay, my bad. Ah Ma, can I talk to you?" I asked, pouring a glass of Kool-Aid for myself.

"Sure baby, what you wanna talk about?"

I took a seat in the living room on my favorite swivel chair and proceeded to tell my mom about the offer that Venus' folks made to me about raising their grand children. I wanted to see how my mom felt about it. To my surprise, she was somewhat for the idea. I say somewhat because, she felt as though since Lil Man was brought up mainly by my side of the family, and he was more familiar with us. I should keep him with me and let my in-laws raise my baby girl.

Which in a way made sense and I knew that it was my mother's way of letting me know that she wasn't about to take care of another baby and go through the changing diapers and feedings all over again. As far as Khalil was concerned, he was old enough to eat whatever he wanted to and he was potty trained, of course with the exception of peeing in the bed periodically.

"Well, I'm glad you feel that way because I was thinking about keeping Lil Man wit us and let Venus' parents raise my baby girl, whom I named Venus."

"Awe, you named her after her mother. That's sweet, Sean."

"Yeah, I thought that was the least I could do."

"What about the funeral arrangements, are her parents handling that?"

"Yeah, Dad called me this morning to let me know they were going over to Marches Funeral Home today and pick out a coffin and everything."

She had a look of concern. "So, are they paying for it as well?"

"Naw, I'm gonna pay for it."

"With what Sean? You don't have any money to pay for a funeral."

"That's the thing, I do. I spoke to my Commander yesterday and he informed me that I had signed up for the family SGLI program and get this, once I submit all the paperwork, I'll get almost sixty thousand dollars from the life insurance policy."

"Oh, wow, that's good then." My mom thought for a second. "I hope you're planning on giving your in-laws a nice chunk of that money for raising your daughter."

"Yeah, of course I do. I just don't know how much I should give them. What do you think would be a reasonable amount?"

"Well, you can always give them something each month, like an allotment or you can give it all to them at once. My question to you is, do you trust them?" she asked with a raised eyebrow.

"Of course I do. They're good church going people and I believe they would do the right thing."

"Well, Sean, babies can be expensive as you already know," she began while pointing to her grandson. "So I think you should open up a high interest trust fund in your daughter's name as well as your in-laws. That way if they need to, they could go to her trust fund and take out whatever they need and if they don't withdraw anything, by the time your daughter reaches eighteen, and with a high interest account, she would have a nice lil nest egg put aside for her."

"Wow Ma, you know that's an excellent idea, I hadn't thought about that. I will definitely do that and open up an account for Lil Man as well."

"You sound like you're surprised Sean, I didn't live all these years without learning a little something," she replied sounding a little insulted.

"Naw, I didn't mean for it to sound like that."

I knew my mother always regretted not going to college and barely graduating high school and therefore a little sensitive about her lack of education.

"Hmmm, I know more than you think I know, Mr. Military Man."

"I know Ma; again I didn't mean it that way. But look, I'ma head out because I have to drop this paper work off to my Commander and stop at the hospital. I'm bringing your grand daughter home today," I said, while getting out of my seat and heading toward the door.

"You want us to go with you?"

"Yeah Daddy, can we go with you, please," Lil Man begged, while looking up at me with puppy dog eyes.

"Sure, why not. Go put your coat on." No sooner than I said why not, he had ran in the bedroom to find his coat.

"Okay, Sean, why don't you go wait in the car and we'll be right out."

"A'ight Ma, don't take all day. I know how slow you can be," I joked while running down the stairs before my mom had a chance to slap me upside the head.

◎◈◈◈◎

After dropping of the paper work to my Commander, we stopped at Wal-Mart to pick up a few things for Venus, such as a new car seat, diapers, canned milk, under garments, and a few cute outfits, and finally, we were on our way to the hospital. We scooped up lil Venus and headed towards my in-laws house.

"She's beautiful, Sean," my mom replied, while holding her granddaughter in her arms.

"Hey, what can I say, I make pretty babies," I stated proudly. "Did you notice how much she looked just like her brother when he was born?"

"She sure does. Look Khaili, meet your new sister. This is how you looked when you were born."

He sat in the back seat with his seatbelt on and almost broke his neck trying to get a better look at his sister.

"Oh, I forgot to tell you, guess who called me late last night?" I asked, looking at my mom.

"I don't know, who?" she asked while still staring down at the baby.

"Cameron."

"Oh, how's he doing?"

"He's doing well and crazy as ever. He had me laughing so much that my jaws were sore. We talked until the sun came up."

"Good, I'm glad to hear he's doing ok. Did you give him my love?"

"Yeah I did. He's feeling a lil' home sick but he says he's having a good time over there."

"Where is he again?"

"Korea."

My mom had a sad look on her face. "Well, I guess you'll be leaving soon as well, huh?"

"I hope not but you never know."

"Well, I hope they don't send you to Iraq or Pakistan or wherever they're fighting."

"Me too, Ma."

On that note, we pulled up into my in-laws driveway. I knew they were home because their car was parked out front. Lil Man was the first to jump out of the car and race up to his grandparent's front door.

"Hi, how's my baby doing?" I heard my mother-in-law ask him, while picking him up. She seemed to be hugging the life out of him.

After all the initial greetings and the introduction of their new granddaughter, we all sat down and discussed Venus' funeral and the raising of our daughter. My in-laws had decided that Venus' wake would be this Friday morning at 11:00 a.m. and the funeral services would follow directly afterwards, and Venus's body would be buried at Woodlawn Cemetery. My in-laws stated that's were they had plots themselves and they wanted Venus to be nearby. They also showed us a picture of the coffin that they had picked out for their daughter. It was a pink champagne color with a rose imprinted on top. I really didn't look at it that hard because never in a million years did I think I would be burying my wife at such a young age. The emotions that flooded my body were overwhelming to the point were I didn't know whether I could actually attend the funeral or not.

As I tried to pull myself together, I looked over at my son sitting on Venus' mother's lap with his head buried in her chest, and looking like he was about to cry.

"Come here son," I said, softly with my arms stretched out to pick him up. He hopped down from his grandmother and ran into my arms. "It's okay," I whispered into his ear as I rocked him back and forth in my arms.

All eyes seemed to be focused on us, as I heard my mother in-law and my mom began to weep. I knew other than the obvious pain they were going through; they were also feeling sorry for me and my children.

My father-in-law broke the tension. "Son, I can't even imagine what you're going through. Lord forbid, if I were to lose your mother-in-law, I wouldn't know what I would do. Now, Venus was our little girl and we loved her deeply but we all have to be strong, son. God has His reasons for all that He does and even if we don't understand them, it's His will, not ours!"

I didn't respond to my father-in-laws comment. I knew he was trying to get me to understand that God has his own way of doing things but I truly wasn't in the mood to hear what God's will was and what it wasn't. All I knew was that God wasn't being fair to me or my children and I will never forgive Him for taking my children's mother away from them. "Are you listening to me son?" my father-in-law asked.

"Yes sir," I said, in a tone that was a little louder than a whisper.

"Good. Now, the funeral Director also informed me that Venus' body will be able to view, by noon. He wants us all to be there to view the body and get our approval. Is that ok with you?"

"Yes, sir."

"Sean, this little baby is an angel," my mother-in-law interjected as she began cooing at her granddaughter.

"Indeed she is," my mom agreed.

"Again, I know this may be a bad time son, but have you decided what you were going to do about the children?"

"Yes. My mom and I talked about it and if it's okay with the both of you, I wanna keep Khalil with me since he's always been with me and leave the baby here with you guys to raise, at least until I decide whether or not to re-enlist or just do the remaining four years and get out of the service." I looked over at my mom while she smiled at me and nodded her head as if to give me her approval.

"Oh, Sean, we would be so honored to raise our granddaughter. I know it's not an easy decision to split up your children but the fact of having this precious little girl with us would give us comfort in losing our own child. I hope you can understand that and realize just how happy you have made us," my mother-in-law stated with new found tears in her eyes.

"Yes Ma'am, I do. I'm also gonna set up a trust fund for her so that if you need financial support, you will be able to go to the bank and withdraw whatever you need."

"No, Son, that won't be necessary. Your mother-in-law and I are very comfortable in our old age. Besides, you're going to need that money to raise your son over there," he said pointing to Lil Man, who was on the floor playing with his truck. "We have also paid the funeral director in full for his services as well."

"You really don't have to do that, Dad. I had family life insurance through the government and I have more than enough to pay for Venus' funeral."

"Nope, that won't be necessary. Now, like I said, it's already been taken care of. Again, you use that money to take care of your son."

"I will, Dad and thank you."

"No need to thank us Son. It's something we feel we must do. Besides, you have just blessed us with this beautiful granddaughter of ours. And remember what I told you, we are still a family, and if you need anything, anything at all. You come to us. Our door is always open."

"Thanks Dad, I really appreciate that."

Chapter 9

I laid in bed that night thinking what a huge weight that was lifted from my shoulders. For once, I felt at peace. I'd left my baby girl with her grand parents whom I knew would love her and do right by her. Even Lil Man was in good hands being with my mom, even though he got on her nerves. As much as my mom complained about him, I knew she loved having him around. Other than him being a handful, he was also excellent company for her. My mom had been single for over twenty years and even though she dated here and there, she always said that she wasn't about to get caught up with some old skeezer and play a nurse. My mom would also say, *what's the point of having some old skeezer who couldn't get it up where all she needed was a fresh pack of double A batteries.* My mom was too funny, often times I would have to tell her, Too Much Information Ma…TMI.

I'd awakened the next morning drenched in sweat. I had that same nightmare I had been having ever since Thomas' death. I knew who killed Thomas, but I didn't know how I could prove it. The nightmare seemed to become more and more real, each time I would have them. But I wondered who would believe me and then I thought, *once Venus' funeral was over with and things somewhat get back to normal, maybe I could meet with Justin and explain everything to him and maybe he would be able to advise me. After all, he was an attorney for the army and he should know what to do, right?* I had less than an hour to meet my in-laws down at Marches Funeral Home to view Venus' body. I called my mom on my cell phone to see if she was going with me. She picked up on the second ring.

"Hey baby, you ready?" my mom asked.

"No, not really but what other choice do I have?" I said yawning into the phone. "Hey Ma, you think we could drop Lil Man off with your friend Mrs. Betty?"

Mrs. Betty was a friend of my mom's who lived in the next apartment complex and would sometimes baby-sit when Venus and I wanted to go somewhere and my mom was too busy. She loved him as though he was her own grandson. She was the type of person who loved all children and even though she had two grandchildren of her own, she very seldom saw them because her daughter and her husband had moved to California because of his new job.

"No, I think he should go since this would be the last time he would get a chance to see her."

"Do you think he'll be able to handle it? I mean, I don't wanna traumatize my own son."

"He'll be fine, Sean. I talked with him last night and he understands that his mother is in Heaven now, playing the organ and singing in God's choir."

"Ma, I swear, you always had a way with gettin' children to understand the most complex things. I remember when I was four and you told me the same thing about grandma when she died."

"And it worked, didn't it," my mom laughed into the phone.

"Yeah, it did. I'll meet you and Lil Man down at the car in fifteen minutes."

I hung up the phone, jumped out of bed and took a quick shower. I stood in front of my closet with a towel draped around my waist and water pouring off my body, trying to figure out what I should wear.

Should I wear a suit or would that be too much, I thought to myself.

Seconds later, I finally decided on a pair of black Kenneth Cole slacks, my Florshiem burgundy loafers and a black turtle neck sweater. After getting dressed, I took one last look in the floor length mirror. As good as I looked and as young as I was, I couldn't believe I'd become a widower.

Lil Man and my mom were already in the car waiting for me as I exited our apartment complex.

"Hi Daddy!" he screamed out the window as he saw me coming toward the car.

"Hey. I see grandma dressed you all up, huh?"

"Umh huh, Granny let me wear my church clothes, see." He opened his coat so I could get a better look.

"I see. I'm scared of you," I responded pulling off.

Within twenty minutes we pulled into the funeral home's parking lot. My in-laws were there because I saw their Black Chrysler 300 parked right in front. Dad didn't get around too well and said he had something called gout. I'm not sure what that was, but a few years ago, he was able to get one of those handicap signs for his car. As we got out of the car, heading toward the entrance, I grabbed Lil' Mans' hand. I don't know whether I grabbed his hand for support or making sure he didn't start running around the funeral home. Either way, I wasn't gonna let him go.

As we entered, I notice a reception desk in the middle of the lobby area and walked right up and asked the receptionist, "Which room is Venus Mathews in?"

After checking her computer, she said, "Mrs. Mathews is in the second room on the left, down this hallway. I believe her parents are in there with her now."

"Thank you," I replied, as we headed toward the room.

As we entered, I stood in the doorway because for some reason, I couldn't go in. My mom and Lil Man walked right in and greeted my in-laws and then stood over Venus' coffin. The piped in music they play in funeral homes didn't make the situation any better. I began to feel nauseous. All I could smell was the aroma of flowers, death and formaldehyde.

"Come on in, Sean. No need for you to hold up the door," my father in-law said standing on the right side of Venus' coffin. With his Sunday's best on, he looked like he was the funeral director.

"Naw, I'll stay right here."

"Are you alright?" my mother in-law asked while dabbing at her eyes with a handkerchief.

"Naw, not really," I answered. I leaned over and grabbed my stomach.

My mom came over to me and noticed that I was panting and sweat was pouring off of me as though I'd just finished a marathon. Then Lil Man suddenly did something strange. He stood back from his mother's coffin and then kneeled down on both knees, clasp his hands together and appeared as though he was praying. Whatever he was doing, it snapped me out of what I was going through. And the more we tried to listen to his prayer, we realized he wasn't praying at all. It actually sound as though he was having a conversation with Venus. I took a seat in one of the wooden chairs up front so I could hear exactly what he was saying. It broke my hurt to hear my son telling his diseased mother that everything was going to be alright and that he would take good care of me. Being that as the father, I should be taking good care of him.

On the way home, I decided to treat my son to McDonald's since he had been so brave at the funeral home and considering we all were starving. The more I thought about it, I realized I hadn't eaten much of anything within the last few days. Lil Man wanted a happy meal, while my mom and I got a Big Mac, fries and a chocolate milk shake. We ate our food there because I didn't want Lil Man to make a mess in my car and I couldn't get him to hold out until we got home to eat. After all, by the time we would make it home, the food would be cold. Lil Man had wolfed his food down so quickly, I knew he had to be starving.

"Daddy, can I go play over on the sliding board?" He pointed to the Playland area.

"Sure, just be careful, a'ight?"

"Okay I will," he replied while running off.

My mother smiled. "He seems to be his own self."

"Yeah, he does. That's wild how he just started talking to Venus like that though. It scared me to death."

"Do you think he was actually talking to Venus?"

"I don't know, Ma. It was just weird the way he just kneeled down in front of her coffin and started talking like that."

"Well, Sean, I had a similar experience myself when my mother, your grandmother died."

"Really, what do you mean?" I asked with raised eyebrows.

"I never told you this but the night your grandmother passed, she called me around ten o'clock that evening and at the time, I was watching my favorite news show. So, I told your grandmother I would call her back. By the time the show went off, I decided to go to bed, thinking that she really didn't have much to say, so I told myself I would give her a call first thing in the morning when I got to work. Anyway, the next thing I knew, Dad called me around 6:00 o'clock that morning to let me know that my mother had died in her sleep."

My mom stopped for a second as she dug in her purse for a tissue to wipe the tears from her eyes. Remembering as though it was yesterday, she continued. "The evening we were to go view her body, I really didn't want to go. I was tired, so I laid down to take a nap and that's when your grandmother came to me."

"Came to you? What do you mean, like in a dream?"

"Even though it was a dream, I think it was much more than a dream. I believe it was your grandmother's way of saying goodbye," she said with a smile.

"Why, what did she say?"

"I don't know if you remember, but that night before she died, she had called not only me but my brother, Rufus and my sister, Janet. Of course I didn't find out about this until after her funeral but in her own way, she was saying goodbye to them and when she called me, to say goodbye, I was too busy."

I could tell she felt bad about that. "So, what happened in the dream?"

She cleared her throat. "Well, my mother told me that she wanted to say goodbye and not to fear death. I told her that I was sorry that I hadn't called her back and that I would always feel guilty about that. She told me not to and that even though she wanted me to come with her, it wasn't my time. I then asked her, how did she know it was her time? She replied by saying that God called her name and she answered. After that, I suddenly woke up."

"That's a wild story. Why you never told me that before?"

"I don't know Sean, I guess I just never really thought much about it until now," she replied with sadness on her face. I reached for my mother's hand to let her know that everything was going to be alright. My mom then gathered up all of our trash and disposed of it as I went to get Lil Man, so we could make our way home.

Chapter 10

I kept Lil Man at my apartment that evening because I didn't want to be alone for the night. For some reason, I had this eerie feeling as though something bad was gonna happen. While giving him a bath, I decided to ask about what had occurred earlier.

"Son, do you remember when we went to go see your mommy earlier today?"

"Umh huh," he replied, splashing water all over the place.

"Did your mommy talk to you?" I asked, bracing myself.

"No Daddy. Did Mommy talk to you?" he asked, still splashing water.

He caught me off guard with his reply and I had to laugh, "Naw, she didn't.

He obviously didn't remember any of what happened to him and I began to worry whether or not this was a one time thing or whether or not Venus would be coming back to have conversations with her son. It began to remind me of the movie *The 6th Sense*. I didn't want my son going around talking about *he sees dead people*. And even though he was only two, he was as smart as any five year old.

After bathing and putting him to bed, I laid next to him and thought about the story my mom had told me about my grandmother. Because of what I was going through, I was beginning to doubt that God even existed, but after listening to her story, I believed it really happened, so God must exist.

"But why was he putting me through all this hell?" I asked myself.

It was strange that my mom would have such a dream that bordered on the *Super Natural* as I too was having dreams about Thomas and his murder, along with what happened to Lil Man earlier that day.

This shit was getting really creepy and made me nervous. So, as I clung on to Lil Man and began to drift off to sleep, I heard a knock at the door. Considering it was so late at night, it immediately caught me off guard. As I got out of my bed to answer the door, I looked around to see what I could possibly use as a weapon. Unfortunately, I couldn't find anything to use, so I crept to my front door as quietly as I could and peeped out the peephole to see who it was. I couldn't believe who it was and had the nerve to be smiling from ear to ear.

"What are you doing here?" I asked, with much attitude after opening my front door halfway.

"Sean, I know this may not be a good time but is it okay if I come in and talk with you?" he asked.

"What's there to talk about?" I was becoming angrier by the second.

"Look, Sean, I don't wanna stand out here in your hallway and talk, can I please come inside, just for a few minutes," he begged.

With hesitation I opened my door so that he could enter. While entering, he tried to hug me in the process but I pulled away.

"Damn Sean, that's cold man."

I didn't bother to offer him a seat. "Look, I don't have all night, what do you want?"

"I know its late and I know Venus' funeral is tomorrow, that's why I stopped by."

"What does Venus' funeral have to do with you?"

Again without offering, he decided to make himself comfortable and took a seat on my couch.

"I don't know why you're sitting down, you're not gonna be here that long," I spat.

"Sean, I just stopped by to ask you two questions."

"Well, I suggest you start asking so you can hurry up and leave."

"Before I do, can I have something to drink?"

"No. That's your first question. What's your second question?" I questioned, still standing by the front door with my arms folded.

"You're not being fair Sean. Me asking you for something to drink was not the reason I came all the way over here."

"Stop beating around the bush and get on with your questions."

He took a deep breathe and asked, "I wanted to know if you mind if I attend Venus' funeral tomorrow?"

"So, you're asking for my permission?"

"Well, yeah. Something like that. Although, as a minister, I can go without your permission but because of the things that have happened between the three of us, I just wanted your approval of me being there. I don't want to cause any other problems than I already have."

"I don't know why you think you need my permission. You didn't ask for my permission when you fucked my wife, now did you?" I asked, as my nostrils began to flare.

He didn't respond, he just sat there with his face in the palm of his hands and sounded as though he was crying. I knew he thought I would be a little more sensitive and pity him but I didn't. Venus was my wife, not his. Hell, I should be the one crying, not him. He was supposed to be a man of the cloth, a preacher man. How dare he have an affair with me and my wife? Again, I refused to pity him but as he sat there weeping, I began to think back to the time when we first met.

Venus had practically begged me for permission to cook dinner for this new young preacher and his family and since his family was coming from out of town and he didn't cook, Venus took it upon herself to offer her services. I met Gabriel at church while attending services of this new young preacher and found out that he was this new young minister's older brother.

The first time I laid eyes upon Gabriel, he reminded me of a white lab mouse. He was so light skinned, with coal black wavy hair and slanted eyes; a white lab mouse is all I could think of. I also remember his solo he sang that morning, *His Eyes are on the Sparrow,* and once he was finished, there wasn't a dry eye in the house. And now he sits before me, with tears of his own.

"Sean, I didn't come here to cause you anymore hurt or pain than I've already caused. I just wanted to see you and talk to you and apologize for what I did and hope that you could forgive me," Gabriel stated while sniffling.

"Look Gabriel, I don't know what I'm feeling right now. I just want all this to be over so I can move on wit my life," I said, taking a seat next to him on the couch.

"So, can I come to the funeral?" he asked, again rubbing the tears from his eyes.

"It doesn't matter, if you want to, that's fine."

I'm not sure what happened, but after thinking about when Gabriel and I first met, my defenses were crumbing down. I wasn't angry anymore; I realized that even though he was a man of the cloth, he was still a man, which meant that he was not perfect and subject to sin as much as I was. I don't know why we as ordinary people put ministers on a higher plane and expect more from them than we do ourselves.

"Thank you, Sean. Now, can I ask you my second question?" He had a devilish look.

"Go ahead," I replied in a nonchalant tone.

"I know you have every right to be upset and angry with me but I've been doing a lot of thinking and I know how wrong I was for doing what I did, but do you remember that night at the hotel?" he asked, with his head hung low.

"Yeah, how could I forget," I replied, as the thoughts of that horrible night brought an end to my marriage.

"Did she ever tell you what happened that night after you left?"

"No. Venus and I hadn't talked very much since that night. As a matter of fact, after that night, I never went back home, other than getting some of my clothes. I've been living in the barracks on base."

"Would you like me to tell you what happened?"

"I'm listening."

"Well, after you left, Venus and I had a huge argument. She called me everything but a child of God. I was shocked to see that side of her because I had never seen that side of her. She was actually more upset with me than she was with you. I couldn't deny to her that you and I weren't sleeping together; she had practically caught us with our pants down. No pun intended. So, ultimately, she demanded I make a choice between her and you. And do you want to know who I chose?" he asked, looking dead into my eyes.

"Is this your second question?"

"No, its not," Gabriel spat. "I'm being serious."

"And you don't think I am?"

"I don't know, Sean, but just to let you know, I hadn't seen Venus since that night, except when she called me the other day to tell me that she was in labor and wanted me to take her to the hospital."

He stopped, took another deep breath and reached out for my hand and said, "I hadn't seen Venus because I chose you, Sean."

At that point, looking into his eyes, I didn't know who or what to believe. "Why are you telling me this now?"

"I thought about telling you the next day after it happened but you were so angry and upset and I understood you had a right to be. I just didn't think you would see me or take any of my calls. And the other day at the hospital, I wanted to talk with you then and let you know how happy I was that Venus' baby turned out to be yours, but again you got so upset and stormed out of the doctors office, I thought it would be best to wait until things calmed down," he stated in a genuine tone.

"I'm burying my wife tomorrow and so you think things have calmed down?" I questioned. I stared at him as if he was crazy.

"Look, Sean, I'm just trying to make peace with you because the truth of the matter is, I've missed you. I miss being around you, I miss talking with you and I miss being with you," he said tearing up.

"What do you expect me to do? Am I supposed to forget all that has happened? I mean, I haven't heard from you since that night and all of a sudden you come knocking on my door in the middle of the night, the night before my wife's funeral, telling me that you've missed me. You know, this is really beginning to sound like a soap opera and I can't stand fucking soap operas."

Gabriel was really beginning to upset me all over again as I sat there looking at him bawl like a child. I'd never seen him cry before until tonight, but I could tell he was in pain. He'd slouched down on the couch grabbing and hugging one of my throw pillows for comfort. I honestly sat there, watching him and didn't know what to do. I got up and went into the kitchen to get us both a cold glass of water.

"Here drink this," I said, handing him the glass of water.

"Thank you."

"Look, I know you're hurt but you're gonna have to calm down with all that noise. Lil Man is in the room sleep, and I don't want you waking him up." I took my seat back on the couch.

"I'm sorry, Sean, I just can't help how I feel," he babbled.

Fortunately, Lil Man slept like a rock. However, I still wanted Gabriel to chill with all that noise because I didn't want my neighbors listening and start to wonder what was going on. Another truth about me is, I couldn't stand to see anyone cry and therefore, I reached over and held him in my arms, hoping to soothe his spirit and comfort him.

Gabriel and I sat on my couch for most of the night trying to hash out our anger toward one another. We also shared a few laughs as well as a few more tears. I knew deep down inside, all of this wasn't his fault. We all played a part of this including Venus. And I believe that if you couldn't forgive someone, how can you expect God to forgive you for the sins that you commit? I may have sounded like a contradiction, considering that within the last few days my faith had been wavered but ultimately, I knew there was a God. I also had to give Gabriel his props for being man enough to come to me and apologizing for what he'd done.

Most men wouldn't have given it a second thought and moved on to the next victim. Being that I wasn't there, I would never know what really happened between Gabriel and Venus or whether or not what he was saying was true, and it really didn't matter now. It was all about forgiving someone and moving on with my life. My mom always said, there's no fool like an old fool. So, whether Gabriel continued to be a part of my life didn't really matter either. I needed to get over this and move on with my life for me and my children.

Chapter 11

It was Venus' Funeral and my in-laws, my mom and me pulled up in front of St. Tabernacle Baptist Church in an all white Chrysler Limousine. My mother's friend, Mrs. Betty was nice enough to watch my son and my in-laws had one of their good neighbors to watch my baby girl. My mother-in-law had requested that as the immediate family, we all should wear white. So even though it was fall, it took me a minute to find a winter white suit, but I did. I had to admit, we looked good as we entered the church, with me upfront and my mom at my side with her right arm clutched to my left arm as she escorted me down the center aisle heading toward my late wife's coffin.

I couldn't stop heaving, I felt like I was about to throw up and my chest began to rise and fall rapidly against my mother's chest. I felt like I was about to lose it, my body began to shake as though I was about to go into convulsions and all I wanted to do was run out of there so I could get some air. The closer I got to Venus' coffin, I felt my legs buckling. My mom sensed I was about to fall and asked Gabriel who was right behind us to help her escort me to my seat. They seated me in the first row of the pew. My mother sat on my left and Gabriel sat on my right. As I sat there trying to get myself together, all I could see was Venus' body lying there motionless.

Before the service even began, I realized that I couldn't handle this, so I began to rise from my seat and try to make a break for it, my mom tried to hold me down but couldn't and I heard her say, "Gabriel, hold him down."

Gabriel grabbed me from the back and placed his arms around me while trying to stop me from swinging.

"Get off me Gabriel!" I yelled, as I fought to release myself.

"Sean, you need to calm down," he said in a stern tone.

Before I knew it, I was literally tackled down to the floor by four or five brothas, who I assumed were members of the church.

Then I heard my mom yell, "Don't hurt my son."

As I laid there penned to the floor and tears flowing down my cheeks and barely being able to breathe, Reverend Wilson came and kneeled beside me and asked everyone in the church to get up and come and form a circle around me and hold hands. Reverend Wilson then asked everyone to close their eyes as he began to pray a special prayer for me.

"Heavenly Father, we come to you today with hurt felt hearts. We ask you to look down on Brother Sean today and bless him Father. His heart is heavy and burdened Lord, speak to him, let him know that through you, he will find his peace. Watch over him Lord and his motherless children. Give him the strength and the love to go on Lord, so that he can raise his children so they may know your mercy and your love, Lord Jesus."

After Reverend Wilson finished praying over me, I was helped up and escorted back to my seat. Reverend Wilson had one of the nurses of the church get me a cold glass of water. I had to admit, Reverend Wilson's prayer worked because after gulping down two glasses of cold water, I felt so much better.

Reverend Wilson began the home going service for Venus as I sat and skimmed through the program that my in-laws had printed and noticed that on the front cover, they'd used the picture that Venus and I had taken professionally less than a year ago. We'd gone to The Picture People in the mall and took pictures together as well as some that were separate. Venus wore her hair up with teased bangs that covered the majority of both eye brows. She sported a pair of small diamond studs in both ears and a navy blue Michael Kors dress that I'd gotten her for Christmas the year before. This was one of Venus' better pictures that I even carried around in my wallet. It brought a smile to my face immediately.

While Reverend Wilson preached the life that Venus lived and praised her for her hard work with her gospel music ministry, I began to scan the audience, just to see who'd come to pay their respects and who hadn't. St. Tabernacle Baptist was a huge church and it was filled to its capacity. Not trying to be so obvious, I turned to my left and was pleasantly surprised to see my new roommate, Ty. All I could do was smile and shake my head as I noticed some female sitting next to him with his arm around her. I couldn't help but think how much of a hoe Ty was, that he had the nerve to bring a date with him to a funeral, but that's Ty.

I also noticed that most of my co-workers were also in attendance which made me feel good that they cared so much. As I turned facing front, The St. Tabernacle Baptist Choir took center stage and began singing one of Venus' favorite songs, *Never Would Have Made It* by Marvin Sapp. Closing my eyes and listening to this choir, I had to give them props because they sung the hell out of that song. People were standing up, clapping, and swaying from side to side as they sung along with the choir. Afterwards, the choir received a thunderous round of applause which was very deserving.

Minutes later, cards and telegrams giving their condolences and heart felt blessings from family members and friends who were unable to attend were read, and finally, Reverend Wilson approached the podium and began Venus' Eulogy.

❧❦❧

Three hours and a few more tears later, I escaped upstairs to one of my in-laws guest rooms as they greeted guest downstairs for Venus' repass After watching her coffin being lowered into the ground at Woodland Cemetery, I really wasn't in the mood to be around a crowd of people. My mom and Gabriel kept me company as they took turns waiting on me, hand and foot. Personally, I think they both thought I would spaze out again and therefore, tried to keep a close eye on me. My mom had fixed me a plate and begged me to eat something, but I wasn't hungry and refused to eat. Gabriel tried to keep my mind focused by talking to me about everything under the sun, including telling me a few lame Christian jokes that I wouldn't dare repeat. And even though my mom had given the guest and well wishers my apologies for not being sociable, they still continued to come upstairs to personally give me their condolences. What I really wanted to do was pick up my kids and go home to some peace and quiet. I guess in my own way, I really did love Venus.

To help occupy my mind and time, my mom had bought me all the cards and notes that people had given to her. She must've known I wanted to be alone, so after she went back downstairs, I sat up in the bed thumbing through everything and began reading them, one by one. Most of them all seemed to say the same thing, *you have to be strong for your children, we'll keep you in our prayers, God doesn't place any pain on us that we can't bare, etc*... But there was this one small blue envelope that had not been opened. As a matter of fact, whoever sent it had sealed it tight. I opened the envelope and immediately became so angry after reading it that I got up, marched downstairs, and told everybody there, "To go fuck themselves." Then got in my car and drove home.

Chapter 12

Two weeks had passed since Venus' funeral and I was still angry as hell at the note I had received from one of the so called well wishers. The day after the funeral I'd shown the note to my mom because she couldn't believe the way I'd acted. But after showing her the note, she too understood and informed me that she'd apologized to everyone on my behalf.

It was my first day back at work in hopes of trying to move on with my life, but I found myself just going through the motions. I didn't feel as though I was living, I felt as though I just existed. I'd received several calls from family and friends who were concerned with my well-being, but as much as I appreciated their concern, I wished they would just leave me alone. At this point, I didn't trust anyone. I sat in my chair not being able to concentrate on anything other than that damn note. I carried it around with me as though I would soon discover who it came from. I pulled it out of my pocket and read it for what seemed the hundredth time:

You think you're in pain now, wait until I get a hold of your Faggot punk bitch ass!

For the life of me, I couldn't figure out who could've been so cruel as to send me a note like this on the day I buried my wife. Needless to say, I thought maybe Jamaal might've written it or had someone do it for him. But even Jamaal being the asshole that he was, didn't really mean me any harm. He just wanted me out of the military, or did he?

Just as I had done for the past couple of weeks, I had gotten off from work and headed to the barracks to take a quick shower and go straight to bed. An hour or so later, I tossed and turned in my bed as I heard my roommate Ty enter the room with one of his female friends. I don't know why, but I lay in my bed playing sleep as I heard moans and groans coming from what used to be Cameron's bed. This of course wasn't the first time Ty had brought some ho into our room. Ty and I had worked out a signal of putting a sock on the outside doorknob of our room to let the other know that we had company or we were there. I hadn't remembered to put a sock out on the door this evening and the room was dark, so I don't think Ty knew I was in the room. I swear I didn't know what was worse, having another gay roommate or someone like Ty who was a serious womanizer. Nonetheless, this was the first time I had actually been there to listen to Ty's love making.

Most would think that I was just getting a cheap thrill but what else did I have to look forward to. Besides, Ty was a hot dude and talked more shit about what he could do. So, I thought it would be interesting to hear what Ty had going on in the fucking department. However, the longer I laid there and listened to what was going on, the more confused I became. Now, I'd had my share of the women and I knew who was supposed to be moaning, but this was different.

I kept hearing Ty moaning shit like, "Dats right bitch, fuck dis shit" and "C'mon baby deeper."

Since I was facing the wall, I quietly turned over to try to see what was going on. Fortunately, Ty's bed was located near the window and the shade was drawn, which allowed the streetlight to shine through.

What the fuck, I thought to myself.

I thought my eyes were deceiving me as I noticed Ty in the doggy style position being banged out by some dude.

I laid there shaking my head in disbelief all awhile being turned on as Ty backed up his perfectly muscled shaped black ass on this brotha who was doing some serious stroking. Still having my blanket over me, I slowly pulled down my boxers and began to pleasure myself. Ty, with his head buried into his pillow was so busy moaning and groaning, he hadn't noticed that I was even in the room but the dude fucking Ty unmercifully did. I'd never had sex with a dude with tits but dude was kinda hot from what I could see of his silhouette.

Dude was a little taller than Ty and his frame was smaller but appeared to be well toned. He sported shoulder length dreadlocks and with every stroke he took, his dreads would flow in and out of his face. For a minute or so, it appeared that dude was looking in my direction and because the light in the room was so dim, I wasn't certain until I actually saw him gesture to me wit his hand to come join them. Talking about having to make a split second decision and Lord knows, I hadn't come close to having an erection or being aroused for the past couple of months.

What the hell, I thought.

I climbed out of bed completely naked as my manhood stood at attention and swaggered my way over to have a threesome.

Dudes dreads hung in his face. I still couldn't get a good look at him but as he continued to plow away at Ty, I took position behind the lil' dude and began to grind my manhood against his small silky smooth ass. I reached around and cupped lil dudes small breast with my hands and began massaging them. As I stated before, I've never had sex wit a dude wit tits before, who was considered in the gay lifestyle to be transgender. But feeling all over his smooth silky body I noticed he had on a black G-string and that shit was turning me the fuck on. My dick was hard as a rock and since I had not gotten off in months, I seriously wanted to tear up some shit.

Just as I was about to slide my Johnson up into this transsexual's ass, Ty threw the pillow off of his head and looked over his shoulder and saw me behind the dude.

"What the fuck are you doing, man?" Ty yelled as he slid from under dude and stood up facing us both.

As Ty stood there in the dark, I really didn't know who he was talking to so I didn't respond but to be honest, I thought he was talking to lil dude because Ty wouldn't have talked that way to me.

"Sean, I said, what the fuck are you doing?" he yelled again. By this time, both me and lil dude was sitting on the bed looking up at Ty as though we were kids being scolded for something we shouldn't have done.

"Ty, chill with all that noise, a'ight?" I replied as I got up and walked past him to find my boxers to put, and turn on the lamp that sat on my night stand.

"Sean, I asked you a question. Why you tryna fuck my girl, man?" He walked up behind me.

Your girl, I thought to myself. I spun around in disbelief and I could see over Ty's short muscular frame a dark skin, slim, nude shawtie with dreads that had on a "strap on" posing before me.

"Yo niggah, who said anything about being your girl?" Shawtie protested as she began putting her clothes on. "This here was for my financial gain or had you forgotten?" She snapped, while holding her hand out as though she was expecting to get paid.

Ty stood there butt naked looking like a deer caught in head lights. I knew he had to be embarrassed that his game was let out. The thought of Ty paying some hooka to fuck him blew my mind as I lay on my bed and watched this whole thing play out before me. Ty finally snapped out of it, picked up his pants off the floor, pulled out his wallet, paid the hooka some money and yelled, "Now, git da fuck out, Bitch!"

Shawtie was already at the front door ready to leave as she put the money in her pocket and like most women who feel the need to have the last word, opened the door, turned around, put her hand on her hips and said, "Niggah you paid me to fuck you and I'm da biotch, I don't think so." Which was followed by our front door being slammed shut.

Ty began to mumble some obscenities as I watched his short smooth muscular frame bending over. He was still nude with lube running down the crack of his ass, digging in his dresser drawer looking for some clean underwear and a towel to take a shower. I'd never really checked out Ty's ass before, but it took everything inside of me not to run up behind him and rape his ass. My thoughts were getting the best of me because I figured, hell, it ain't like Ty can't take some dick because the strap on that shawtie had on had to be at least ten inches and Ty was taking that shit like a champ.

Not to mention, Ty had a pretty muscular ass and he didn't need to take a shower because I would have been more than willing to slop up that lube running down his ass wit my tongue and fuck him like he stole something.

Ty didn't say a word or even look at me as he headed out the door heading toward the bathroom. My dick still stood at attention as I fantasized about fucking him. I remember the many nights Cameron who was more than willing to do whatever I wanted him to do, slept in this very room and due to my denial, I would fall asleep with a major hard on and I refused to let that happened again. I needed to devise a plan to have Ty so turned on that he wouldn't refuse my advances, but how?

Ty entered the room with the towel wrapped around his waist and I noticed that he had his underwear still in his hand. I think I shocked him as he looked at me butt naked lying on my bed and stroking my dick. Ty just shook his head and walked over to his dresser and tossed his underwear back in the drawer. He then snatched off his towel and lay across his bed on his stomach.

Within minutes, he began to slow grind against his mattress and I could softly hear him moaning. I watched his silhouette slowing move up and down on the bed and the perfect muscled V-shape curvature that Ty had in his back was one of the reasons why so many men stayed in the gym five to six times a week. My right hand started to become moist as I felt the pre-cum slowly oozing down from my erection. This is going to be way too easy.

Several minutes later, I noticed Ty seemed to have stopped moving. I didn't know whether he had dozed off to sleep for real or whether or not he was just playing possum, as they say. I was hoping I didn't blow my chance, so I got up from my bed and tiptoed over to the foot of Ty's bed and stood over him while still stroking my joint. I watched him as he laid there face down and his legs spread apart. My mouth actually began to water as I kneeled down anticipating sticking my tongue in his ass. Just before entering Ty with my tongue, he began to squirm around a bit which was a good thing because he opened his legs further apart and his booty hole became easier access.

I froze; waiting for him to fall back off to sleep. Within seconds, Ty was back in never never land and my drooling tongue was less then an inch away from what was going to be the best nut I had had in months. I closed my eyes, tightened the grip around my dick wit my hand and Ty let out the loudest, funkiest farts I had ever heard or smelled.

As I leaned back to escape the foul odor, Ty fell out all over the floor with laughter. And I don't mean just a regular laugh, I mean one of those laughs where you seem as though you can't stop laughter.

"Yo, niggah, that's fucked up," is all I could say, while getting up and going back over to my bed. Ty continued to laugh hysterically while still lying on the floor in a fetal position and holding his sides. I was tempted to pee on his ass as he laid there but with my dick still slightly aroused, peeing was the last thing on my mind. I put on my boxers, grabbed my wash cloth, toiletries and headed out the door to the bathroom.

When I returned back to the room, Ty was on his bed pretending to read a book. He looked up at me as I entered and began chuckling. "Dats what yo ass get, muthafucka," breaking out into laughter once more.

"That wasn't even necessary," I replied climbing into my bed.

"Why wasn't it?" he asked with a chuckle.

"Because, I thought that's what you wanted."

"Well, you thought wrong niggah. I ain't gay. I'm not into that shit."

"Oh, really? Well, answer me this, why would you pay some hooka to fuck you with a strap on, when you can get the real thing for free?" I asked, sitting up on the side of my bed.

"Fuck you Sean, a'ight!" Ty spat, as he threw his book on the floor and turned over in his bed facing the window as though he was going to sleep.

"Oh, you don't wanna talk about that, huh? I guess you don't find that funny, huh? Yeah well, fuck you too Ty!" I yelled, while turning off the light.

I was suddenly startled out of my sleep when I heard my cell phone go off. I looked at the clock on the wall and it was almost four in the morning. I grabbed my cell phone off my nightstand, opened it and didn't recognized the number that appeared, although it was a local number.

"Who's this?" I asked groggily.

"Hey, Sean, this is Cameron," he replied softly.

"Hey, Cam, where are you?" I sat up in my bed.

"I'm here on base in the Stock Aide."

"What do you mean, in the Stock Aide?" I said, almost shouting into the phone.

"Do you mind," Ty said sounding irritated.

"Shut da fuck up," I spat at Ty.

"Who are you talking to?" Cameron asked.

"My new roommate, don't worry about him. Anyway, why are you here in the Stock Aide?"

"Your boy, big mouth Jamaal had gotten a warrant for my arrest because they claimed to have found my DNA at Thomas' house. So, now they tryna say I killed him and brought me all the way back here to put me on trial," he answered though tears.

Chapter 13

I sat in my office the next morning just going through the motions as I have been for the past couple of weeks. However, this morning was different. After receiving that call from Cameron last night, I couldn't wait for this day to be over so that I could pay my friend, my love a visit at the Stock Aide. I was blown away when Cam said that he was brought back here because big mouth Jamaal thought Cameron actually killed Thomas and therefore, had found his cousin's murderer. I knew without a doubt, Cameron had nothing to do with Thomas' death. But in a way, I was overjoyed with Jamaal's ass backwards decision. It had brought Cameron back into my life and I'd missed him more than I ever thought possible. Also, if my nightmare about Thomas' death had any truth in it, Cameron would be out of the Stock Aide in less than 72 hours.

In order to get the ball rolling for Cameron's release, I desperately needed to talk to Justin. I pulled out my cell phone and dialed his work number.

"Adjunct General's Office, can I help you?" the female voice on the other end asked.

"Yes, can I speak to Lieutenant Glover?"

"Who may I say is calling?"

"This is Private First Class Mathews."

"Is he expecting your call?"

"Yes, he is," I replied, knowing it was a lie.

"Hold on, please."

Within a matter of seconds, I heard Justin say, "Hey Sean, how are you? I was wondering when you would get around to giving me a call."

"Hey Justin, I need to talk to you about something very serious."

"What's going on Sean?"

"I was hoping that I could meet with you, later. That is if you didn't have any plans."

"I do have something to take care of later, but what time are you talking about?"

"How about nine thirty this evening?"

"Okay, I'll be home so give me a call when you're on your way."

"A'ight cool, I'll see you then."

"Hey, Sean."

"Yeah."

"Are you going to give me some chocolate?"

"You're a crazy white boy, you know that," I chuckled.

"Hmmm, you should let me show you how crazy I can be," he said devilishly.

"I'll see you later," I responded with a smile and hanging up.

⁕⁂⁕

The day couldn't end soon enough as I quickly gathered my things to leave. Cameron had been on my mind all day and I couldn't wait to see him. Cameron had only been gone for a few months but it seemed like a life time. The anticipation of seeing him again had butterflies in my stomach as I walked the few blocks to the Stock Aide. I stopped and pulled out my cell phone because it started to buzz. I forgot I had turned the ringer off earlier; I looked at the caller ID and it said PRIVATE.

Out of curiosity, I picked up and said, "Hello."

The caller didn't say anything right away. All I could hear was what sounded like paper rustling around in the background and then I heard the voice say, "Homosexuality is a sin and for that, you must die."

The person then hung up. Again, I was so upset, I couldn't think straight. What made matters worst is that I couldn't tell who it was because the caller had obviously distorted their real voice. I couldn't believe someone had just threatened me. This had to be the same person who'd sent me that fucking note.

Who in the hell would hate me that much, I thought as I continued to walk.

As I approached the Stock Aide building, it brought back memories of when I was first brought here, all because Jamaal thought I was Thomas' murderer. The butterflies in my stomach seemed to be getting worse. I became nauseous and I felt like I had to throw up. Once I made it up the steps and entered the building, I was kinda happy to see that SFC Roberts was on duty.

"Hey Mathews, I figured I would be seeing you soon," Roberts said smiling, sitting behind his huge desk.

I smiled and leaned across his desk. "Hey, Roberts."

"Now let me guess, you're here because you've lost my number and you came to invite me out on a date, right?"

"Maybe some other time Roberts but for right now, I need to see Cameron."

"Hmmm, I figured as much. Now let me see, what's Cameron's last name again?" he said, looking at his computer.

"Jenkins, PFC Jenkins."

"Awe, here we go," he said laughing.

"What's so funny?"

"I see your man, Jamaal had him put in the same cell you were in."

"Whatever. So can I see him?"

"No can do, Sean."

"Why not?"

"Your name is not on the visitors list," he said, looking at his computer once more. "And it looks like Jamaal left strict orders here in the system that no one sees him other than immediate family, Cameron's attorney and himself."

I was becoming frustrated. "Look Roberts, I need to see Cameron, it's very important."

"I wish I could Sean but I can't."

"Look man, I'm sure I can make it worth your while," I replied, licking my lips and grabbing my crotch.

Roberts looked at me with a serious expression. "You gonna owe me big time, if I let you in!"

"I got you, a'ight," I replied with a sexy smile.

"Okay, stay here. I'll be right back."

When Roberts got up and made his way down the long corridor, I took a seat in one of the steel folding chairs that lined the sides of the wall. As I waited to see Cameron, I called my voicemail just to see who'd called. My answering service said I had one message, **MARKED URGENT**.

Ty's message was, *"Hey Sean, this is Ty man. I just wanted to first of all apologize for what happened last night. I know what I did was kinda foul bruh but what you did to me really turned me the fuck on man and to be honest, it scared me. So I did what I did. Well anyway, I wanna talk to you lata this evening and maybe you can help me understand this shit I'm going through. I figure at some point you must have gone through this yourself and maybe you can help me through it. So, I'll see you lata this evening, a'ight? PEACE."*

I couldn't help but laugh to myself thinking that he had a lot of nerve. I erased his so called urgent message and gave my mom a call to see how she and Lil Man were doing.

"Hello Ma."

"Hey Sean, you okay?"

"Yeah. I was just calling to tell you that Uncle Sam brought Cameron back here to Fort Meade because they now think he was the one that killed Thomas."

"What? You got to be kidding me."

"No, I wish I was."

"Where is he?"

"They have him locked up here at the Stock Aide, that's where I am now."

"So, how is he?"

"I don't know, Ma. I haven't seen him yet."

"That's a damn shame! Uncle Sam doesn't have anything else better to do but waste my tax dollars in locking up innocent people?"

"Yeah well, that's Uncle Sam for you." I looked up and saw Roberts coming down the hall. "Hey Ma, I gotta go, I'll call you lata a'ight?" I hung up as he headed in my direction.

"A'ight Mathews, come with me," he said, gesturing with his hand.

I followed Roberts down the long corridor through another door that led down a flight of stairs. By the time we reached our destination, Roberts turned to me and said, "A'ight Mathews, Cameron is in that room there," he said pointing to a closed door. "Don't take too long and remember you owe me one."

My heart raced a mile a minute as I slowly turned the knob and opened the door. Before me sat Cameron in a metal chair with his head down between the palms of his hands and like the one I was forced to wear, he too had on the Government issued green jumpsuit. I grabbed one of the other metal chairs in the corner and placed it in front of Cameron and took a seat.

"Cam, you a'ight?" I asked waiting for him to look up at me." Cameron didn't respond, he just sat there with his head down and then began to cry. "Cam, look at me," I said, reaching out and holding his chin up. I couldn't believe what I saw as I held his chin up wit my hand. Cameron had two black swollen eyes as though someone had been beating on him. I stood up and grabbed Cameron into my arms as he continued to weep. "Who did this to you?" I asked, raising my voice.

He looked up at me. "Who do you think?"

"I'm so sorry Cam, I really am," I replied, hugging him tightly. "But look, I'm gonna get you outta here, so don't worry, a'ight?"

"And how are you gonna do that, Sean?" he asked, not believing I could.

"I have one of the military lawyers here on base that's gonna take on your case. His name is Lt. Justin Glover. He helped get me outta here and he's gonna help you too," I stated confidently.

Cameron backed away from me. "Sean, you just don't get it do you."

"What are you talking about, get what?"

"I was there Sean. I was there the night Thomas died. Why do you think they found my DNA there?"

"What are you saying? Did you kill Thomas?" I asked dumbfounded.

Cameron turned and walked over to the other side of the room and leaned against the wall. I stood there waiting for him to respond but he didn't. I don't know what got into me but I leaped over to where he stood and grabbed him by his shoulders and yelled, "Did you kill Thomas?"

"No, but I wish I had!" he yelled back as spit flew out of his mouth and onto my face.

"Look, just calm down and tell me what happened?" I said wiping my face.

"Where do you want me to start?" He sat back down.

"Okay, why don't you start by telling me what in the hell you were doing ova at Thomas' house?" I asked curiously while taking my seat across from him.

"Thomas called me that afternoon. I was in Baltimore helping Chauntel wrap up some finishing touches on our wedding. When I answered and realized it was him, I started to hang up until he said that you were in trouble."

"And what kinda trouble was that?"

"He said that he saw you walking out of the NCO Club and that you were drunk. He said that you were so drunk that you'd literally passed out right outside the club and the MP's came and were going to arrest you but they were friends of his and they allowed him to take care of the situation. He said that he'd brought you to his house and that you were sleeping it off in his spare room. But since it was the night before my wedding, he thought he would call me and that I would come and get you, mainly to make sure you made it to my wedding in the morning."

"Sounds like something Thomas would do. Go on."

"So, I came out to Thomas' house thinking you were there and to make a long story short, he tried to pull the same shit when he came to the barracks that morning looking for you."

"You're saying he tried to rape you again?"

"Yes."

"So did he?" I asked cautiously, not wanting to make the situation worse.

"Fuck no, he did that shit once and I wasn't about to let him do it again, ok!" Cameron said, moving his head from side to side.

"So how did they find your DNA at his place?"

"Chile, we started fighting and somehow ended up in his kitchen; he grabbed a knife lying on the counter and started swinging the knife at me. And that's a good thing because I was wearing his ass out. Anyway, I tried to take the knife from him and in the process, the knife scraped against my arm and it started bleeding. It really wasn't that bad of a cut but I wanted to kill him so I looked around and saw a toaster oven sitting on the counter and picked it up and busted him over the head with it."

"Only you Cam," I replied, laughing while trying to imagine my friend picking up a toaster oven to defend himself.

"Humf, don't laugh, that shit worked, knocked his ass out right then and there. He fell to the floor like a ton of bricks," he said, snapping his fingers and moving his head from side to side.

Even though the circumstances weren't good, it was nice sitting there talking to Cameron. It felt like old times because Cameron hadn't changed one bit, the feminine side of him was coming to the surface. It made me smile.

"What you smiling for?" Cameron asked, looking at as though I was crazy for finding anything under these circumstances to smile about.

"Nothing. So what else happened?"

"Like I said, he fell out and I thought maybe I did kill him. So, I kneeled down to check whether or not he was breathing and he was, so I got the Hell outta there!"

"Where's the knife? Did you take the knife with you?"

"No, like I said, I got the hell outta there."

"Hmmm," I said, thinking to myself. "So Jamaal must have the knife that has your blood on it as well as you might have dripped some of your blood on Thomas when you kneeled down to see if he was breathing."

He smiled. "Well, aren't you the one and only Mr. CSI, Poppi."

"Yeah well, first I need to talk to Lieutenant Glover and see what he can do about getting you outta here."

"And what makes you so sure he'll help me?"

"Oh yea of little faith, you're not under estimating me are you?" I said, standing up and pulling Cameron into my arms.

"Hmmm, so you're fucking this Lieutenant Glover?" he questioned, sounding jealous.

I kissed him softly on the lips. "Why, are you jealous?"

"Maybe." He pulled away.

"Don't be," I said, pulling him back and looking into his eyes. "Well sir, let me go, so I can hurry and get you outta here," I said, heading toward the door.

"Hey, Sean!" Cameron called out.

I turned around. "Yeah."

"You know I still love you and more than a brother!"

"You betta," I replied, pointing my finger at him as I took my exit.

Chapter 14

I finally made it to my car and within minutes I was speeding down route 198, heading toward Justin's house. As I drove around in the secluded neighborhood Justin lived in, I knew I was on the right block, but I couldn't remember the exact house number until I saw someone coming out of what looked like Justin's house. I thought my eyes were playing tricks on me so I slowed down and parked my car several doors down the street. I then hunched down in my seat and adjusted my rearview mirror to watch this familiar brotha that came out of Justin's house go into a house just a few doors from where I was parked.

"Unfucking believable, what in the hell would big mouth Jamaal be doing coming out of Justin's house?" I stated out loud to myself.

But after thinking about what Justin told me the first time we met, he said that he lived right down the street from his SIR. Things were beginning to make sense to me as I got out of my car and walked up to Justin's house. I opened the screen door and knocked.

"Good evening, Sean," Justin said, as he opened the door to allow me to enter.

"What's up."

I entered and noticed that everything looked pretty much the same as it did the first time I came to Justin's house. It reminded me of my grandmother's house with little knick knacks and dollies everywhere.

"Please, have a seat," he said, pointing to his couch. "I was delighted that you got around to calling me, but it sounded serious. What's going on with you?" He sat next to me.

"First of all, who was that who just left here?" I asked curiously.

"Oh, so you're stalking me now, huh?" Justin replied jokingly.

"Naw, I had just pulled up and saw this brotha leave your crib. So I was wondering who he was?" I said as a matter of fact. I also didn't want Justin to know that I knew who Jamaal was.

"Well, if you must know, that was SIR. Would you like something to drink?" he asked, getting up to fix himself something to drink.

My mouth almost hit the floor when Justin said that it was his SIR that had just left. Now, I knew Jamaal when I saw him and there was no doubt in my mind that it was him but I needed to know SIR's real name. "Naw man, I'm cool for now but can I ask you a question?"

"Sure," he answered as he came back over and sat on the couch next to me.

"This SIR of yours, what's his name, if you don't mind me asking?"

"His name is Eric, why do you ask."

"What's his last name?"

"What's with all the questions about SIR, Sean?" he asked, becoming defensive.

"Look, I'm just trying to figure sumf'n out. So, what's his last name?

"Watson, his name is Eric Jamaal Watson. Is there anything else you want to know?"

"I knew it, I knew it was him!" I yelled. I then sprung up from Justin's couch as I began to pace around in his living room.

"Sean calm down, take a seat and tell me what you're talking about?" He patted his hand on the couch next to him.

"Don't you get it? That's the Bastard that had me locked up." I took a seat next to Justin as I continued to say, "You were my attorney. Why didn't you tell me he was the one you were having an affair with?"

"Look, Sean, when I first met you, I didn't want my involvement with my personal life to interfere with my work. I never have and never will and even though I knew SIR was the lead investigator for your case, he always signs his name as Eric Watson, not Jamaal Watson. Besides, once I started working your case and realized you couldn't have killed Specialist Thomas, I had to make a decision as to whether or not to let my personal life take precedence or do my job.

Again, I chose to do my job and don't think that didn't cause problems between SIR and I. After all, Specialist Thomas was Eric's cousin." Justin stopped, took a breather and continued to say, "And to be honest, I didn't want it to ruin my chances of getting to know you. That's why I didn't tell you."

I sat there in utter disbelief; this whole situation was getting more and more fucked up by the minute. And knowing what I knew, how could I possibly expect Justin to help me with Cameron's case? "Sean, do you forgive me?" I heard Justin ask.

"Ah look Justin, I need a favor from you," I said, looking as sexy as I could.

"Hmmm, you wanna take me here or shall we go upstairs?" he asked laughing.

"You're so silly," I responded. "Anyway, before you say no, I want you to think about it, a'ight?"

"Sounds serious, what is it?"

"Jamaal, I mean Eric is up to his old tricks again."

"What are you talking about, Sean?"

"Remember my friend, Cameron who got married and left and went overseas to Korea?"

"You mean the wedding you tried to stop?" he asked chuckling.

"Yeah, well anyway, Jamaal I mean Eric had Cameron arrested and had him brought back here to the Stock Aide."

"For what," he asked curiously.

"For killing his cousin Thomas and because he's an asshole."

Justin sat back on the couch and downed his drink then quickly refilled it. "Are you sure you don't want something to drink, Sean?"

By this time I was getting a little thirsty myself and asked for a beer. Justin went to his kitchen and brought a Heineken back.

"Thank you," I replied.

"You're welcome," he said, taking his seat back on the couch. After what seemed to be a pregnant pause as they say, Justin looked at me and asked, "So, what do you want me to do?"

"I want you to take on Cameron's case."

"And why should I do that?" he asked facing me.

"Because Cameron didn't do it!"

"And how can you be so sure?"

"Because I know who did," I said confidently.

"Well, if you know who did it, you don't need me. Why don't you just go to the MP's and have the muthafucka arrested?"

"It's not that simple Justin. Hell, if it was that simple, I would've done that when I realized who did it," I said, finishing off my beer.

"So, who do you think did it?"

"In order to answer that, I have to first tell you about this nightmare I've been having."

"Can't you just skip the commercials, and tell me who you think did it?"

"No, I can't, so can I please tell you about my nightmare?"

"Okay fine, but before you start, can I get another drink?"

"Sure," I said, handing him my now empty bottle.

"Would you like another beer?"

"Yes."

Justin went to retrieve me another Heineken as he refreshed his own drink and came back and sat across from me, handing me my beer.

"Thank you."

"You're welcome. So tell me about your dream, Sean," he said, sitting back on the couch getting comfortable. I began telling Justin about my nightmare and fifteen minutes later after explaining my dream, Justin began laughing at me.

"What's so dayum funny, Justin?" I asked becoming angry.

"Oh come on now, Sean. You can't expect me to take on a case according to some nightmare you had," he said sarcastically and continued to laugh.

"Fuck you Justin, a'ight," I said, getting up to leave.

"You can't be serious?" He tried to stop me from leaving.

"Yes, I'm serious. Do you see me laughing?" I asked staring at him.

"Do you understand what it is you're asking me to do?"

I leaned against the front door. "Yep."

"And what is it that you understand?"

"I'm asking you to get my friend out of prison and put the person who's responsible for Thomas' death behind bars."

"It's more than that, Sean. You're asking me to take on a case based on your dream that wouldn't even be considered circumstantial evidence and to top things off, the person you want me to try to convict is my SIR," he replied raising his voice.

"I thought you said that you wouldn't let your personal life interfere wit your job?"

"That's not fair Sean," he said, walking back over and taking a seat on the couch.

"What's not fair is that muthafucka getting away with murder," I said angrily while taking my seat next to him.

"Sean, I know you want to get your friend out of the Stock Aide but why would Eric wanna kill his own cousin? That doesn't make sense."

"I don't know, why do children sometimes kill their parents and why do parents sometimes kill their children?" After thinking about Jamaal's possible reason, it dawned on me that he might have done it to get back at Thomas. "Have you ever considered that maybe Jamaal killed his own cousin to get back at him?"

"Get back at him for what?"

"Love or maybe hate."

"What are you talking about?"

"Look, in my dream, Thomas was fucking Jamaal. So maybe when they were young, Thomas might have raped Jamaal and now Jamaal is the way he is and blamed Thomas as a result of it," I said, trying to make sense of Jamaal's actions.

"Alright, that's it. You have lost your fucking mind; get out of my house Sean!"

"Look Justin, I know this might sound a little crazy, but Jamaal ain't wrapped too tight anyway."

"I said get out of my house Sean, or would you like me to call the police and they can escort you out?" he said angrily, while standing at his front door wit his arms folded.

"A'ight man, but at least think about it?"

Justin opened his front door and I walked out into the cold night air feeling that I had let Cameron down. Maybe Justin was right. Why would he want to try a case that could possibly put his Lover or his SIR behind bars forever? I got in my car and while driving back to the barracks, I came to terms with possibly having to have a truce with Jamaal. Whatever it took, I was willing to do in order to get Cameron out of Uncle Sam's prison.

Chapter 15

The next morning, I wasn't looking forward to this day considering that the highlight only would have been me getting a chance to see Cameron over at the Stock Aide after work. As I pulled up to my job, I sat listening to one of Cameron's favorite songs, *Lady Marmalade*. Boy, I really did need to get a grip. I turned off my car and headed up toward my office building.

I walked the long corridor to my office and before entering I heard someone say, "Good morning, Private Mathews." I turned and standing behind me was Cat, the Caucasian, red haired bombshell that I had forgotten all about.

I smiled. "Well, good morning to you too, Specialist Dobbs."

"Where have you been hiding yourself?" she asked. It seemed as if she was flirting with me.

"And what makes you think I've been hiding?" I replied, flirting back.

"You've been hiding because I haven't seen you in a while and you hadn't called me."

"Yeah, well, I've been kinda out of it. I don't know if you knew but I lost my wife a month or so ago."

"Oh no, I'm so sorry to hear that."

"Thank you. I appreciate that."

"Well, look, here's my number again, so when you're ready to have company or if you're in the need to just talk, give me a call," she said, handing me her card.

"Thank you Cat, I'll do that." I took her card and put it in my pocket.

Cat's flirtation brought a smile to my face as I entered my office. But it quickly disappeared when I saw all the work on my desk that needed to be processed. Like I'd done every morning before getting started, I picked up the phone to call my mother and check on Lil Man.

"Hey Ma, how you doing?"

"I'm fine, Sean. I'm glad you called. I was worried all last night to find out how Cameron was doing?"

I explained to my mother about what happened when I went to see Cameron and how hard I was trying to get him out. I also spoke to Lil Man. God, I didn't realize how much I missed him. Before hanging up, I told my mom that I might have to stay on base that weekend because I needed to work on Cameron's case.

"Kiss Lil Man for me, a'ight."

"Okay. Call me later if you get a chance."

"Will do Ma." I didn't want to worry my mother about the phone call I'd received the day before, so I just hung up.

I began my work day and there were sixty new recruits that had come in last night and they all needed to be slotted in positions. That's the only thing I don't like about my job. The military will sometimes hold off and process many recruits at one time which made it harder for me to do my job in a timely manner. There was one in particular that caught my eye and that was Cameron's. He'd received permanent orders to be slotted in the Stock Aide. I sat there staring at his orders for more than thirty minutes and I just couldn't do it. I placed Cameron's orders in my bottom drawer, hoping that I could get him out before having to process it.

At lunchtime I ran into Jamaal over at the mess hall. I actually was glad to run into him because I wanted to talk to him about Cameron's case and hoped he would try to work out a deal. I also wanted to find out if Jamaal would slip up and say something about the card I received or that crank phone call. Jamaal sat over in the corner at a table by himself. I gathered up my tray and headed in his direction.

"Do you mind?" I asked, standing over top of him.

"Well, if it isn't Private Mathews. Sure, why not," he replied, gesturing with his hand.

"I guess you didn't expect to see me, huh?" I asked taking a seat across from him.

"Actually, I knew it would only be a matter of time, Sean," he said with a smirk on his face.

"Hmmm, anyway, I wanted to talk to you about Cameron's case."

"I thought you might. What about it?"

"I thought maybe we could work out a deal or something."

"Are you trying to bribe me Private Mathews?"

"Naw, I ain't tryna do nothing but help my friend."

"You mean your lover, don't you?"

"Anyway, what do you want Jamaal?" I asked, becoming annoyed.

"What are you willing to give Sean?"

"It's whatever. You have the upper hand, so you tell me?" I replied in defeat.

Jamaal pulled out a piece of paper and wrote something on it and handed it to me, "Be at this address tomorrow night at 9:00 p.m. sharp!"

"Tomorrow is Friday Jamaal; you know I go home on the weekends."

"I guess you need to change your plans for the weekend then, huh?" he smirked, while leaving me sitting there alone.

For the rest of the afternoon, I sat at work, thinking about what Jamaal had planned for me tomorrow. I wasn't afraid, if anything I was more curious than afraid. I wondered what he could possibly have up his sleeve. I opened my cell phone to give Justin a call, if anybody would know, I'm sure he would. Unfortunately, he didn't answer and my call went directly to his voicemail, so I left him an urgent message to give me a call back as soon as he could. As soon as I hung up the phone, my cell rung. I looked at the caller ID and saw that it was Ty.

"What's up negro?"

"E'rythang is e'rythang."

"I see someone has been listening to too much Michael Baisden," I said, laughing through the phone.

"Yeah well, don't act like you don't. But anyway, I wanted to know what you were doing lata?"

"I have to make a stop once I get off from work and I don't know how long that will take, why?" I looked at my computer and began to map quest the address Jamaal gave me.

"I thought we could spend some time alone and I could talk to you about what I've been going through."

"Okay cool. Like I said, I don't know what time I'll get there, but it should be before eight o'clock, a'ight?"

"A'ight. I'll check you out then. Peace"

Fortunately I made it through the day without any mishaps. I remembered to grab the directions lying on my desk of the address Jamaal gave me and placed it in my back pocket of my fatigues. I hopped in my car and drove over to the Stock Aide hoping that I would be able to see Cameron. If Roberts wasn't there, I knew my chances of seeing Cameron was slim to none. I parked my car right in front of the building and made my way inside. Much to my dismay, Roberts wasn't on duty. Sitting in Roberts's seat was a white dude who I didn't know, so I took a deep breath and walked up and asked, "Ah, I'm here to see PFC Cameron Jenkins."

"And you are?" he asked, while checking to see if my name was on Cameron's visitor's list.

"I'm PFC Sean Mathews but my name…" before I could finish, he interrupted.

"Yes, here we go," he said, handing me a visitor's pass and giving me directions to Cameron's location.

Since I was never one to look a gift horse in the mouth, I took the pass and proceeded to locate my friend. Seconds later, I came upon Cameron's cell and he was lying on the old beat up cot, reading a *For Sisters Only Magazine*. He looked up as I stood starring at him through the bars. He began to smile ear to ear as he got up and walked over to the bars to greet me.

"Kinda different than it was yesterday, huh?" he said, gesturing at the bars that now separated us.

"Its cool, you seem to be in a better mood." I tried to force a smile.

"Well, I guess I have you to thank for that."

"Oh yeah, what did I do?"

"I don't know, but child what I do know is that Jamaal came by here a couple of hours ago to let me know that my case was being reviewed and there was some new evidence found that may exonerate me. Shit, I might be getting out soon," Cameron squealed, while jumping up and down, like some teenage girl.

"That's great news, Cam. Did he say what kinda evidence?"

"I didn't ask him all that. All I heard was exonerate and getting out soon. And I have you to thank for that."

"Well Cam, as much as I would like to take the credit for that, I have to be honest and let you know, I had nothing to do with that. But I'm happy for you nonetheless."

I didn't want Cameron to know I had anything to do wit whatever Jamaal was up to just in case it didn't go through. Besides, I didn't know whether or not I could trust Jamaal, especially not knowing what he had planned for me the following night. And if it didn't go through, I couldn't take the responsibility and the hurt Cameron would go through.

But I do give Jamaal credit, that muthafucka always seems to stay one foot ahead of me.

"Sean, hello. Are you even listening to me?" he asked, snapping his fingers.

"Ah, I'm sorry Cam. What did you say?"

"I asked if you were getting any rest cause you looking kinda shabby, Poppi!"

"Listen at you. You got the nerve to talk wit two black eyes," I said laughing.

"Ain't shit that a lil' cover girl can't cover, okay! My girl Tina Turner proved that."

"You know Cam, you'll never change and I appreciate that about you," I said as seriously as I could.

"Oh damn Poppi. You getting me all moist and everything, you better stop sweet talking me like that before I do sumf'n you might regret," he said, talking like Ms. Chi Chi while trying to grab my dick.

"Yo, Cam, cut dat shit out. Trust me, once you're out, you'll definitely get your chance." I pushed his hand away. "By the way, I meant to ask you, have you talked you Chauntel? Has she been here to see you?"

"Yeah, she came out here to visit me this morning and brought Junior. He has grown so much, have you seen him?" Cameron inquired, switching from a Ms. Chi to sounding like a proud father.

"Naw, I hadn't, but look man, I gotta run, I'll stop by over the weekend to check on you. You need me to bring you anything?"

"Nothing you don't already have on you," he responded with a wink.

Chapter 16

After parking my car in my barracks parking lot and heading towards my room, I knew Ty was in the room, not because of a sock being on the door handle but because he had his music blasting. I opened the door and just as I met Ty like the first time, he was working up a sweat with his Crunking routine. Being in a fairly jovial mood, I decided to join in while Lil Wayne's voice blast through Ty's Bose Surround Sound System.

"Go Sean, go Sean, it's yo birthday," Ty sang, urging me on.

I jerked and gyrated for at least fifteen minutes showing Ty that I too could make my body do what it do. Ty soon joined in, showing me some new moves he had just learned himself. At one point, I had worked up such a sweat that I had stripped down to my wife beater and Calvin Klein boxers.

Another hour or so passed and not only had we worked up a sweat, we also worked up a serious appetite. "Yo Ty, I'm through bruh," I said, wiping sweat from my body and passing out on my bed.

"Shit, you can't hang, huh?" Ty boasted as he continued to jerk, gyrate and grind his body in front of me.

"Awe man, it ain't like I can't hang. There's just not enough room in here for me to do what I do. I need room, niggah."

"Ah, that sounds like a challenge," he said, turning off his sound system.

I wasn't gonna back down. "Anytime, any place."

"A'ight. How about tomorrow night? There's a club called The Paradox in Baltimore, we can go there and show out."

"You ain't said nothing but a word niggah, then again, I can do betta than that. How about tonight? There's a club in DC called The Mill, they party there on Thursday nights. We can go there, that is if you ain't scared and got some game."

I challenged Ty because I had plans to meet with Jamaal the following night and besides, I was just curious as to whether he'd heard anything about The Mil or not

"Sounds like a plan. I'm in the mood to work it out anyway," Ty replied jumping off his bed.

"Cool. Well, I don't know about you but I'm hungry as shit. Let's go get some grub," I said getting off my bed and looking for some sweats to put on.

"I feel ya. Where you wanna go?" he inquired.

"Wherever, my treat, now hurry up." I put on my Puma jacket that matched my pants and headed out the door.

"I'm right behind you."

✉✉✉

After finishing our dinner, we made our way back to our room about two hours later. On the drive back, Ty became quiet as though something was bothering him.

"You cool?" I asked.

"Yeah, I'm cool. But I do have a lot of questions to ask you."

"Shoot," I replied, before pulling back into the barracks parking lot.

"It can wait 'til we get in the room," he said, exiting the car.

When we entered our room a few minutes later, the first thing I did was fall onto my bed. I was so stuffed that I couldn't see straight. Ty began taking off his clothes and sat along side of his bed.

"Sean, tell me sumf'n. You were married and have children, why are you gay?"

Ty kinda caught me off guard with his question. I thought this was supposed to be about him, not me. But the only thing I could think of to say was, "Look Ty, there are a lot of forms of being gay."

"What do you mean, different forms of being gay?" he questioned with a confused look on his face.

"Being gay is not what it traditionally used to mean. I mean back in the day, being gay meant that you were a top, bottom or versatile, which meant that as a top, you were considered the masculine

brotha who like to fuck dudes in the ass. Being a bottom brotha traditionally used to mean that you enjoyed getting fucked in the ass and
was somewhat feminine. Being a versatile brotha meant sometimes
you felt like a nut, sometimes you didn't. In other words, either you
felt like doing the fuckin' or either you felt like being fucked."

"Where do you fall into that equation?"

"I don't," I said as a matter of fact.

"So, you're sayin you're not gay?"

"Naw, I ain't sayin that. I am gay but I don't fall into the tradi-
tional meaning of being gay. Are you gay?" I asked, being curious as
to his response.

"Hell naw," he said becoming offended.

"And why not, you like getting fucked," I retorted challenging
him.

"Because I like being with women."

"So, I'm gay and I like being with women as well."

Ty became quiet as though he was trying to think of an answer
to come back with. I knew it was difficult for him feeling this way
about his own sexuality, hell, I've been there and done that. And if it
wasn't for Thomas and Cameron, I don't know where I would be.

"What kinda gay brotha are you?" Ty asked looking for an-
swers. I guess he was hoping to be able to define himself.

"I'm a gay brotha because ultimately I enjoy having sex with
other men as well as I have better relationships with men more so
than with women. But don't get it twisted, I enjoy having sex with the
ladies as well. I don't consider myself as a DL brotha because first
and foremost I'mma man but I don't hide what I like."

"What do you mean?"

"What I mean is, I don't go around sashaying or nothing but
I'm not on the DL either because if I'm interested in being with a
honey, I'm upfront. I tell her what I'm about and by doing that; I've
given her a choice."

"Okay, I feel ya. But that don't get you very far telling them
upfront like that, does it?"

I smiled. "I haven't been denied yet. As a matter of fact,
there's this fine Caucasian honey, right here on base that's dying for
me to fuck her and I told her the first time we met practically."

"Oh, I know you're not talking bout that fine bitch Specialist
Dobbs, are you?" he asked with a hint of jealousy.

"That's the one."

Ty rubbed his dick. "Ah man, what I wouldn't give to tap dat."

"Anyway, I'm more of a bi-sexual brotha. But I'm not into getting fucked, that's just not my thing. But you obviously seem to enjoy it, so what's up wit that?"

"Man it's hard to put into words. I guess it all started when I was at Juevy. I practically lived at the gym and the pain I put my body through actually turned me on. So even though I enjoy having sex with bitches the regular way, I get off better after fucking them, they turn around and fuck me back."

"You sound like a versatile brotha, so why does it have to be with a shawtie? Why can't it be with another versatile brotha?"

"Because I like the feel of a shawties body, I like eating pussy and I love tits. I love feeling them, sucking them and having them banging against my back while they're fuckin'' me."

"You're such a freak," I said, laughing to myself. "So what about being fucked, don't that shit hurt?"

"Yeah it does, but that's what uhm sayin, my body enjoys the pain of them penetrating me, ya know, pulling it in and out? Kinda like the pain and pleasure thing going on."

I couldn't help but think how much Thomas would have loved fuckin' Ty as well as being fucked by Ty in return. "So, would you now consider yourself as being gay?" I was curious.

"Yo, man, I don't know about all that because you said that ultimately being gay meant having sex with another man and under those terms, I've never had sex with another man."

"But some would say, by you enjoying being penetrated, regardless as to whom is doing it, would still consider you as being gay." Ty didn't respond to that comment but looked like he was giving it some thought. I guess I was giving him some things to think about. "So, do you think you would someday enjoy having sex with another dude?"

Ty looked confused and disappointed. "I don't know."

"We're still hanging out tonight, right?" I inquired looking at my watch.

"Hell yeah, you ain't getting out of this ass whipping that easily," he said springing out of bed to prepare for our outing.

I was glad The Mill was a good thirty or so minutes away down on BWI Parkway, which gave me a chance to school Ty as to what kinda club we were going to. I didn't think it would be a problem but I think people should always be forewarned.

"So, Ty, have you ever been to a gay club before?"

"Ah man, is that where we're going?" Ty asked, slouching down in the passenger side seat.

"Is that a problem?"

"Naw, I guess not. As long as them muthafuckas don't put der hands on me and I can get my groove on."

"Yeah, I feel you," I said, thinking about the first time Cameron brought me to this same club. "But because I like people to be forewarned I said, "You can definitely get your groove on but just so you know, if you're in a gay club, most of the gay brothas gonna assume you're gay and therefore, will try to push up on you, on and off the dance floor."

"I wish a muthafucka would try something," Ty said with major attitude.

"Look Ty, you're a good looking, dark-skin, buffed shawty and with a nice phat little ass, I might add, whom they've never seen before and hell yeah, they gonna push up on you. Just look at it this way, if you were gay, would you push up on you?"

"Fuck you Sean."

"Don't get mad at me because yo momma gave you an ass that's begging to be fucked!" I said laughing.

"See, that's what I don't understand, if top brothas like you, like fucking brothas in the ass, why not fuck a female in the ass instead? There are a lot of honeys out here that like that shit."

"Yeah, I know. But it ain't the same."

"What do you mean, not the same?" Ty questioned. He sat up in his seat.

"Logically, I thought the same. An ass is an ass, right?"

"Yeah."

"Wrong bruh. A dude's ass is totally different."

"Ah, come again?"

"It's different. I've since fucked a few honies in the ass but man; it was like fuckin' two pillars, fo real." Ty began laughing as I continued to say, "But fuckin' a dude with a nice ass is different because we as men have a prostate gland that women don't have and when touched, teased and agitated, it begins to sweat with secretion and therefore causes the ass to become wet and juicy.

"Oh wow, so that's why my ass be getting wet and shit when them bitches be fuckin' me, huh?" he asked, connecting the realization to what I've explained. "Oh shit, that's wild. I thought it was just me."

"Naw man, it's not just you. Why you think there're so many gay people out here."

"Cause that shit feels good."

"That's what they tell me," I said, pulling up to the club and looking for a parking spot.

Chapter 17

After ten minutes or so, we finally made our way into the club. I'd remembered the dude at the door looking at ID's and I knew you had to be at least twenty-one to get in and I knew Ty was only nineteen, so I paid the brotha an extra twenty to let Ty in. He didn't have a problem since both Ty and I were in the military. Most people always felt that if you could go in the military and sacrifice your life for our country, why couldn't you buy a pack of cigarettes, buy alcohol and go to a club?

I escorted Ty around the club so that he could see how the club was set up and if he wanted to venture out on his own, he would know where the bar was and where the rest rooms were located. We hadn't been in the club no more than a hot ten minutes and while at the bar putting our order in, comes this brotha up in my face, asking me my name.

"What's your name, sexy?" the brotha asked.

"His name is not important, besides he's with me," Ty said, coming to my defense.

"Whoa, my bad, I didn't know he was with you," the brotha responded with his hands in the air.

"How could you not know he wasn't with me, we been standing here for the last few minutes talking and waiting for our order, muthafucka!"

"Ty, chill bruh." People started to hear Ty and look in our direction so I needed to squash this before it got out of hand. "Yo man, you have to forgive my boy here. This is his first time in a gay club. Lemme buy you a drink and forget this ever happened, how's that?"

"Oh a'ight," he said, looking Ty up and down. "Its cool man but you need to keep your little pit bull locked up at home or on a fuckin'' leash," the dude said, as he trailed off into the crowd.

Personally, I found what he said to be funny, but Ty didn't. He started to go after the dude, until I pulled him back and walked him over on the other side of the club.

"Ty, what's yo' fuckin' problem?"

"How that niggah gonna walk up on you like that and I'm standing here? He don't know who I am, fuck that muthafucka. For all he knew, I coulda been yo niggah and he just totally disrespected me by approaching you, in front of me."

"A'ight man, I hear you but you can't be flying off like that. I don't know any of these brothas in here and I am not getting my ass whooped by a bunch of homosexuals because you felt disrespected. Let's go with the flow, have a couple more drinks, dance and have a good time, a'ight?"

"Cool. My bad."

For the next hour or so, Ty and I danced our asses off and had a ball, especially during our CRUNK dance off. Now, I'll admit Ty did beat me and the crowd agreed but in my defense, Ty had been crunking a lot longer then I had. After awhile, I just passed the dance floor over to Ty and stood back along with the crowd and watched him show off. I knew he was having a good time as the DJ put the spotlight on him and blasted the old school favorite, *Yeah*, by Usher. Ty jerked, shaked, twitched, and gyrated his entire body as the crowd cheered him on. There were a few brothas who tried to take Ty on, but to no avail.

Ty had everybody screaming and cheering him on as he sat down everybody who challenged him. Truth be told, the brothas only tried to challenge Ty just so they could get a quick feel here and there. The first brotha that tried bumping against Ty's ass bothered me, but Ty just looked at me, winked, smiled and continued dancing. I was so proud of the fact that, he'd went wit the flow.

When it was time to leave, I had to damn near drag Ty off the dance floor. As we made our way outside, I noticed that people were standing around mingling and trying to get those last minute phone numbers.

"What's your name?" this brotha asked as he approached us. Ty and I looked at each other because we weren't sure who he was talking to. He then stood directly in front of Ty. "You shawty, what's your name?"

"People call me D, why, what's up?" Ty replied checking the

brotha out from head to toe.

"Nice to meet you D, I'm Mike," he replied, extending his hand.

"This here is my niggah, James," Ty said, referring to me as he shook the guy's hand.

"Oh my bad. I didn't know." Mike sounded disappointed while looking in my direction.

I displayed a devious smirk. "Not a problem."

"Well, I just wanted to come over and let you know that I was checking you out on the dance floor and compliment you on your skills," Mike said to Ty.

Ty couldn't help but smile. "Thanks bruh."

"A'ight, you brothas have a good night," Mike said as he headed up the street.

"You, too," both Ty and I said in unison.

As we stood there checking everything out, Ty had obviously made a few fans because practically everybody who walked by complimented Ty on his dancing. Some had stopped to ask Ty for his name and number. And just like the first guy, Ty didn't give out his real name or real number. I looked at my watch and saw that it was almost three o'clock in the morning so Ty and I headed back to my car and began our destination back to the base.

⌘

On the drive back, I was curious to know what Ty thought about the club so I started the conversation. "So Ty, what did you think of the club?"

"It was cool yo, when can we go back?"

"Well, check you out. I guess you wanna keep your fan club happy, huh?"

"Awe niggah, it ain't even like that. I had a good time, so why not?"

"Yo, man, I saw a lot of them brothas cruising yo ass, too. I saw a few of them touching and freaking on you too, while you were dancing and you didn't stop them either."

"You told me to go with the flow, right?"

"Yeah, and I'm proud of you man. I know my first time there, I was paranoid as hell."

"By the way, how did you find out about this club, who brought you?"

"My friend, Cameron."

"Is that the brotha you kickin it with?"

"Naw, although I used to."

"Where is he, why aren't you kickin it with him now?"

"You are asking a lot of questions. But if you must know, he's in the Stock Aide."

"Fo real? What happened?"

As we continued our ride down 295N, I told Ty all about Thomas and Cameron and how I first met them. I also told him about how I fell in love with Cameron and how I tried to stop his wedding. Ty thought it was funny and started laughing as though I just told him a joke. Of course, I didn't find it funny at all. I told Ty about how I found Thomas dead in his bedroom and how his cousin Jamaal had me falsely locked up. And because I had an alibi, I was released but now Jamaal has evidence against Cameron that linked him to Thomas' murder. So as a result, Jamaal had Cameron brought back all the way from Korea and locked up.

"You sound like you're still in love with Cameron?"

"Yeah, I am."

"Wow man, that's deep. So, what are you gonna do? Is Cameron still married?"

"I'm talking with one of the lawyers on base to try to help Cameron out because he didn't do it and to answer your last question, yes, Cameron is still married."

I knew Justin wasn't going to help me, but I didn't want Ty to know that I was willing to do whatever I had to do to get Cameron out, even if it meant having to deal wit Jamaal. My mom always said, "Don't let your right hand know what your left hand is doing."

"Can I ask you a question?" Ty asked.

"Shoot."

"How can you be so sure that your friend didn't do it?"

"Because I do, now can we drop it?" I replied, becoming annoyed.

"Damn Sean, my bad. That niggah must of seriously put it on you, huh?"

"Whatever," was all I could say as we pulled into the barracks parking lot.

Ty and I both took quick showers, as soon as we got back and crashed out in our beds. Just as I was about to doze off, Ty spoke up.

"Yo Sean, you sleep?"

"I was about to, why?"

"Can I ask you a question?"

"You know what Ty, instead of you asking if you can ask a question, you should just ask the dayum question!"

Ty seemed to hesitate before asking his question as though he had to think of a way to phrase it.

"Have you ever, you know, given a brotha a blow job?"

"Are you just being curious or is dat an invitation?"

"Just being curious yo, dats all."

"Yeah, I have. Is there anything else you wanna know?"

"Yeah, but I'll ask you some other time," he said, laughing and turning over to go to sleep.

Chapter 18

Fridays were days we wore our Dress Greens and had Inspection. Our Inspection consisted of Captain Randall walking through formation, looking at each one of us to make sure our uniform was sharp, our hair was cut according to military guidelines and our belt buckle and shoes were spit shined. Captain Randall stopped in front of me and said,

"Good morning, Specialist Mathews, how are you doing today?"

"I'm fine Sir, but I'm Private First Class Mathews, Sir," I said, standing at attention and starring him eye to eye.

"Are you saying I'm wrong Specialist Mathews?"

"No Sir, but as you can see by my insignia I'm a Private First Class, Sir."

"Well, then Specialist Mathews, you're out of uniform, aren't you," he said, pulling out a pair of Specialist insignias. The guys in my battalion started laughing and applauding as it dawned on me that I was being promoted, right then and there.

"Thank you Sir," is all I could say while accepting my new Specialist Insignias.

But as happy as I was, I couldn't help but think if Jamaal had something to do with my promotion. Things seemed to having been going a little too well lately and I could only imagine how this day would end after my meeting with Jamaal.

No sooner than I had entered my office building a few minutes later , I heard a familiar voice say, "Congrats, Specialist Mathews."

I turned around. "Well, thank you, Specialist Dobbs."

"I guess I can't tell you what to do anymore since we're the same rank, huh?" Cat said flirting.

"That depends," I replied flirting back.

"On what? Wait don't answer that. Besides, you never called me so you never took any orders from me to begin with."

"Hold on, that's not fair. Besides, I take orders in person betta than on the phone, so what's up wit you, ah, tomorrow night?" I stated, knowing that my Saturday evening would be free.

"Oh, so now you wanna take me out?"

I smiled. "Something like that." .

"Well," she said thinking for a moment. "Unfortunately, I'll be out of town this weekend but I'll be happy to give you a rain check for next Saturday."

"Oh, going back home to visit family?" I inquired as I opened the door to my office.

"You could say that. Well look, I got a lot of work to do today, how about we have lunch today and talk?" she asked, standing in my doorway.

I sat a few things on my desk. "Cool, what time?"

"I'll call you, how's that?"

"You do that, Ms. Lady." I leaned back in my chair and looked up at her with pure lust in my eyes. Cat just smiled and exited my office while closing my door behind her.

As I began my day, I couldn't help but think about my new promotion and not being called a Private anymore. Anyone having been in the military would definitely understand what that feels like. Being excited about my new rank, I was going to take all of my uniforms to the cleaners so they could change my insignias to my new rank at lunch time but I guess I'll have to do it tomorrow morning since I have this date with Cat.

My desk phone rang, interrupting my thoughts. "Good morning, Specialist Mathews speaking, how can I help you?" I answered with pride.

"Specialist Mathews?" my mom questioned.

"Hey Ma, you must have ESP, I was just about to call you."

"What's with this Specialist stuff?"

"Yeah, that's why I was gonna call you. I got promoted this morning."

"That's wonderful, Sean. I'm so happy for you. So that means more money right?"

"I should hope so."

"Well good. I just called to say good morning and let you know that I am so proud of you."

"Thanks Ma, I love you too."

I was unsure as to whether my mom would feel that way if she knew what I was trying to do to get Cameron out of the Stock Aide.

"I didn't say anything about love," she said, laughing into the phone.

"Anyway, how's my son doin?"

"I'm just joking with you baby, you know I love you. Your son is right here driving me crazy. You wanna speak to him?"

"Yeah, put him on the phone." After waiting for a few seconds and my mother fussing at Lil Man in the background, I finally heard my son say, "Hi Daddy."

"Hey Lil Man, how you doin?"

"Fine," he said sounding so grown up. "Daddy you coming home?"

"I'll be home next weekend. I can't wait to see you, you know I miss you."

"I miss you too, Daddy," he said sounding kinda sad.

"Hey, next weekend, we'll go somewhere special, okay?"

He screamed into the phone. "Yeeeeeeaaaaaah."

"A'ight son, put Granny on the phone and I'll talk to you later. I love you."

"Love you too, Daddy," he replied while handing the phone back to my mother.

"Yeah, Sean, I'm here."

"Okay, Ma, but before I go, how has Lil Man been? I mean after what he did at Venus' viewing, is he having nightmares or acting strange?"

"No, he seems to be fine."

"Hmmm okay, well keep an eye on him and let me know if he does start acting differently."

"Yeah, I will, don't worry, he's in good hands."

"Yeah, I know. Well, I'll talk to you later. Love you."

"Love you too, baby."

After hanging up with my mom, I turned on my computer and navigated to the army.gov website to see exactly how much more money I would be making as an E-4 Specialist. Much to my surprise and after calculations wit being an E-3 PFC married wit a family vs. now being a single/widower my pay really hadn't changed that much. Those that were in the military and being married were paid more, kinda like getting a stipend but being single, I will no longer get that stipend. So in a sense, I kinda broke even.

Ain't that a bitch, I thought to myself.

I sat at my desk for the next few hours trying to straighten out several data entries that someone had put into the system incorrectly. And just when I figured out what the problem was, our computer system had gone down. Therefore, I shut my computer system down and called Cat to see if she was ready for lunch, but I didn't get an answer.

Just as I was about to get in my car, my cell began buzzing letting me know I had a text message. I started up my car and then pulled out my cell to retrieve the message. The message was from a private number that read:

It's just a matter of time faggot!

"Fuck you, muthafucka!" I said out loud while looking down at my phone.

Whoever was doing this was seriously starting to worry me. What made it worst was the fact that I couldn't report it to anyone, especially not Uncle Sam considering my Commander already thought I was gay. I wasn't ready to be put out of the military with a dishonorable discharge.

I have put up with too much shit to go out like that, I thought to myself.

While no longer having an appetite, I decided to go back to my room and take a quick nap.

Chapter 19

After my nap, I headed back to my office but I noticed that most of the cars that were parked in the parking lot earlier where gone. I didn't know what was going on until I got to my office and was informed by one of the MP's on duty that the offices had closed for the rest of the day because the I.T. Specialist couldn't get the computers up and running again so they gave us all four hours of Administrative Leave, which was music to my ears because that meant I could stop by and see Cam real quick.

I got back in my car and pulled out my cell to give Justin a call because I knew that he too would be on his way home like everyone else. Once again, he chose not to answer, so the call went to his voicemail.

"Hey Justin, this is Sean, gimme a call once you get this message, a'ight!"

I knew Justin still must have been mad with me and that's probably why he wasn't taking my calls. I thought about driving over to his house to confront him but I really didn't want to make matters worse, so I decided not to. I pulled up in front of the Stock Aide and parked.

As I entered, I noticed SFC Roberts at his desk, "Roberts, how you doing, bruh," I asked approaching him.

"Hey Mathews, you hear your boy Cameron will be getting out."

"I knew he was getting out, but I didn't know exactly what day."

"Well, I don't know what you did to pull that off but I'm glad we're friends," Roberts replied smiling and winking at me.

"Yeah well, I don't know if I can take credit for that. Anyway, can I see Cameron?"

"Hold on for a second."

I took my seat over in the steel chair along side the wall as Roberts went to inform Cameron I was there to visit him. As I sat there, I looked around and noticed how dreary this place really was.

"Hey Mathews, Cameron just got finish eating his lunch and is expecting you. So you can go on through," he replied giving me a visitor's pass.

"Thanks, Roberts," I responded, getting up from my seat and making my way down the long corridor.

"Hey Mathews, I couldn't get a private room like I did the last time."

I walked by Roberts. "That's cool thanks anyway."

"Mathews, don't forget, you still owe me one," Roberts whispered in my ear as I walked by him.

"I won't."

I made my way down the stairway and couldn't help thinking how much this place looked like a dungeon. I approached Cameron's cell and he was standing there butt ass naked and smiling from ear to ear.

"What are you doing, Cam?" I asked, while looking around.

"I wanted to thank you, Poppi for all you've done for me," Cameron said turning around showing me his body.

"And how can you possibly thank me? You're inside that cell and I'm standing out here." I was becoming aroused.

Cameron still had it going on, the swelling in his eyes were going down and his 5'5 hundred pound smooth shapely frame was begging to be touched, but taking into consideration of where we were, all I could say is, "Put your jumpsuit on Cam, we'll have plenty of time for that," I said licking my lips.

"Oh, you're no fun, Sean," Cameron said, sounding disappointed while putting his jumpsuit on. "You know I'm getting outta here Monday morning, just as soon as the adjutant general comes in."

"Yeah, I heard. So is Chauntel coming to pick you up or what?"

"Her ass betta be here. Hell she so happy, she might be camping out here on Sunday night."

"That's good, Cam," I said, looking into his eyes.

"What's wrong Sean?"

"Nothing. Why you ask that?"

"I know that look, Poppi, this is me, remember?"

"I know who you are," I said laughing and trying to play everything off. "Oh by the way, check it out," I said showing Cameron my new rank.

"Oh my God. You got promoted!" Cameron screamed. He started jumping up and down.

"Niggah, chill with all that noise."

Deep down, I knew Cameron would be happy for me and to be honest, I appreciated him showing so much enthusiasm. So often we want to jump up and down or shout for joy about something but we don't. Cameron is one of those individuals that do and don't care who knows or sees him.

"You betta work, Ms. Thang," Cameron said, snapping his fingers.

I grabbed my crotch. "Yeah, well I got your Ms. Thang right here."

"And I know this, trust and believe...okay!" He replied licking his tongue around his lips.

"You so silly, but look, did Jamaal say how he was getting you out? Were they gonna drop the charges or what?"

"Yeah, I talked wit him this morning and he said that they were gonna let me out on my own recognizance, and that I couldn't leave the state because ultimately, I'm still considered a suspect. Me a suspect, puh-lease," Cameron replied with his hands on his hips.

"But what about this DNA evidence he had?"

"He said something about it got mixed up with some of the other stuff they had and was now tainted. Why you asked about that Sean, you're not happy that I'm getting out?"

"Of course I am. I can't wait to hold you in my arms again man, for real," I said smiling and leaning up against his cell, showing my dimples.

"You know Sean, you are so fuckin" sexy, yo ass betta be lucky I'm in here and you're out there," Cameron replied while trying to grab for my dick.

"Anyway," I said backing away. "The computer systems went down this morning so Uncle Sam let us off with four hours of admin. So, I'm going back to the room and take a long over due nap. But, I'll be back tomorrow afternoon, a'ight?"

"Alright Poppi, I'll be here. By the way, don't make no plans for next weekend because we gonna party, alright?"

"Yeah a'ight," I said, walking away thinking how I was going to be in three places at one time.

I'd already promised Lil Man that we would hang out for the whole weekend and then I promised Cat we would definitely do something next Saturday and now Cameron. Needless to say, Lil Man would take precedence. He needed me more now than ever and I couldn't expect my mom to raise my son for me. As I headed to my car I thought, *may be I can just go home tomorrow morning for a surprise visit and spend time wit lil man this weekend.*

I made it back to my room and fortunately, Ty wasn't there. He worked in the same office but his job did not require him to use computers, he was just a file clerk and therefore I guess Uncle Sam thought there was no need for him to be off. I stripped down, wrapped a towel around my waist and took a quick shower.

After my shower, I went back to my room and found that Ty had come in and began playing his rap crap. "Hey Sean, how's it going, bruh?"

"It was going well until I noticed you here," I said falling out on my bed.

"Damn Yo, what did I do?"

"Nothing man. I'm sorry. I just thought I could get some peace and quiet that's all," I said yawning into my pillow.

"My bad. But hey, you don't have to worry about me because it's the weekend and I'mma be out in a few."

Ty turned the music off and headed for the shower.

"A'ight cool."

I laid there in my bed and the next thing I knew, I was knocked out.

When I finally awoke, the room was dark. I grabbed my cell off of my nightstand and noticed that it was 6:45 p.m. I hadn't even heard Ty when he came back into the room and left out. I must have been really tired, two naps in one day! I laid there for a few because my dick was hard as a muthafucka, so I began playing with myself but then I realized I might as well keep what I had for Jamaal's ass. I thought if he wanted the dick, that's exactly what he was going to get. Besides, I had just enough time to get dressed and grab me something to eat before my meeting wit his conniving ass.

I jumped up, grabbed my toiletries and headed to the bathroom. I took a quick bird bath, shaved, brushed my teeth and brushed the waves I had going on. Once I got back to my room, the thought of fucking Jamaal began to appeal to me. All of the good and bad he has put me through, I thought I would finally get some revenge. I turned on Ty's music system to Howard University's 96.3 FM listening to the Quiet Storm while getting ready. I then pulled out some baby oil from my dresser and began putting it all over my body as I grooved to the sounds of Prince's International Lover, coming from Ty's sound system.

I then opened my closet to look through my clothes to decide what I was going to wear. I thought the best thing, to do is wear something that was pretty much easy on, easy off, since whatever I decide to wear, I wouldn't have it on long. Jamaal strikes me to be about his business, no long drawn out conversation or beating around the bush. Therefore, I decided to just wear my 501 baggy boy jeans, my timbs, and no underwear. I threw on my black biker leather jacket with no shirt. And just as a finishing touch, I sprayed on some of my Dolce & Gabbana Cologne. I then took one last look in the mirror before leaving and thought to myself, *you are just too phyne, playa.*

Chapter 20

After leaving the mess hall and eating that crap they called food, it dawned on me why it's called the mess hall, because it's nothing but mess. I jumped back in my car and started my journey to Columbia, Maryland to meet with loud mouth Jamaal. I looked at my clock on the dash board and it read, 8:15p.m. I had at least forty five minutes to make it there on time. The directions weren't that difficult but once I got in the area, I began to wonder whether I was in the right neighborhood.

Most of the houses were old and looked like they hadn't been lived in in years. Matter of fact, they looked haunted; I couldn't help but think of the house from the old T.V. series, *The Monsters*. I checked the address on the piece of paper that Jamaal gave me and I looked at the street sign and I was definitely on the right street. I pulled up to the address and saw this huge black iron gate that surrounded the property but it didn't look like anyone was there. I didn't see any other cars parked anywhere.

I sat in my car thinking whether I should even get out or not. I didn't have Jamaal's number to call and confirm whether I was at the right spot or not. And to be honest, the place looked rather spooky. It was a huge old Victorian type home that had bars up to the windows like the ones on the house in all the Freddy's movies. There was one very dim street light that made the house look even creepier. Looked like the house was in need of some serious repairs, the window shutters were only hanging on by a thread, and the house was screaming for a fresh paint job.

As I sat in my car, I looked up into the driveway that led up to the front door and there were about six huge trees on each side of the driveway that lined the entrance of the front door. There was a good hundred feet or so from the iron gate to the front door and the closer I looked, it appeared to be tombstones coming out from the ground.

I didn't know what kinda game Jamaal was playing but I had to go through with whatever his game was. After all, Cameron's release depended upon my going in or turning back. Before getting out my car, I checked to make sure I had my cell on me just in case. I then slowly opened my front door and got out. I stood there for a minute or two just looking at how creepy this house was. Of course I knew that if Jamaal was here, he was probably looking out of one of those windows wit binoculars having a good laugh as to how scared I was.

"Get it together Sean," I said to myself out loud.

I slowly began walking up to the gate and saw that it had a simple latch that was easily unlatched. I walked with swagger and confidence as I made my way up the long driveway, knowing deep inside that if someone had of said boo, I would have shit on myself right then and there.

After swallowing the fear down my throat several times, I finally made it to the front door and much to my surprise, there was a note attached to the door wit my name on it. I snatched the note off the door and it read:

Dear Sean,

I'm glad you made it in one piece. The door is open so just come in and have a seat at the dining room table. There is a bar in the corner, so feel free to make yourself a drink and I'll be down in a minute.

Jamaal

I opened the door and the place completely blew my mind. It looked nothing like it did on the outside. I walked into the black and white checker board foyer and was stunned to see the huge rooms to the left of me as well as to the right of me. All the rooms were painted pure white as I took my own little tour of this mini palace. I walked into the living room area and marveled at the glass coffee table, surrounded by all white leather sofa, loveseat and chaise. There was a white brick fire place and on top of it sat a huge trophy. I leaned closer to read it's engrave caption and it read, SIR of the Year 2006 "Jamaal Watkins." All I could do is shake my head and laugh to myself. There was also a gigantic plasma screen T.V. on the left side of the wall. I then walked around the center staircase and found my way into the kitchen. The kitchen was also done in all white except for the stainless steel appliances. The stove, refrigerator, the dish washer and the washer and dryer, all were stainless steel. The kitchen island was done in white cedar wood with white and stainless steel matching bar stools.

Dayum, where did Jamaal get all this money from to afford all this shit, I thought to myself.

I walked out of the kitchen and into what appeared to be the dining room area. The white stoned glass dining room table sat in the middle of the room with matching white cloth covered chairs. As Jamaal mentioned, there was a bar that sat over in the corner filled wit some of the best liquor money could buy, Veuve Clicquot, Moet, Dom Perrion…you name it. Even fifths of numerous other liquors such as Ciroc Vodka, Remy Martin, Hennessy, Jack Daniels and E&J. Not being much of a drinker, I mixed myself an E&J and Coke. I then took a seat in one of the side chairs waiting for Jamaal to make his appearance.

Suddenly, I heard footsteps coming down the foyer stairs, and a familiar voice saying, "Thank you for coming to my home, Sean. I hope you found everything you were looking for." Jamaal came around the corner with a red silk and suede smoking jacket wit matching pants.

"I wasn't looking for anything in particular, just admiring the place. Although, the house could use some attention from the outside," I said, not phased by Jamaal's presence.

"Are you trying to be funny, Sean?" Jamaal asked, taking his seat at the head of the table.

"Naw, not at all, it was just an observation."

"Do you have any idea as to why I invited you here tonight?"

"To wine and dine me, perhaps," I said sarcastically.

"Not quite but there will be some wine involved. Would you like some?" he asked, getting up from the table and going to the bar.

"Sure, why not."

"I'm glad to see you're being in such a festive mood. I've known you for a couple years now give or take and this is the nicest you've ever been to me," he said handing me my drink.

I was losing my patience. "A'ight Jamaal, cut the crap, what do you want."

"Damn Sean, I thought you knew."

"Knew what?" I asked demandingly.

Jamaal took his seat and smiled. "I want you."

"What do you mean, want me? Want me how?"

"The same way my cousin had you."

"Look Jamaal, if you did everything you've done so far for me, just for some dick, we can do this here and now and get it over with." Jamaal leaned back in his chair and began laughing as though I had just told a joke. I didn't get what was so funny and I asked, "What the fuck is so funny?"

"Sean, you're a funny guy, you know that? Now, let me explain something to you, I invited you here for the entire weekend to do with you what I will and to initiate you into my family."

"What do you mean, initiate me into your family?"

"Yes, initiate you into my family. From this point on, you will belong to me. You will be my BOY and do as you are told," Jamaal said adamantly.

"You know what Jamaal; fuck you and your family. I'm outta here," I replied, getting up and heading for the door.

"A'ight Sean, the choice is yours but if you leave this house without my permission, your little boyfriend Cameron will stay locked up," Jamaal said, angrily while staring me face to face. "Now what is it gonna be?"

I returned to my seat. "Fine. We'll play your little game."

"Now, as I was saying, you're going to be a part of my family and this is your initiation weekend. I guess the best place to start is to introduce you to your new brothers and your new sister, as a matter of fact, I believe you already know them. Jamaal reached in his pocket and pulled out an object that appeared to be a remote control of some kind and pressed it. Within a matter of minutes, one by one they came down the stairs.

The first person to come down the stairs and enter the dining room in nothing but a black G-string and a dog chain around his neck was Justin. I looked at Justin but he just stood there with his head down and back against the white wall. He didn't look like himself, not the assertive attorney I knew him to be, instead he looked weak and submissive.

The second person to come down the stairs and entering the dining room was this familiar looking brotha, wearing the exact same black G-string and a dog chain around his neck as Justin wore. The more I looked at him, the more I began to realize who he was. This brotha's name was Mike. He was the guy that introduced himself to me and Ty last night at the Mill. He too looked submissive as he took his place beside Justin against the wall.

The third person to come down the stairs threw me for a loop. This brotha's name was Rick. I'd met Rick the first time Cameron took me to the Mill. He talked so much trash about how he could give me a serious blow job that Cameron and I went home with him. Rick allowed Cameron to stay in his guest room while Rick and I stayed in his room to take care of business.

Unfortunately, Rick wasn't as good as he said he was and therefore, Cameron and I snuck out of his apartment while he was still asleep. However, Cameron felt as though he needed revenge so before we left, Cameron poured white glossy paint that Rick had in his closet, all over his newly polished hardwood floors. Rick wore the same outfit as Justin and Mike and took his place along side the wall wit his head hung low as well.

And last but not least was Cat. *What the fuck,* I thought to myself.

Cat came down the stairs with the same black G-string, dog chain and black tassels glued to her nipples. Cat didn't stand beside Justin, Mike or Rick, instead she took her place, I guess as the first lady, and stood along side of Jamaal's chair wit her arms around his shoulder. She hadn't once looked up and noticed me; it appeared as though she was just going through a normal ritual.

So many thoughts went through my head as I sat there looking at these four individuals that I was attracted to. I found it to be interesting that Jamaal and I seemed to have had the same kinda taste when it came to both men and women. I wondered if they too would be shocked, once they looked up and saw who I was.

"Family, this is your new brother, Sean. Sean, meet your new family," Jamaal stated wit authority, while interrupting my thoughts.

All at once Justin, Mike, and Cat lifted their heads and stared at me with approval in their faces, all except Rick. He seemed to have remembered who I was and looked at me as though he wanted revenge for what Cameron did to his floors. Although, I didn't do it and it was Cameron who did it, I knew he didn't know that it was Cameron. As far as Rick knew, I was the one who destroyed his floors.

"So, what do you want from me Jamaal? Am I supposed to fuck all y'all? Is that my initiation?" I asked wit a smile, knowing that this would be easy for me to do.

"I see you are full of yourself, huh, Sean?" Jamaal asked while laughing and feeling all over on Cat's ass.

I was becoming impatient. "Well, what do you want Jamaal?"

"This is not about you fucking anybody Sean. This is about me fucking you and you being able to satisfy me."

Jamaal stood up and walked over to the side chest against the wall and pulled out a G-string and dog chain and sat them in front of me and said, "Put these on, this is all you will be wearing all weekend."

"You must be fucking jokin'. I ain't wearin' that shit and you ain't fuckin'' me," I stated angrily, while throwing everything on the floor.

"Sean let me tell you one fucking thing, I run this shit a'ight and you'll do what you're told and if not, your boy Cameron will stay in prison. Now you decide what you are going to do because I don't have all night." Jamaal banged his fist down on the dining room table.

Jamaal wasn't giving me much of a choice; I couldn't see Cameron in prison for something he didn't do. So this is what it came down to, either I let Jamaal fuck me and get his little cheap ass thrill or I walk the hell outta there. I looked up at Justin to see if I could get something from his expression but he just turned his head the other way as though he was feeling sorry for me. I looked over at Cat but she didn't have any expression at all. I looked at Mike and he just kept smiling as though he was flirting wit me. And as for Rick, he looked like he couldn't wait to see me tortured in some way.

"A'ight Jamaal, if I do this, Cameron will be out first thing Monday morning?" I asked, sounding defeated.

"At 0900 hours, Monday morning your boy will be a free man," Jamaal replied with a smirk.

With that being said, I stood up and began to disrobe. All I had to take off was my leather jacket, my timbs and my jeans, which I let fall on the floor and I stepped out of them. I stood there totally nude as I saw them all look upon me with lust in their eyes. I was never ashamed of my body; I had worked hard maintaining it. I wasn't what you called buff but I do have a six pack, with a smooth toned ass body and a nice cut dick that any man or women could drool over. I picked up the G-string and dog chain that I threw on the floor. I tried putting on the G-string but had a problem in stuffing my dick into this tiny garment.

"Help your brother," Jamaal ordered.

All at once, Justin, Cat, Mike and Rick came to my aide. As Cat, Mike and Rick seemed to enjoy stuffing my dick into the small garment; Justin clamped the dog chain around my neck. Once all was in place, they stood back and just stared at me. I wasn't used to this G-string all between the crack of my ass but I knew I looked good, just by the look in their eyes. Even Jamaal began to drool and look at me with lust in his eyes.

"So, does this please you Jamaal?" I asked standing there looking down at my body and then at him.

"Yes, it does, very much so."

"Well, let's get this shit poppin then." I walked and stood within inches of Jamaal's face.

"As you wish. Take Sean downstairs and prepare him," Jamaal ordered.

"Come this way, Sean," Justin spoke.

I followed Justin, Mike, Rick and Cat to the back of the house and down some steps leading to the basement. We entered into an area that seemed to be an adult's play room. There was a huge leopard skin rug on the floor wit a king size bed that sat up on a platform of some kind in the center of the room. There were about twenty different sizes of pillows that decorated the allure of the bed. There was also a stripper's pole that stood from the ceiling to the floor on the left hand side of the room and some kinda contraption on the right hand side that had a leather harness made into it. Another huge flat screen T.V. that hung on the wall and a small round dining room table wit four leather chairs. There was also a fireplace on the opposite side of the bed that gave the room a warm and cozy glow.

"Would you like something to drink?" Mike asked, while walking over to the bar that stood next to the stripper's pole.

"The strongest thing you got," I said standing and looking at everything in amazement. "Are those whips?" I asked as I noticed a few of them hanging on the wall.

Mike smiled while pouring me a drink. "Yes, they are."

"Why don't you come and have a seat here?" Cat asked while patting on the left hand side of the bed, where she now was lying.

"So, is this all a part of preparing me?" I asked while taking a seat next to Cat.

"Not quite," Mike replied while handing me my drink and sitting on the other side of me on the bed.

"What do you mean not quite?" I asked, gulping down my drink.

Justin kneeled in front of me. "Have you ever been screwed?"

"Naw," I responded, looking at him with a surprised look on my face.

"Then, I think you're going to experience some pain, so take this and when SIR begins to enter you, take a sniff of this. It will be less painful that way," Justin said, giving me a little brown bottle with some kind of liquid in it.

I was very familiar with the little brown bottle, it was called "Rush" and Thomas used to sniff this shit all the time when I would fuck him. I remembered sniffing this shit before and didn't like it because it left me wit a serious headache. But since I have a very low tolerance for pain, this was going to be my new best friend.

Mike massaged my shoulders. "So, what we have to do Sean is get you relaxed."

"Can I have another drink?" I asked, while showing my empty glass to Justin.

Justin took my empty glass. "Sure."

"Here, have some of this," Cat cooed while handing me a blunt.

I sat there drinking and smoking a blunt while Cat, Mike and Justin did everything they could to get me to relax except for Rick. He stood over in the corner and looked on as though he didn't want any part of this whole thing. After ten minutes or so, I was more than relaxed. I laid back on the huge bed getting my freak on as Mike and Justin took turns sucking my dick and licking my nuts as Cat squatted over my face as I ate her out. I hadn't had a nut in so long, I felt like I was about to explode. I was having the time of my life enjoying what they called the best of both worlds.

Cat was amazing, she grinded her womanhood up, down and

around my face as I ate her up as though she was my last meal. She moaned, groaned and purred like a true feline as her firm full breast bobbed up and down before me. At this point I was so aroused; I wanted to fuck the shit outta Cat. So, I pulled Justin and Mike away from my dick and threw Cat down on the bed missionary style and shoved all ten inches of me right into her hairless love tunnel. Cat threw her arms around my back and started clawing me while Justin continued licking my nuts and Mike kneeled behind Cat as she began licking his nuts and while Mike impatiently waited for me to suck on his manhood.

I wasn't much into sucking dick mainly because a lot of brotha's dick look like they had Down Syndrome or some shit, but Mike was a cool. Even though he wasn't as big as I was, he had a good looking dick. Besides, I was attracted to him when I first saw him and even though I never thought I would be doing this, I thought what the hell. I took Mike in my mouth like a pro and slobbered on his shit forcing out whatever juices he had building up inside. He looked down at me with one of the sexiest smiles I'd ever seen, along with plowing in and out of Cat's pussy while Justin moved from licking my nuts to licking out my ass. I lost all control. I pulled myself out of Cat just in time because I began squirting my hot sperm all over her breast. I sat there shaking and jerking my body as Mike leaned over Cat and sucked up the last bit of sperm I had left.

"Dayum," I moaned, trying to catch my breath as the sweat poured off my forehead.

"You okay," Cat asked, while lying there playing wit herself.

Justin smiled. "Oh he's fine."

"Yo Rick, why you still standing over there? Come on over here and do what you do best niggah," Mike demanded.

"Come on Sean, let's go over to the bar and have a drink and chill out for a minute and watch the show," Cat directed.

As instructed, I got up and followed Cat over to the bar and took a seat at one of the bar stools butt naked as she poured us both another drink. And just as Cat said, within minutes both Cat and I sat there and watched Justin and Mike double team Rick. Mike had Rick in the doggy style position and plowing his ass with slow grinding humps as Rick kneeled on all fours moaning and groaning and begging for more. Justin kneeled down in between Rick and Mike then sucked his dick vigorously. I sat there trying to talk to Cat about all of what was happening but truth be told, I couldn't concentrate at all. Looking at Rick giving up the ass so freely and easily only made my dick rise. And with Mike's hard muscular smooth dick squirming in and out Rick's ass. I wanted some, too.

I didn't know whether to just get up and go over to join in or ask or what? I tried my best to cover my now hard on wit my hand but that wasn't working as I began to squirm around in my seat and bite down on my lower lip.

"You want some of that, don't you?" Cat asked. She could see that I was ready once more.

"Hell yeah," I replied with eyes wide opened.

Cat took the drink out of my hand. "Go for it Sean, we're family now."

I walked over to join in and grind behind Mike as I squeezed his nipples as he still continued to give Rick his pipe. Rick seemed to be in another world as he humped back on Mike's dick wit ease. Mike then turned his head around and began kissing me on the lips. I must admit, Mike had some kissable lips and my dick began to grow as stiff as a board.

"You want some of this, Sean?" Mike whispered between kisses.

"Some of what, you or him?" I whispered back.

"Take your pick, my niggah," Mike said.

"I want some of you," I replied, while digging my finger up in Mike's ass.

Mike pulled himself out of Rick and stood there. "How do you want me?" I jerked my dick. "Doggy style is my favorite position."

"Cool, mine too," he agreed, while propping down on all fours on the bed.

Rick on the other hand didn't seem too happy about the turn of events. He gave me an evil eye as he stood up and walked over to the bar where Cat and Justin now sat drinking and smoking another blunt. On the other hand, I really didn't give a shit. All I knew was that I was enjoying myself.

Hell, I hadn't had any sex for months and considering all I had been through, I earned and desired all the sexual gratification I could get. Mike was definitely a turn on. He didn't look like the average brotha who enjoyed being dicked down. He had one of those street looking faces, kinda hard like but attractive. He was about my height six feet, one hundred and eighty pounds give or take, bald, dark brown skin, with a thin mustache, muscular built and had a nice plump muscular ass.

As I began to slowly enter Mike from behind, I watched as he began to sniff some of the "Rush" that he held in his right hand. Much to my surprise Mike pushed back up on me and I watched as all ten of me slid up inside of him. Mike let out an eerie sound at first which kinda scared me but after a minute or so adjusting, he relaxed and began gripping my dick with his ass muscles. Mike's ass was hot and I could feel his prostate gland as it began to sweat and juice up his ass with each movement I made going in and out of him.

"Do that shit, Sean," Mike said, breathing heavily and panting. "Yeah, right there, awe damn niggah, do that shit."

"You like that, huh?" I replied, while slowly grinding my torso around in circles.

"Yeah, awe shit, dats my spot niggah, dats my spot."

Mike was a straight up niggah and his talking shit was turning me the fuck on even more. I looked over at the bar at Cat, Justin and Rick and they were over there getting there life as I noticed Justin fucking the Hell outta Cat, while Rick sucked on Cat's breast.

"Mike, you got some good ass, bruh," I whispered in his ear as I went back to handling my own business.

Mike laughed. "You could've gotten this shit last night, Sean, if you and your friend had some sense."

"Yo Mike, I thought your interest was in my friend," I stated.

Mike continued to wiggle his ass up on my dick. "No, my interest was in you. I just tried to use your friend to get to you."

"Mike, you betta slow that down. You gonna make me nut a little too soon," I admitted.

Mike just smiled from ear to ear as he continued to grind and wiggle up on me. I started thinking that if this brotha could actually get into this and enjoy it; maybe I too could get into it and enjoy it. Therefore, the thought of Jamaal wanting to fuck me didn't seem all that bad. Although, if I had the choice, I would prefer Mike being the first one to fuck me, since I was actually feeling him. I guess after watching Mike fuck Rick and seeing how chill and smooth Mike was with his fucking skills. He fucked, kinda the same way I do. Unlike the way I'd seen Jamaal fuck. I then began to feel Mike getting wetter and wetter as he squeezed his ass muscles around the edges of my dick head and without any control, my love juices squirted out into Mike's ass before I had a chance to pull out.

"Dayum Mike, my bad. I didn't mean to do that," I said jerking my body and pulling out of him.

Chapter 21

"Don't worry about it Sean, he like that shit. Don't you, Mike?" Jamaal questioned, while standing over in the corner.

"Yeah, I do," Mike responded, with a huge smile on his face as he got up to go into what looked like a bathroom to clean him self off.

Jamaal took off his smoking jacket and silk pants. "Well, Sean, looks like it's your turn."

"Wait, hold up, I'mma need another blunt for this," I said, staggering toward the bar where there were several blunts sitting on the counter.

I picked one up and lit it as I took a seat and watched Cat, Rick and Justin, still going for it on the floor in front of me.

"You know Sean; I'm surprised you never got fucked man. I mean after all, look at all that ass you got," Jamaal stated, as he walked around me and felt me on my ass.

"Well, I hadn't. So let's get this shit over wit, a'ight," I said, putting out the blunt and stumbling over to the bed.

"For someone who has never gotten fucked, you sure are in a hurry for this, huh?" Jamaal smirked, while holding his little seven inch dick in his hand.

"Whatever dude, just do what you gotta do," I said getting in the doggy style position that I had just seen Mike do. Besides, at this point, I was just ready for this to be over. I saw Mike come from out the bathroom with a towel draped around his waist as Jamaal demanded him to lube me up.

"Sir, first don't you think I should lick him out for a minute to get him in the right frame of mind?" Mike asked.

"A'ight, go ahead, I'll take a couple hits off this blunt while you do that," Jamaal replied, while taking a seat over at the bar. I then noticed Justin, Rick and Cat stopped what they were doing and began catering to Jamaal. Both Justin and Rick began licking and sucking on Jamaal's little dick while Cat started planting kisses all over Jamaal's face.

"Just relax, Sean?" Mike said, as he took his position kneeling behind me and slowly began licking the crevices of my asshole. My initial reaction was to tense up and Mike must've noticed. "Relax. It's just me," he said again.

I don't know whether it was Mike's touch or voice, but I suddenly began to relax and enjoy his hot thick tongue sliding up and around my ass. I believe Mike also began to notice how much I was enjoying it as he began to lick, slobber and push two of his fingers up in my ass.

"Dayum Mike, that shit does feel good," I said, while biting on my bottom lip and stroking my dick in my hand.

"You do have a nice ass, Sean. I would love to fuck you," Mike whispered.

I didn't want Jamaal to hear me, so I also had a low tone. "Well, go ahead, I want you to."

"I can't do that," he said. "Ah, Sir, he's ready." Mike stood up and walked over to Jamaal.

"Good," Jamaal said, as he stood and walked his way over toward me.

Jamaal stood behind me as I watched him squeezed out some "Wet" and rub it all over his manhood. Mike and Justin came up along side of me on the bed as though they were going to coach me through this ordeal.

"Sean, take a sniff of this in each nostril as he slides up in you, a'ight?" Justin said, while handing me the bottle of Rush.

"Sean, remember, just relax, okay," Mike said, as comforting as he could.

Just as I felt Jamaal entering into me, I did exactly as Justin told me and sniffed some of the Rush into each nostril and mixed wit the alcohol and the weed, it didn't hurt as bad as I thought it would. Although, I knew Jamaal wasn't all the way in. I wished that it had been Mike instead, so the further Jamaal went up inside of me, the pain was becoming excruciating. I felt as though my insides were being ripped out of me, tearing and burning. All I could do was look in Mike's face as it seemed to soothe me for some reason. I guess that's because I wished it was him and by the look on Mike's face, he too looked like he wished it was him as well.

Jamaal humped, humped and humped like he was going to a fucking race. Fortunately, the pain was subsiding enough for me to at least bare it but when it came to fucking, Jamaal had a lot to learn. I closed my eyes and lowered my head into one of the pillows as I bit down as hard as I could.

"You okay, Sean?" Justin asked.

"Does it look like I'm okay?" I tried not to yell.

"You're doing good Sean. Just relax and hang in there man," Mike said, with that comforting voice of his.

"You know Sean, I've wanted this ass since the first time I saw you. And just like I thought, you got a phat ass bruh and just so you know, it's the best I ever had," Jamaal said, panting and pumping up and down in me.

I don't know whether that statement was to make me feel good about what he was doing or not, but all I wanted was his ass to stop. Jamaal had been pumping in and out for the past fifteen minutes or so and the shit wasn't feeling any better. I thought at some point it was supposed to feel good but this shit was just getting down right annoying. So, to get the shit done and over with, I did what Thomas, Cameron and Mike would do and I started gripping his dick wit my ass muscles and just like that, Jamaal starting yelling obscenities, pulled out his dick and squirted his nut all over my back.

Jamaal then stood, picked up his smoking jacket and silk pants and grabbed Cat by the waist as they headed up the steps without a word.

"Is that it?" I asked, rolling over on my back, trying to catch my breath.

"You wanted it to last longer?" Justin laughed then got up to pour me another drink.

"Hell no," I said, feeling nauseous.

"Here, rise up some. Let me put this under you," Mike said, placing his towel up under me.

"Dayum, that shit hurt. How y'all deal with that?" I asked no one in particular.

Of course they all laughed at me, even Rick couldn't help but laugh. Although, I believe his laughter was because of the pain I went through more than anything else.

Mike laughed as he went to go have a drink at the bar. "It gets better with time and practice"

"I don't think this is for me man," I said as I balled up in a fetal position on the bed still holding onto my stomach.

Something didn't seem right, I felt like I had to throw up and as soon as I tried to get up and run into the bathroom, I vomited everything out right on their leopard skin rug.

"Damn, Sean. What the fuck is wrong with you? I know I ain't cleaning that shit up," Rick said with an attitude.

"It's cool Sean, I got you man," Mike said, as he held my head up.

"Rick chill the fuck out. Give the brotha a break asshole," Justin spat, while getting some wet towels in the bathroom. "At least he didn't pass out like your ass did the first time!" Justin yelled from the bathroom. He and Mike began to laugh.

"Fuck all y'all, a'ight!" Rick yelled, while putting his G-string back on and heading up the steps.

As Mike held my head up, I couldn't help but start laughing as well. Rick passing out and sounding like a little bitch brought out the humor of what had just happened. I for one, never thought about getting screwed, looked way too painful for me. As well as I never met anybody that I would want to even do it wit, but here I am kneeling on this basement floor while Mike held my head up from my vomit and I began to seriously think about him being inside of me. Mike seemed so different than everyone else, he was masculine yet gentle and passionate. He was kinda on the thuggish side but yet calm and tender. He was sexy as shit wit a banging ass body and thick full lips that people actually paid to have.

After my bout with regurgitating, in one smooth motion, Mike picked me up and laid me on the bed. Now, I never had a dude pick me up before and that shocked the shit outta me. Mainly because it turned me on.

Mike put his G-string back on. "You hungry?"

"Yeah, Sean, we can go get you something to eat if you like," Justin reiterated, while cleaning up the mess I made on the floor.

"I'm starving, I feel like I can eat a dayum cow, for real," I said, trying to stand up.

Suddenly, I began to feel something run down the side of my leg. I looked down and noticed I was bleeding from my ass. "Oh shit!" I yelled, while looking at the blood I now had on my finger tips after rubbing in the crack of my ass.

"Hey Mike, why don't you stay here and put Sean in the shower and I'll go get us something to eat," Justin said.

"A'ight, cool. Come on Sean let me put you in the shower."

For the second time tonight, Mike scooped me up in his arms like a rag doll and put me in the shower.

I stood under the shower washing the sweat, blood and everything else off as Mike just stood outside the shower watching me. I wasn't sure of the attraction we had for one another but I knew he wanted to join me just by the way he was looking at me.

"Why don't you come in and join me?" I asked seductively.

"I thought you would never ask," he replied, as he ripped off his G-string and entered the shower.

I stood behind him against the wall and marveled at his body as he stood under the shower head as water cascaded down his brick hard body. I couldn't help but cup his ass cheeks into my hands. I heard him began to laugh. He then turned around exposing his erection that pointed directly at me. I kneeled down to take him in my mouth. Mike was truly bringing something out in me. I guess most brothas would say it was the bitch in me but it wasn't that. My desire was definitely a man on man thing and had nothing to do with feeling like a bitch, such as the way, Cameron or even Thomas might've felt. And even though I still loved Cameron with all my heart, what I was feeling toward Mike was pure lust in its finest form.

Mike was packed with about nine inches of dick and seemed to fit perfectly in my mouth. I think the attraction for Mike was that there was no role playing. I felt as though I could do whatever with him and he could do the same wit me. Mike then leaned down to pull me up and we started grinding on each other as the water from the shower head sprayed upon us.

I never was one for the whole bumping and grinding because I'd always seen that as a part of foreplay and after a minute or so of that, I wanted to fuck something. But with Mike, the grinding and bumping sent chills through my body that words couldn't describe. I wanted it to last forever; his body matched mine, muscle for muscle, six pack for six pack, dick for dick and ass for ass. Maybe there was something to this versatility thing after all.

"C'mon Sean, fuck me again," Mike said, while moaning in

my ear.

I squeezed his ass cheeks. "Only if you promise to fuck me in return."

"I can't do that Sean, I'm sorry," he said backing away.

"What do you mean you can't?"

"This is your initiation weekend, Sean. Only SIR can do that to you."

"Who do you mean, Jamaal?"

"Yeah. I mean…I'm not allowed."

"We're the only one's here. He's upstairs doing God knows what. How is he gonna know?"

"That's a part of the rules, Sean. A new BOY can not be touched that way during initiation weekend," he said, climbing out of the shower.

"Mike, first of all, I ain't no BOY and secondly, fuck the rules!"

After turning off the water, I exited the shower and followed Mike back into the room.

"Sean listen, I would like nothing more than to do whatever you wanted me to do but this is not a joke to me. I take this very seriously, this is the lifestyle that I lead, I'm a BOY and Jamaal is my SIR and I have to respect that. And even if you don't respect the rules, at least respect me and my choice," Mike said, sitting alongside the bed wit his head down.

"Okay, I feel ya, bruh. No, I don't respect Jamaal or the rules of this lifestyle but I do respect you, so it's cool, a'ight." I stood in front of him and slapped my dick up against his face.

"You betta stop before I bite that shit off."

Playing around, Mike lifted my ass up off the floor and threw me on the bed. At that point, we began wrestling but after letting him get the best of me, we started feeling, touching, licking, and slapping on each others body. The chemistry between us was insatiable. I couldn't get enough of him. I loved every thing about his body, the scar on his left arm and even though I hate to admit it, his integrity as well. I guess I always wanted what I wanted. But as crazy as it was, how could I get upset about a brotha not fucking me when just hours before, I had never wanted it done.

Mike and I continued fucking around with one another up until I was at a point of wanting to nut so Mike stood over top of me and slid his muscled ass right down on my throbbing pole. I grabbed his waist and rammed my dick up into him as far as it would go.

"Damn son, what you tryna do to a brotha," Mike said, between breaths, while trying to keep his balance.

"Fuck you the way you should be fucked."

"Hmmm, you ain't lying, damn Sean, your shit feels so good."

I continued to pound into his ass while holding on to his waist as he humped up and down on my throbbing pole. I could feel the grip of his ass muscles wit each stroke and I was on the verge of cuming for the third time. I knew I was backed up but I had never cum so much in my life. Just as Mike began to squirm his ass around my dick, I felt someone licking on my nuts at the same time, I couldn't see who it was because Mike's backside was blocking my view. Although it didn't matter because almost instantly, my nut shot out of me so fast, I didn't have time to lift Mike off of me.

All I could do was hold on tight to Mike's waist and let out a loud grunt as my toes began to curl while every bit of sperm in me, squirted up into his ass wit a vengeance. Within seconds, I heard Mike let out a faint moan as I noticed Justin sucking and lapping up every morsel of Mike's nut.

"Damn Justin, between you and Sean, y'all gonna drive a brotha crazy," Mike replied, while trying to catch his breath and getting up off me.

Both Justin and I laughed as Mike wobbled and almost fell while making his way into the bathroom to clean himself off. As I got up to follow Mike into the bathroom, I couldn't help but think, *I could definitely get used to this, even if I did have to deal with Jamaal in the process!*

After a quick shower, Mike, Justin and I sat up until daybreak eating fast food from McDonald's that Justin had brought back as they explained more to me about this lifestyle of being a BOY and serving Jamaal as their SIR. I already knew Justin's story of how he met Jamaal, so I was more interested in listening to Mike's side of the story and how he first met Jamaal. Mike told me he first met Jamaal about three years ago at a club called "The Eagle" in Washington DC where this club holds several events yearly for the "SBI" which stands for: SIR's & BOY's Incorporated.

Mike said he had gone to this club because someone had told him that on Sunday nights, they had a thing called, "Lights Out," which meant if you met someone there at the club you were interested in physically, you could have sex wit them right then and there and no one could really see because the club had all their lights out. Mike said on that particular Sunday, he was feeling kinda horny and decided to go. However, the club was hosting an "SBI" event instead, so he decided to stay and see what it was all about.

That night, there was a contest between ten contestants who were all BOY's and the winner of the show would be crowned a SIR. Needless to say, Jamaal had won, thereby giving him not only the honor of becoming a SIR and wearing the crown, he also had first pick of anyone in the audience he chose to be his BOY.

Mike said he was shocked when Jamaal noticed him standing over in a corner drinking a beer and pointed right at him saying, "I want him." Mike said he almost shitted bricks when Jamaal pointed at him and the club's spotlight circled the club and then glared right at him as the MC of the show asked Mike to come up front on stage. Mike said he really didn't know what to do but thought he would go along wit the program for fun. So, long story short, he and Jamaal have been together ever since.

Mike said the reason he continued to be a part of the SBI was because the organization was like that of a fraternity and that there were SBI groups all over the country. Mike said he traveled a lot wit his job and that he had met a lot of other members from different parts of the world who he was able to do business wit that allowed him to become one of the top consultant's at the firm he works for. And also because he was a true freak at heart, he loved sex with men whether it was being a bottom or a top, as well as wit women. Mike also said he enjoyed wearing leather G-strings wit leather arm bands and ultimately being controlled and satisfying people's fetishes. Mike said that there was ultimately nothing he wouldn't do to please someone sexually other than being peed on, "Golden Showers" or being defecated on.

As Mike continued to talk, I realized that we had a lot in common. Although, I wasn't into being controlled by anybody, Uncle Sam already had that covered and I didn't like that. But, I do enjoy having sex with both men and women it appears and the leather G-string really wasn't all that bad. I guess after having a dick up in your ass, I could hardly feel the thin piece of leather that lined the crack of my rectum. And I also didn't see myself as being no one's BOY. I was definitely a SIR in the making because the idea of calling anybody SIR was crazy, other then those officers who were a part of Uncle Sam's Army. Jamaal was a Non-Commission Officer the same as I and the idea of calling him SIR was Bullshit. If anything, Jamaal was a murderer and it was only a matter of time until I proved it.

Chapter 22

I'm not sure what time I'd awaken the next morning but I found myself handcuffed to the bed by my wrists as well as my feet, face down. I tried to break free but I couldn't. I turned my head around to see what was going on and noticed Jamaal standing behind me butt naked and grinning.

"What the fuck?" I yelled, as I tried once again to break free but couldn't.

"Good morning, Sean. I was told you had a very exciting evening last night," Jamaal said, while putting some lube on his semi erect penis. "I also heard you wanted to be fucked, so I thought I would give you the pleasure, once again."

"Pleasure, you got to be joking."

"Oh, so you don't like being fucked by me? What, you rather it was Mike instead of me, huh?" he asked with a smirk on his face.

"Hell, I'd rather be fucked by anybody other than you, truth be told," I laughed.

"Is that right?" Jamaal asked, as he walked in front of me holding a huge black dildo in his hand. "Let's see how you feel about this."

"Wait a minute Jamaal, don't do that."

"Do what Sean? You said you'd rather get fucked by anyone other than me, right?" He walked behind me and began squirting lube up in my ass.

"I said anyone, not anything." I tried my best to break free.

"Sean, you say tomato, I say tomoto, it's all the same, right?"

I knew I was fighting a losing battle and thought I could relax enough like Mike told me to do last night and I would be able to handle it. "Hold up Jamaal, before you do that, can I at least have some of the "Rush" there on the table?"

"Now why would I wanna help you, Sean? Your ass should be lucky I took the time to lube you up," he replied, while ramming the plastic dildo up into my ass.

I let out a yell so loud that within seconds I heard footsteps coming down into the basement. The tears that fell from my eyes made it kinda blurry for me to see straight but the pain was excruciating. Every part of my body seemed to be burning as my insides began to tear. Jamaal showed no mercy as he continued to ram the dildo further and further up into my rectum as I closed my eyes and bit down on the pillow I laid my head on. The anger I had in me caused my nostrils to flare and I began to perspire rapidly. I felt the sweat forming on my brow as it began to fall; I felt the sweat from my back, run down the spine of my back and onto the sides of my waist.

"What's my name muthafucka!" I heard Jamaal yell, as he continued to push the dildo in out of the bloody gush that was once my ass.

"Fuck you," I responded through the pain.

"See Sean, you gonna have to learn my name and until you do, I can do this for the next few hours if you like."

With my eyes closed, I felt someone with a cool wet towel wipe the brim of my forehead. I looked up to see who it was, and it was Justin kneeling in front of me with pity in his eyes.

"Sean, just say what he wants you to say and he will stop," Justin said in a low tone.

"I can't and I won't," I replied between the pains that shot through my body.

"Sean, here, sniff on this," Mike said, as he held a bottle of "Rush" up to my nose.

"Y'all get the fuck away from him!" Jamaal ordered. "He's gonna learn to respect me and call me by my name and until he does, he will stay down here in this basement wit this dildo up his ass!"

"Jamaal, why don't you just let him go, baby? Don't you see how much pain he's in?" I heard Cat ask.

"Why are you muthafuckas so concerned with his ass anyway? I'm the head niggah in charge here. I'm the SIR, or have y'all asses forgotten about that?"

"No SIR," they replied in unison.

"The only one here who hadn't seemed to forget is Rick."

"No SIR, I hadn't forgotten and I think Sean does need to

learn how to respect you because if I was you, I would be doing the same thing," Rick said, sucking up to Jamaal.

Jamaal continued to shove the dildo up in my ass and just before I thought I couldn't take it any longer, I whimpered, "Ok Jamaal, you win."

"What's my name muthafucka?" he yelled.

"Sir," I responded in a weak tone.

"What's my name?" Jamaal asked, shoving the dildo in harder.

The pain was unbearable. "Sir."

"Louder muthafucka, I can't hear you!"

"SIR!" I yelled as loud as I could.

And much to my surprise, Jamaal actually stopped and pulled the dildo out of my ass. Of course along with pulling the dildo out came a gush of blood and shit that ran out of me like a waterfall. I laid there thinking I had never felt so defeated in my entire life. I felt as though Jamaal ultimately wanted to take away my manhood and he had succeeded. I laid there crying, whimpering and shivering like a five year old just as I had seen Jamaal do in my dream.

"Okay, y'all can release him," Jamaal ordered with a smirk, as he left the scene of his crime.

Justin, Cat and Mike had come to my aide and began releasing my hands and feet from the handcuffs. Rick had followed Jamaal up the stairs as Mike picked me up and carried my limp, aching body into the bathroom and sat me into the tub as the warm soothing water began to cover my body. I didn't have enough strength to even wash myself but Mike kneeled along side the tub and began to gently wash my aching body. I leaned my head back against the porcelain tub as the tears slowly ran down my cheeks.

"Sean, its okay, you gonna be a'ight," Mike said, while wiping the tears from my eyes.

I knew Mike was trying to be comforting but I didn't feel like talking and even though I was really getting into Mike, all I wanted to do was get up and leave. I knew he was just trying to make me feel better but all I could think about was how I was gonna get Jamaal back for what he did to me and if it took everything I had, he was going to pay, even if it meant wit his life.

"Sean, listen to me. You're gonna be fine. Just focus on my voice," Mike kept saying over and over.

I guess I had such a deranged look on my face, Mike probably thought I was going to pass out or something, so I answered softly, "I know."

Mike rubbed my face. "Look Sean, you got less than twenty four hours left because Jamaal is going to let you go at noon tomorrow. He told us that. Just do what he says and everything will be a'ight."

"Yeah Sean, just do what he says and you'll be out of here. Remember, this is your initiation, so after it's over wit, you'll be one of us," Justin chimed in.

"And you think that's what I want, to be one of you?" I questioned, while staring into Justin's eyes. Justin saw the hurt and anger in my eyes and just turned away as though he was hiding something.

"Sean, I know you might not believe this, but the worst is over. You see, it's been worse on you because you're a threat to Jamaal. You were a full pledge Top like he is and he just wanted to break you but he hadn't. You're still here and you're the same phyne ass muthafucka I saw the first time I laid eyes on you. Don't let him take shit away from you," Cat said, softly, while standing in the bathroom doorway.

I thought about what Cat had just said and realized she was absolutely right. I couldn't let Jamaal take away my manhood or anything else. I guess he'd won this battle but the war wasn't over. Maybe I was still out of it but I suddenly began laughing hysterically. But I guess the old saying is true and that if you start to laugh, people around you will start to laugh as well because even though no one knew why I was laughing, Justin, Cat and Mike began to laugh along wit me.

"Y'all muthafuckas don't even know what y'all laughing for," I said, while cracking up.

Mike was still laughing. "Does it really matter?"

Cat smiled. "Looks like you're feeling better and that's all that counts."

"Yeah, I guess. Anyway, let me get the Hell out of this tub before my shit start wrinkling up and shit," I said, while climbing out the tub.

"You sure you don't need any help?" Justin asked, while trying to help me.

"I got this, a'ight? I just need to eat something and get some rest," I said drying myself off.

"Okay Sean, why don't you lay down for a minute and I'll fix you some breakfast. How does that sound?" Cat said, while going up the stairs.

I climbed back on the bed. "That'll work. Thanks Cat."

"Sean, we're going to let you get some rest and someone will be down to bring you your food, a'ight?" Mike replied as he and Justin ascended the stairs.

I guess I must have been asleep for an hour or so but I felt someone standing over me, so I opened my eyes and standing before me wit a tray of food was Rick. Now Rick and I had not been alone since I walked in this bitch and I knew he had an attitude wit me but I thought since I was going to be a part of this "SBI" group and he would soon be my brother, that all would be forgiven. I thought wrong!

"Here's your muthafuckin food," Rick replied, while placing the tray down on a nearby table.

"Dayum Rick, what's your problem?"

"What's my problem? Niggah you don't think I remember who you are?"

"So, you do remember me?" I questioned.

"Yeah, I remember you fucking up my hard wood floors. That shit was foul and totally unnecessary. Then again, fuck you, you getting everything you deserve, you Bitch!"

"Wait, hold up, for the record, let me inform you that I wasn't the one who fucked up your floors, it was my friend but I wished I had, you punk ass muthafucka."

"Oh, so I'm the punk ass muthafucka but yet you were the one being fucked wit a big ass dildo no more than an hour ago!"

"That may be true, leprechaun, but trust and believe you will never have the opportunity to do it. And once this shit is over, I'm gonna make your life a living Hell."

"Fuck you Sean, and fuck your friend who messed up my floors as well."

"Don't get mad at me because you don't know how to suck a dick!"

Rick mumbled some obscenities while storming back up the stairs but I really didn't care how he felt. Although at the time when Cameron poured the white paint on his floors, I thought that was wrong but now, I'm glad he did it. I looked at my watch and realized it was two fifteen in the afternoon. I turned on the flat screen TV and sat down to grub. The food wasn't that great but I was starving so I ate it like it was my last meal. Cat had fixed me some scrambled eggs, link sausages, hash browns, toast and a glass of orange juice.

One of the channels played one of my all time favorite movies I used to watch as a kid called, *The Enchanted Cottage*. The movie was about this attractive pilot played by Robert Mitchum who brings his bride- to- be to this cottage were they planned on spending their honeymoon. I guess deep down, I was a romantic at heart.

As I continued to look at the movie, I heard someone descending from the stairs and just as luck would have it, it was Jamaal.

"I see you're looking better," he said, taking a seat across from me at the table.

I didn't say anything as I continued to eat my food and ignore him.

"So, you're not talking?"

"What do you want me to say?" I asked sucking my teeth.

"You could start by thanking me," he said wit a smirk.

"Thank you for what?" I asked, looking at him like he was crazy.

"For your new life."

"My new life?"

"Yeah, your new life," he said wit a smile. "I've nominated you in tonight's show."

"Show, what show?"

"The SBI is having their annual competition and I've nominated you."

"What the fuck are you talking about?"

"Look, Sean, I know you don't like me and that's cool but would you rather stay and deal wit me as my BOY or would you rather win this competition, get from under me and have your own little harem. Besides, you think you're as good as I am and if you really think that, you would win this competition and prove me wrong."

"So, why would you want me to do this, what would you get out of it?"

"Seniority, I get seniority within the organization."

Jamaal began to explain that within the organization there were different levels of being a SIR. He was at level one and there were four levels to reach the top. As a fourth level SIR, you could ultimately run for the groups Presidency which meant, he would make over five hundred thousand dollars a year just by holding the title of President. Jamaal had informed me that the organization had never had a black President and that he wanted to be the first. And the reason why he was so gung ho about having me in his little group was because he thought I could help him move one step closer to his goal. Unlike Rick, Justin and Mike, neither one of them had the balls or the leadership skills that I had. Unlike them, he informed me that I had the looks, the body and the aggressiveness to be a SIR. The rest of them were too comfortable being passive and submissive in their roles.

The thought of getting out from Jamaal did appeal to me, although I wasn't sure if I wanted to parade around some stage or platform almost naked in front of a lot of people I didn't know. I wasn't ashamed of my body or anything; I just wasn't what you call an exhibitionist.

"What about it Sean, you think you can win and be on my level?"

"What time does this thing start?"

"Midnight, but we have to be there by ten pm if you want to compete."

"How many others are going to be in this thing?"

"They try to have at least ten contestants, so you'll be number ten."

"Okay, let's do this," I replied before I realized what I'd actually said.

"Good, we have a lot to do. What size suit do you wear?"

"Forty-four long, why?"

"What size shoes do you wear?"

"I wear a size ten. Why you wanna know?"

"Sean, we need to get you a tuxedo, some shoes, a nice G-string, swimming trunks and something ghetto to wear for your casual wear, and what's your shirt size?" Jamaal asked, while writing down my sizes.

"Sixteen and a half by thirty-five sleeve."

"Cool, I'll be back later this evening. Justin, Mike and Rick will explain more to you about the show and all you need to know. Cat and I have some shopping to do," Jamaal stated as he rushed up the steps.

I couldn't help but sit there thinking, what in the hell I'd gotten myself into. But I thought, if this would get me out of a night of torture dealing with Jamaal's ass, it might be worth it. Within moments of Jamaal's departure, I heard several footsteps descending from the stairs.

"Yo Sean, is it true man?" Mike questioned, with a surprise expression on his face.

I smiled. "Is what true?"

"Stop playing Sean, Jamaal told us already. Are you going to seriously compete in the SBI competition?" Justin asked excitedly.

"Sure why not?" I said, throwing up my arms as though I was surrendering.

"Humf, you must really think you're all that don't you?" Rick asked wit sarcasm.

"Yo, Rick, why don't you chill the fuck out man," Mike said coming to my defense.

"Yeah," Justin agreed.

"It's cool, I don't know if you guys know but Rick and I go back a little ways."

"Niggah please, we don't go back no where," Rick replied, while sucking his teeth.

"Anyway Sean…" Justin began while rolling his eyes at Rick. "We are going to school you on how you can win this."

For the next several hours, both Mike and Justin explained to me what and how I should walk, talk and act while being judged. The judges were made up of six SIR's and one BOY who had just recently been crowned as BOY of The Year. They also explained the different scenes that included the formal wear portion, the casual wear portion, the G-string portion, the swim suit portion and the final Question and Answer portion.

"What, no talent portion?" I asked laughing.

"Your talent is your looks and how you carry yourself as a man," Justin informed.

They also informed me that I had to come up wit a name because it was prohibited for any of the contestants to go by their real names. I wasn't quite sure as to why but thought I would just go wit the flow.

"How about the name, "Equipped?" Justin said drooling. He looked me up and down.

"Hmmm, how about asshole," Rick said, standing off to the side.

"Look Rick, if you're not here to help, why don't you carry your short punk-ass upstairs somewhere!" Mike barked.

"Whatever," Rick spat, while leaving the room.

"Now, where were we, oh yeah, Sean stand up and take the G-string off. Let me look at you totally nude," Mike said, as though it would help him more to come up with a name.

I took off the G-string and stood in front of them in my birthday suit. As strange as it was having both Justin and Mike walk around me, checking me out from the front and back, I began to get aroused and my dick began to rise.

"See, that's what I like about you Sean, you're always ready," Justin proclaimed, while pulling on my dick and smiling from ear to ear.

I smiled showing my dimples. "You betta stop that before he spits on you."

"Yo Sean, you know you have some sexy ass dimples?" Mike stated.

"So, I've been told once or twice."

"That's good man, because every time you come out on stage tonight, I want you to show them every chance you get. You need to flirt with them as much as possible," Mike said, while nodding his head up and down and smiling at me.

"And even though you're competing to be a SIR, don't be shame to show that beautiful muscular ass you got, damn, you got it going on in the front and back," Justin said, still drooling at the mouth.

I laughed. "You so silly."

"Don't laugh Sean, not only do Tops like a nice shaped ass, so do Bottoms and trust me, once they see you come out there on stage, work what you got man and act like you know," Mike said, in a confirmative tone.

"Well, if that means getting away from Jamaal, I'll do the best I can."

"Let me see you walk, Sean," Mike requested.

"Walk, what for?"

"Contrary to popular belief, a Top's walk as well as a SIR's walk is very important to the judges and if they see you walking feminine or goofy looking, that within itself can cause you to lose."

"You ain't gotta worry about that because I don't walk like no punk," I spat.

"Well, playa, walk," Mike reiterated.

To satisfy Mike's concern, I walked back and forth, from one side of the room to the other. I did this for at least a couple of minutes as Mike and Justin looked me up and down.

"That's sweet," Justin chimed in with approval.

"Yeah, you got a nice swagger Sean, kinda like my man, Denzel Washington," Mike complimented.

"That's it, that's your name, Sweet Swagger!" Justin yelled.

"Hmmm, Sweet Swagger, I like it," Mike agreed.

"So, what do you think, Sean?" Justin asked excitedly.

I thought about it for a moment and had to agree, it had some flava to it. "Sure, why not," I replied.

"Sean, you got this man. Just don't be nervous, show them you the man and ain't nobody there betta then you. You gotta show them confidence and that your shit don't stink, a'ight?" Mike suggested.

"Stop worrying Mike, I got this a'ight?" I said, giving him a big hug.

Justin began pouting. "Hey, you guys just forgetting about little ole me, huh?"

"Come here white boy, you know I got mad love for you, too," I said, putting my arm around Justin.

We all shared a group hug.

Chapter 23

"Well, I'm glad to see you guys getting along so well," Jamaal said as he stood there watching us having a group hug.

"Yes, they are," Cat cooed, while smiling in our direction.

"So, you guys finally made it back. What took y'all so long?" Justin asked, sounding startled as he was the first to release from our group hug.

"Well, it takes time to have a designer Tuxedo made," Jamaal said, holding up a suit garment bag in one hand and four other shopping bags in the other.

"Wow, you going all out, huh SIR," Mike said, sounding surprised at Jamaal's gesture.

"Definitely. Sean's going to get me one step closer to where I want to be, right Sean?"

"I guess."

"Look, there's no guessing here. I got a lot at stake here besides, you have to win. I have a very special surprise for you tonight," Jamaal said, smiling at me.

I was curious. "What are you talking about?"

"All in due time Sean, just go out there and win a'ight? Justin and Cat, I want y'all to help Sean wit his make-up…"

"Hold up, I ain't wearing make-up," I stated angrily.

"Don't worry Sean, it's not a lot, it's just enough so the stage lights will pick up on that gorgeous face of yours," Cat said assuringly.

"Anyway, before I was rudely interrupted, Rick, I want you to help Sean with his outfits to make sure they fit and Mike, I want you to trim his hair and you know what parts I'm referring to," Jamaal said as he walked around me looking me up and down.

"Now we don't have much time, we have to be there by ten

pm and it's already a little after eight."

"Well, I don't know about you guys but I'm hungry. Don't we get a chance to eat first?" I asked. looking at each one of them.

"Sorry Sean, everybody knows that before doing a show, you can't eat. So I guess you're gonna have to wait until after the show," Rick said sarcastically, as I watched him pull out a chicken leg from the KFC box that Jamaal and Cat brought back wit them.

"What do you mean, why?" I questioned as my stomach started rumble.

"Unfortunately, he's right Sean. It's a known fact that people perform better when they're hungry. They try harder because psychologically the brain can't tell the difference if whether you're starving for food or whatever it is that you're trying to accomplish," Justin informed me.

For the next hour or so, I had endured Cat and Justin plucking my thick eyebrows, and trying to find the right color foundation for my skin, while Mike shaved every part of my body, even the thin tiny hairs were gone. He also trimmed my pubic hair down to a V-shape that appeared to be pointing at the end of my dick which was kinda interesting. Then Rick had me try on all the outfits that Jamaal brought back wit him. The first was the so called designer tuxedo, it was made out of some kind of white material that was silky but wasn't made of silk. It came up to my neck in a Pegasus Style and buttoned across my left shoulder as the full length tail out from the start of my six pack and down to the floor. The pants were made of the same material and had a draw string sash that fit tightly around my hips with wide pant legs and cuffs.

I must admit after staring in the mirror looking at myself, I looked good, I mean really good. The casual outfit just consists of a white wife beater, a pair of Calvin Klein button down bootleg jeans and a new pair of rust colored Timberlands. The swim suit was an off white silky material like the tux and had a draw string on each side, which showed the sides of my thighs.

Last but not least was the black leather G–string that was two sizes to small. I looked inside to check the size and it read small. The problem other than it being too tight. I couldn't fit my dick inside the cup. Of course Cat, Mike, Justin and even Jamaal got a big laugh out of that.

"Don't worry Sean, that's Rick's G-string, that's why it's so small. But we'll tuck it if we have to," Justin said laughing.

"Tuck, tuck what?" I asked with raised eyebrow.

"Tuck this, Mr. Sweet Swagger," Justin reiterated as he walked by me and grabbed my crotch.

"Why can't I just wear a bigger one? Mike, why can't I wear one of yours?"

"I see he's missing the point," Rick replied in yet another sarcastic tone.

Mike smiled and winked at me. "Yo Sean, you look great bruh, don't worry about it. The audience will love it, trust me."

"I guess."

"Well, let's get ready to go, it's that time," Jamaal said, looking at his watch.

∞

Within minutes we were in Mike's new charcoal gray 535i BMW going down 295 headed for our nation's capital Washington, DC. I sat in the back seat with Cat and Justin while Rick sat up front with Mike. Jamaal stayed behind and said he would meet us there, I don't know why he didn't come wit us but I truly wasn't going to miss him. For the past few years, I had driven up and down this rode so much that my thoughts began swimming in and out of my head so fast that I could barely hold onto a thought for more than a few seconds.

"You okay, Sean?" Cat leaned over and asked.

I shook my head. "Yeah, I'm cool."

"You sure, you kinda quiet," she replied, while stroking my hand for comfort.

"Naw, I just have a lot on my mind, that's all."

She smiled. "Oh, just making sure."

We drove for another thirty minutes or so and finally Mike pulled into club "Eagle" parking lot. As I looked out the window, I noticed that they already had a line forming outside the club that almost wrapped around the corner. I looked at my watch and it was exactly ten p.m. We exited the car and Mike led the way up to the front door.

"Ah yes, this here is Sweet Swagger, and he's performing tonight," Mike said to the bouncer while pointing at me.

The bouncer looked me up and down, gave me a wink, unleashed the rope that blocked us off and allowed us to enter.

I'd never heard of this club until yesterday and here I was coming here for the first time to actually perform. This was beginning to sound crazy and I began to get a little nervous. We walked through the small hallway that led to the main club area; the first thing I could smell as we entered the main dance floor was smoke and "Rush". I also noticed that most of the people here were white and the majority of them wore leather.

Leather G-strings of all colors, leather pants with matching vests, leather cock rings, leather, you name it, and they had it. I found it funny that in this day and age, most predominately white clubs still have a huge disco ball hanging from the ceiling.

The DJ was playing, *It's Raining Men* by The Weather Girls and every white sissy was out on the dance floor spinning and turning like they were having a seizure. I did notice a few black brothas who were called snow bunnies. That was a nick name that brothas gave other brothas who were into white dudes. And even though I liked Justin, that didn't make me a snow bunny because I liked brothas, too. Most snow bunnies are called that because ninety nine percent of the time, snow bunnies only like white dudes and won't give another brotha the time of day.

The main dance floor had mirrors that wrapped around the entire room as well as a bar at each end. Justin, Cat, Rick and I followed Mike from one end of the club to the other, traveling together as though we were a click of our own.

"Anybody wanna drink?" Mike asked us, while yelling over top of the music.

"I'll take a Heineken," I said, trying to clear my throat from all the smoke that filtered the entire room.

"Make that two," Rick gestured with his fingers.

"Make that three," Justin chimed in.

"Make that…"

"Yeah, I know, make that five including mine," Mike laughed, while we all headed toward the bar.

After waiting for almost ten minutes, Mike finally got our beers and we stood around just checking out the scene of the white people partying. Of course, Justin felt right at home as he greeted and spoke to most of the guys that were there.

"Damn Justin, you know everybody in dis bitch or what?" Rick spat

"Don't hate. This used to be my old hang out," Justin snapped his head at Rick as he made his way out on the dance floor.

I couldn't help but laugh at Justin's comment at Rick because Justin must have been feeling right at home. I saw the bitch coming out in him, and that was something I hadn't seen before. The DJ then started playing Beyonce's, *Single Ladies* and the place went wild. The white kids were losing their fucking minds, I didn't even know they knew who she was; let alone liked her.

"Come on Sean, let's show them how it's done," Mike suggested, as he pulled me onto the dance floor.

Mike kinda caught me off guard by pulling me out on the dance floor but I figured, what the hell. Much to my surprise, Mike wasn't a bad dancer at all, although he had nothing on me. While Mike did his side to side dance looking all hard and shit, I did a few of my crunking moves that I'd learned from Ty. Mike actually stopped dancing, stood there looking at me with his arms folded and smiled. People were beginning to stare and I didn't wanna make Mike look too bad so I stopped and grabbed him around the waist as I began to grind my body next to his.

"So, you can swing a little bit, huh?" Mike asked.

"Yeah, well what can I say?"

"Sean, ah I know this might not be a good time but I just wanted you to know that I think you're a cool brotha and I like you, a lot."

"Oh really?"

"Yeah really, especially this and that," he said, grabbing my crotch with one hand and my ass with the other.

"How can you say you like sumf'n you never had," I said removing his hand from my ass.

"Well, I never had a million dollars but I know I would like to have it, wouldn't you?"

"Point well made," I said, putting his hand back on my ass.

I couldn't lie. I liked Mike too and there was something about his looks and body that made my dick hard just by looking at him.

The DJ then turned up the lights and turned the music down to announce that all contestants in tonight's contest must report down-stairs in the dressing room to sign in and to bring all of our costumes.

I felt a bit nervous. "Costumes, I don't have any."

"Will you stop worrying Sean, that's just another term for out-fits," Cat reassured me.

"Okay, so Justin, why don't you go downstairs with Sean and I'll go out to the car to get Sean's stuff," Mike said giving direction.

"Cool, come on Sean, follow me," Justin said, leading me by the hand as though I was a small child.

We made our way down to the small dressing room and as I stood in line to sign in, I noticed that all the other contestants were white, I was the only brotha in the bunch. This too made me feel a lit-tle nervous.

"Hey Justin, maybe we should go, I don't think I'm up for this, you know?"

"Oh no. We're here now and you're going to win this shit."

"Look Justin, I don't think I'm feeling well. Maybe we should leave."

"Sean, that's just nerves, here take this," Justin said, reaching in his pocket and pulling out a small blue pill and inserting it in my mouth. "Here, swallow," Justin said giving me a sip of his beer.

Before I knew what hit me or what the pill was, I'd already swallowed it. "What was that you gave me?"

"Something that will give you some courage, stop worrying."

We finally made it to the head of the line and I was asked my name.

I smiled. "Sean, ah I mean, Sweet Swagger."

"Hmmm, Sweet Swagger huh?" the white chubby guy asked as he looked me up and down.

"Yes, "Sweet Swagger." Justin stepped in hugging and kissing all over me. I knew that was just to let the chubby white guy know that I was spoken for.

"Hmmm, yes here we are," he said, looking at the forms in front of him. "Just sign your name here, Sweet Swagger. You can use that dressing mirror and locker over there." He pointed over in the corner of the room.

I signed my name on the form and preceded over to the corner where the last mirror and table sat. Just at that moment, Mike was coming down the stairs with my stuff and Justin started to unwrap everything in the bags and hang them in the locker in order of first to last, and the first outfit being, the casual scene.

"A'ight Justin, I'mma go back upstairs and check out the show but I'mma send Rick down here so he can help you get Sean ready, okay?"

"Okay."

"Sean, remember what I told you on the dance floor, a'ight?" Mike whispered in my ear then kissed me on the cheek before leaving.

"Hmmm, what was that all about Sean," Justin asked, sounding a little jealous.

"He was just wishing me luck. Don't tell me you're jealous?" I wrapped my arms around him.

"I know I shouldn't be, but maybe a little bit," he said, while holding his head down.

"Look at me," I said, holding Justin's chin up with my hand. "I like both of you, a lot. So like you keep telling me, stop worrying, a'ight?"

"Yeah you're right. Oh shit."

"What's wrong?"

"I meant to give Mike your music before he went upstairs."

"My music, I didn't know I had any music," I replied, looking dumbfounded.

"No, silly, it's the music you going to walk out on in each scene. Everybody has their own music to flaunt their stuff with. Stay here, I'll be right back," he said, taking off upstairs with a CD in his hand.

I sat down in the chair and looked at myself in the mirror thinking that this was some wild shit I was about to do. I watched the other contestants getting ready and felt myself becoming aroused for no reason at all and then I became a little lightheaded. I didn't know what the fuck was going on but after seeing my so called competition, I began to relax and I feel good about myself. I mean really good about myself. I was ready for whatever was about to go down. I was gonna give these white boys a run for their money. Suddenly, I heard an announcement from the DJ upstairs that the show would begin in five minutes.

"Come on Sean, what are you waiting for," Justin said, running back down the steps and began pulling off my shirt.

"A'ight, hold up. Let me stand up first, dayum."

"Rick, take his shoes off," Justin demanded, as Rick made his way over to us.

"Okay, the first scene is the casual scene, so it won't take long for this scene," Justin announced as though he was a director on location shooting a scene.

"Can I have all the contestants line up over here?" the white chubby guy requested.

"Wait, hold up. I don't have any underwear on," I said, trying to fasten my button.

"You don't need any Sean, trust me. You look great," Justin tried to assure me.

I threw on the Timberlands without even tying them and took place in line, being the last contestant. Everything and everybody seemed to be in a rush, kinda like Uncle Sam with his motto of hurry up and wait because that's exactly what they had us doing.

We stood in line for at least twenty minutes before they even started the show. But I was cool because I was high as a kite. I was feeling some kinda good and I couldn't wait to get out there and flaunt my shit in front of all those white boys.

Chapter 24

All the contestants had gone before me as I watched in the wings just to see them strut their stuff, but none of them did, except this one white boy. His name was Chad and he did his thing, but still didn't have shit on me.

"Bringing to the stage is our last and final contestant and he goes by the name of, Sweet Swagger," the MC announced as contestant nine walked off stage.

I stood there in the wings for a minute as my music began to play. I was so pumped, my dick got hard instantly when I walked out to the beat of the music. The spotlights were aimed directly at me, and I couldn't really see anybody so I strut and swaggered my way down the cat walk like a professional model. I was in my own world as the music blazed through the ten thousand watt sound system. I realized people were out in the audience because the white children hooped and hollered, especially after I stopped and began to rip my wife beater off of my body.

"You betta work dammitt!' I heard a familiar voice in the audience yell out.

Again, because of the blurry lights, I couldn't see who it was, so I continued to do my thang. I threw my torn T-shirt out in the audience and unbuttoned my jeans so they hung off my ass.

Now to be quite honest, I forgot I didn't have any underwear on but when I heard people in the audience shout, "Take it off, take it all off!"

That's when I noticed my pants were hanging too far off my ass. At that moment, I quickly did a military about face and headed backstage. Even as I ran down the steps to change for the second scene, I kept hearing the crowd scream my name, Sweet Swagger, Sweet Swagger!"

By the time I got down to the dressing room, I noticed the other contestants weren't too happy at all. They mumbled derogatory comments and rolled their eyes as I walked by but I didn't care. I had no idea what kind of pill Justin had given me, but it had my ass feeling good.

"Sean, you were fantastic!" Justin screamed as he jumped up into my arms and wrapped his legs around my waist.

"And I know this," I said very arrogantly

"You're a mess. I didn't know you knew how to work it like that. Damn, you had all those queens out there drooling," Justin replied, sounding like a proud lover. "So, how do you feel, did you enjoy it?"

"Hell yeah, that was awesome man, whew….I feel so pumped," I said, trying to shake it off.

"Well, you got three more scenes to go, so enjoy it. Now come on and let's change into your swim suit," Justin said, leading me back over to our dressing area.

He began pulling off my shoes and then unbuttoned the buttons that I hadn't gotten to while I was on stage. As the jeans fell to the floor, Justin couldn't help but notice that my dick was hard and true to form. He looked around to see if anybody was looking and they weren't because most of the other contestants had gone up stairs to line up. Justin took this opportunity to suck my dick a little, while pulling my pants off.

"Hey, Justin, as much as I'm enjoying what you're doing? I think you better stop."

He stopped and looked up at me. "Party pooper."

Justin then pulled out some baby oil from his bag and I stood there butt naked as he literally poured the baby oil all over my body. My body was so shiny and felt so slippery; I thought I would fall on my ass because I couldn't keep still.

"This would go a lot faster if you try to keep still, Sean."

"I'm sorry, but that pill you gave me got me pumped, for real."

Justin began to wrap the off-white silky swim suit around my body and tie up the sides with the hand-made draw-string that kept the swim suit from falling. Once he was through, I looked in the mirror and because the swim suit was so small, my dick stuck out from the top. Justin just stood there looking and laughing at me as though it was funny. I tried to lay it over my right side but because of the opening of the draw string, you could still see the head of my dick, regardless of whether I laid it on the right side or the left.

Justin was almost drooling at the mouth. "Just leave it like that Sean, besides, it looks sexy as hell."

"You don't think it's a bit much? I mean, I don't want it to seem like I'm trying to hard?" I asked still starring at myself in the full length mirror.

"You don't have to try. You already got what it takes. So, don't worry about it. It looks sexy, so get on up there," Justin said, shoving me toward the stairs.

By the time I got to the top of the stairs, I was next in line to go out on stage. I stood in the wing still feeling pumped while jumping up and down as I heard the DJ announce my name.

"Coming back at you again, contestant number ten, Mr. Sweet Swagger."

I waited to hear the music start up before going out but the DJ seemed to be having a problem in finding the right song, so I stayed in the wing and waited. The audience on the other hand didn't care about the music as I heard them chant my name, Sweet Swagger, Sweet Swagger"

While the DJ and his assistant continued to fumble around and try to find the right song, I walked out in complete darkness and stood center stage front. No one knew I was out there, until I heard the same familiar voice shout, "You betta work, dammit!"

And then I heard a loud snap and I knew without a doubt, that it couldn't be anybody else but Cameron. The lights suddenly came on and as I looked down, right in front of the stage, Cameron was starring up at me smiling from ear to ear. "You betta work, dammit!" he shouted.

Out of my own excitement and not giving a shit what people thought, I jumped down off the stage and picked Cameron up and gave him the biggest, sloppiest kiss I could give. And without saying a word, I put him down and hopped back up on stage and continued to strut my shit like it was all a part of the show. The audience went wild. They clapped, shouted, and stomped their feet as I made my exit backstage.

The G-string scene was pretty much the same except my hard on wouldn't stay in the small cup. Justin tried to tuck it under me but that shit hurt and wasn't gonna work either. I didn't understand how some people could even do some unnatural shit like tucking their dick between their legs, especially when the shit was hard. So I said fuck it and threw the G-string across my shoulder, a towel around my neck and walked out on stage stark naked, while the smooth sounds of R. Kelly sing, "Ain't nothing wrong wit a little bump-n-grind".

Of course there were the usual sounds of gay men oohing and aahing and smacking of the lips but I didn't give a fuck once I looked down at Cameron and he nodded with a smile, and giving me an approval with a wink.

I was so turned on by the response from the audience and the pill that Justin gave me, that by the time R. Kelly got to the bridge of the song, I did exactly what the song directed. I laid the towel down on the stage floor and I laid my body on top of it as I began to masturbate right on stage. The audience must have been in shock because they didn't say a word as their eyes seemed to bug out as they all tried to get to the front of the stage to get a better look. I then turned over in the push up position and began grinding my torso against the floor while flexing my ass muscles.

By the time Mr. Kelly got toward the end of his song, I was so fucking horny, that I turned on my back and watched the crowd as I continued to stroke my dick up and down. As Mr. Kelly sang the last note, I'd nutted more than I ever had in my entire life. The shit squirted out of me with such force that it shot out at least a foot into the air. Not only did it get on me but also on the stage floor. Every person in the audience, even the people sitting at the bar and those sitting at tables were on their feet, stomping and giving me a standing ovation. I eventually got up and began laughing because I couldn't believe I just did that shit right then and there. But like any other arrogant muthafucka, I took a bow, winked and blew a kiss out into the audience as I swaggered my way off stage.

Justin was right in the wing, laughing his ass off and shaking his head in disbelief. "I can't believe you just did that," he said, looking at me puzzled.

"That's what I felt like doing, besides; I couldn't get it to go down no other way. So I figured, why not?"

"Come on Sean, let's get this last scene over with before they lock your ass up," Justin said, laughing and pulling me down the steps.

The other contestants were already on their way upstairs in their tired, black, ordinary rented tuxedos. I started laughing as we went pass them, but Justin hit me on the back of my head, signaling me to stop.

The last scene was the tuxedo scene with the judges asking you questions that we pulled from a jar. Justin had grabbed another towel from his bag and began to wipe all the sweat and baby oil that was still on my body off. I really liked the tuxedo that Jamaal had made for me and I had to give him credit for that, even though he was a jerk and a murderer, he had good taste. Justin had just finished tying the sash of the pants around my waist but it dawned on both of us, I didn't have any shoes.

"Damn, Jamaal didn't get any fucking shoes, shit," Justin spat, while searching through all the bags, hoping to find some shoes.

"Calm down Justin, it's cool. I just won't wear any, kinda sheek, don't you think?" I asked while strutting around barefooted.

"Hmmm, okay, that'll work," Justin agreed as he began nudging me to go get in line. "Go, Go, Go."

"A'ight, I'm goin'," I answered, then climbed the stairs two at a time.

By the time I reached the top of the stairs, there were five other contestants still waiting to go on. So for once, I had a moment to calm down and thank goodness my dick finally went down some. It was still semi hard but I could deal with that, besides, it looked long and thick under the satin-like material of my pants. As I got closer to the front, I noticed that after each contestant strutted around the floor for a minute, wearing their finest, they were being instructed to walk over to where the judges sat and pull out their question from a big bowl. I knew there were ten contestants and ten questions and since I was last, I would be stuck wit the last remaining question, not giving me any others to choose from.

"And last but not least, our last contestant, Sweet Swagger," I heard the DJ say interrupting my thoughts.

Before I even hit the stage floor, the audience was again standing on their feet with applause and admiration. As soon as Justin Timberlake's song, *Sexy Back*. I knew that was my queue.

As I made my way center stage, the lights were flickering and changing colors, thereby changing the color of my tuxedo. I looked down in front of me and Cameron was still there, smiling and cheering me on. The audience loved it and so did I. I had to give Justin his props for the music. The song was perfect. I swaggered my way around the cat walk, just so everybody could see. People were every where. It was so crowded that there were several people sitting on the edge of the stage. After several minutes of showcasing my hand made tuxedo, I walked over to the judges to pull my question out of the bowl.

"Before I read your question to you, I just wanted you know Mr. Sweet Swagger, that if you don't win, I want you to know that you can come home with me, Okaaaaaaaaaay," Judge number three said, fanning himself with a piece of paper.

The audience screamed in laughter. I personally didn't find it funny considering he was old enough to be my father and about fifty pounds over-weight. Besides, I came here to win, not lose.

I stood there and smiled as wide as I could, showing off my dimples and bowing before him.

"Humf, Mr. Sweet Swagger you betta stop that being all gentlemanly and shit because I'll rape yo ass right here and now," he continued to say while fanning himself. The audience once again roared in laughter. Again, I just stood there with my hands behind my back and smiled.

"Hmmm, so so sexy. Anyway, here is your question, Mr. Sweet Swagger. Name the one thing in life that brings you the most joy as well as the most pain, and explain. Let me repeat the question again, Ah, can we have some silence please so the contestant can hear the question please!" the judge said, reprimanding the audience. The audience finally settled down. "Thank you, now back to you, Mr. Sweet Swagger. What is the one thing in life that brings you the most joy as well as the most pain and explain?"

Without thinking, I said the first thing that came to my mind and that was, "I would have to say the one thing that brings me the most joy in life as well as the most pain would be my son and that's because I love him as much as I do. And for those of you who are parents, I'm sure you understand exactly what I'm talking about."

After answering the question, I took my place in line alongside the other contestants and waited for further instructions. It's funny, as I looked out into the audience, they were clapping and I do mean loud and that was before I could really finish the question. I wondered if they really heard all of what I said. I also kept hearing

Cameron hollering and screaming something. I wasn't sure what he was saying but I knew it was love as he kept on smiling at me.

As the applause came to an end, Judge number one stood up and came on stage to inform us that now that we were finished, their work had just begun and that we should go back downstairs to the dressing room while the judges added up the scores. As we headed backstage, it was pretty clear to everyone, including the other contestants that I was the winner and the fact that the audience kept chanting my name didn't hurt.

Chapter 25

I made my way past the other contestants, climbing down the stairs to get something to drink. My throat was so dry, I thought I was going to fall out from dehydration. Justin must have known I was thirsty because he stood in our area smiling proudly and holding out a cold bottle of Heineken in my direction.

"Thank you," I said, while gulping down the cold beer.

"You're welcome, SIR," Justin said smiling.

"Don't you think that's kinda presumptuous?"

"Oh please Sean, you got this and you know it."

"Even if I do, does that mean you can't call me Sean anymore?"

"I can call you anything you want me to call you but in this arena, I have to call you SIR."

"Well, in this arena, you can't even call me, Sweet Swagger?" I asked, while sitting down in the chair.

"I can only call you that in this arena if you lose. However, behind closed doors, I can call you anything you want me to."

"Hmmm, I see. Oh, guess who's out in the audience?" I asked with the biggest smile on my face.

"Cameron," he said sounding disappointed.

I was surprised. "Yeah, how did you know?"

"SIR, the second time you went out on stage, you jumped off the stage and kissed him like you ain't seen him in years and besides, Jamaal told us what the surprise was."

"Why didn't you tell me?"

"And spoil the surprise?"

"You don't sound too happy about it."

"Should I be happy? The great love of your life is right out front and I should be happy?

"Yes. After all, isn't Jamaal the great love of your life?"

"No."

"Damn, my niggah, you wore them muthafuckas out. You got my shit hard a few times," Mike said all loud and excited as he headed in our direction.

"Yeah, well what can I say?" I replied, while standing up and giving him some dap.

"Oh shit, what's wrong with me. I mean to say Damn SIR, you wore them muthafuckas out." Mike burst out laughing.

I punched Mike on the shoulder playfully "Hahaha, very funny negro."

"You performed well, Sean," Jamaal said, sneaking up on us.

"Thank you."

"So, I gathered you saw the surprise I had for you out there?" Jamaal gloated.

"Yes, I did, thank you. How did you get him out?"

Jamaal smiled. "Don't worry about that. However, if you do win, which it appears you will. I have another surprise for you."

"You're just full of surprises aren't you?" Justin asked, sarcastically.

And before anyone knew what happened, Jamaal hauled off and slapped the shit out of Justin. He slapped Justin so hard, that he fell over the chair onto the floor. Jamaal looked as though he had fire in his eyes as he began to approach Justin; I grabbed Jamaal behind his back and held onto him.

"Justin, why don't you go up stairs and chill out, a'ight?" Mike suggested then helped him off the floor.

"Yeah, and I expect a fucking apology, too," Jamaal spat. "Get the fuck off me, Sean!"

"You need to chill out, too," I said to Jamaal, while releasing my hold.

"I don't need to do shit but what you need to do is win this contest, or else," Jamaal stated angrily.

"Or else, what?" I said eye balling him.

"You'll see," Jamaal replied, while going back up stairs.

After that scene, Mike and I just stood there dumbfounded, not knowing what to say but fortunately, we heard the MC announce that all the contestants needed to come back to the stage. So one by one, we followed in order up the steps.

"Okay, Swagger, I'll see you at the winners circle, a'ight."

Mike laughed as he past me on the steps heading out front into the crowd.

"Okay, are the contestants ready?" the MC asked.

"Yeah," someone hollered from back stage.

"Will the contestants please take center stage?" the MC ordered.

We followed each other out on stage and took our spots. I stood there looking out into the audience to see if Cameron was still there. Considering how pissed Jamaal was, I was afraid that he had left and took Cameron back wit him but I was relieved to see that Cameron was still there, front and center screaming, hollering my name while jumping up and down, acting like a pure fool. I couldn't help but smile.

"Alright gentlemen, we have tallied up all the votes and the decision is final. Now, before we reveal this year's winner, let me tell you what the winner will receive…"

The MC began talking about what some of the prizes were as well as the privileges that came with being this year's SIR winner. I on the other hand didn't care about the prizes or the privilege, I just wanted to get Cameron out of the Stock Aide and get Jamaal off my back.

"And this year's SBI SIR of the year winner is, Sweet Swagger!"

The crowd exploded in applause but to be honest, I was so busy thinking about Jamaal and Cameron that I really didn't hear who he said so I just stood there. It took a minute for me to realize that the MC had called my name until I saw people waving at me to come down front. At that point, I swaggered my way down center stage and stood next to the MC as people continued to clap, scream and holler my name.

"Well, well, well, aren't you a fine specimen of a man," the MC said, as she looked me up and down.

But standing as close as I was to her, I realized she wasn't a she at all, he was a dude made up in drag. He was over six feet tall, all of about three hundred pounds, and had the nerve to wear a leather cat suit.

"How does it feel to be this year's SBI winner," he asked, placing the microphone up to my mouth.

All I could do other than smile like a Cheshire cat was to raise my right arm and wave it in the air with a balled fist and yell the dog pound sound of, "Woof, woof, woof."

I wasn't surprised by the response of more than half of the crowd as they gave their, "Meow, meow, meow." That shit made me laugh even harder.

"Alright my sisters, calm yo ass down and let's start the ceremony. So, Sweet Swagger, it says here that your SIR is Mr. Jamaal Watkins," he asked, while looking at some papers in his hand.

"Yes, he is."

"Jamaal honey, are you out there?" he asked, while looking out into the crowd.

The next thing I know, Jamaal came running through the crowd and leaped up on stage grabbing me by the waist and hugging and kissing me as though we were long, lost lovers or some shit.

"Jamaal, you must be very proud of Sweet?" the MC asked.

"Yes, Ms. Ineedaman," Jamaal replied, grinning and looking at me as though we were really tight.

"Well, let's proceed with the first order of business. Wire cutters, who has the wire cutters?" Ms. Ineedaman asked. At that moment someone from back stage brought out some wire cutters and handed them to her. "Thank you, darling," Ms. Ineedaman replied and continued with, "Okay Jamaal, you know how this works. Since you won a few years ago yourself, you have the honor of cutting the dog chain from around Sweet Swagger's neck," she said, while giving the wire cutters to Jamaal.

Jamaal started unbuttoning the top of my tuxedo, exposing the dog chain I wore and began cutting the chain from around my neck. Of course I didn't trust Jamaal wit a sharp object that close to my neck but I didn't think he would do anything stupid in front of a crowd of people and fortunately, he didn't. I watched as the chain fell from around my neck and onto the floor.

"Now that we have that outta the way, the next order of business is the crowning of a new SIR," Ms. Ineedaman replied, while looking out into the audience.

As I stood there waiting to see what would come next, I noticed this really skinny white dude come from behind stage wit a King's Crown that obviously was made up of rhinestones cause it was shining and glittering all over the place. He also had some kind of sash that read, "SIR of 2008".

"Oh, there it is. Well, Jamaal, you also have the honor of crowning our new SIR into our organization, so please do so," Ms. Ineedaman stated, while looking on as Jamaal took the crown and placed it on top of my head.

"I'm proud of you, you know that?" Jamaal whispered in my ear, while putting the crown on my head.

I didn't respond because I knew Jamaal was full of shit and he was doing all this for himself and not for me. This was just another way for Jamaal to get ahead in this organization. He wasn't fooling me at all.

After placing the crown on top of me, the crowd again applauded and roared in acceptance of me as the newly crowned SIR.

"Sweet, can you come and stand a little closer to me, darling? Hell, I won't bite, not unless you want me to," Ms. Ineedaman said, while flirting. I walked around Jamaal and stood next to Ms. Ineedaman and watched as she put the sash around my neck as it hung across my chest. "Alright darling, now this is a token of our appreciation and love for you. You are now one of our SIR's and hopefully this will help you in some small way and if you need anything and I do mean anything, don't hesitate to call on any one of us."

I stood there not really understanding what was going on or what she was talking about until the same white skinny dude came from behind stage with a giant size check in the amount of 10 Gs, made out in my name. The skinny white dude handed the giant size check to me as Ms. Ineedaman asked, "This is for you, Sweet Swagger and even though this is just a replica of the real thing, we do have the real check in the back for you. So how do you feel?"

I was stunned. "Oh shit, is this fa real?"

"Yes, it is fa real," Ms. Ineedaman mocked me.

"Oh shit. Are you serious?"

"Yes, baby, we are serious. Now, calm down because as the last order of business, you need to look out into this crowd and choose your first BOY."

I forgot that Mike had mentioned to me that that was how he met Jamaal and that it was a part of the ceremony for me to actually pick someone out. I didn't know anybody other than those that I came with and Cameron. But I also remembered that I could choose anyone, even if they already had a SIR, I could still choose them. Needless to say my options only consisted of Cameron, Mike and Justin. I wanted Cameron, but since he really didn't know anything about this organization as well as him being married, I didn't think it would be fair for me to throw him in the midst of this. So as I looked out into the crowd, searching for Justin and Mike and noticing them at the bar, I had to choose one of them.

"Alright Sweet, we don't have all night," Ms. Ineedaman said clowning me.

I was about to call Mike's name but to be honest, Mike scarred me a little bit. He made me feel things I never felt before. He made me feel like a top as well as a bottom. In other words, he was the kinda dude that I wanted to fuck as well as get fucked by but after what Jamaal had done to me, and still being somewhat sore, getting fucked was the last thing I ever wanted to do. So I played it safe and said, "Justin, come on up here."

"Justin, you lucky homo, where are you darling," Ms. Ineedaman said, laughing into the microphone.

I watched as Justin jumped up and down as he ran up to the stage screaming like a thirteen year old girl. I also noticed the disappointed look on Mike's face as he turned his back from me, still drinking his Heineken, while sitting at the bar. I knew by not picking Mike that we would never get an opportunity to have sex again. That was also part of the rules, you can not sleep with another SIR's BOY, and Mike was still Jamaal's BOY. I also saw the puzzled look on Cam's face.

However, my thoughts were interrupted as Justin hopped up on stage and jumped right into my arms as his legs wrapped around my waist. Justin didn't weigh that much but he caught me off guard and almost knocked us both down to the floor.

"So, this is the lucky homo, huh?" Ms. Ineedaman asked me.

"Yeah, but I'm lucky, too."

I pulled Justin down and kissed him dead on the lips as Jamaal looked on. *Fuck him,* I thought to myself.

"Well, my children, that concludes another SBI contest of the year and Sweet, now that you've won, we hope to see a lot more of you because your admittance here to the club will be free for an entire year," Ms. Ineedaman said.

I stood there with my arms wrapped around Justin and nodding my head letting her know that I will definitely be coming back.

"Well Mr. DJ, let's get this shit jumping," Ms. Ineedaman

said, as the DJ began to play Beyonce's song, *Single Ladies* again, which I thought was very appropriate.

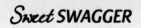

Chapter 26

As the party began, Jamaal, Justin and I made our way off stage into the crowd as people constantly stopped me and congratulated me on winning the title of SIR. While Jamaal walked towards the back where the bar was, I made my way over to Cam and introduced him to Justin, even though Cameron had heard of Justin, he never met him.

"Cameron, this is Justin. Justin, this is Cameron."

"Well, it's nice to finally meet you," Justin said, extending his hand.

Cameron didn't respond nor did he extend his hand back to Justin. He just stood there looking at Justin as though he was crazy. This made me feel a little uncomfortable and I knew I had to take Cameron somewhere and talk to him in private. Fortunately, to break the ice, I heard another familiar voice walking up to me saying, "Yo niggah, you are off the fucking hook." I turned around and it was Ty standing behind me cracking up.

"Yo Ty, what are you doing here?" I asked, giving him some dap.

"Jamaal stopped by the room and told me that you were gonna be in some kind of contest and told me that you wanted me to come."

"Well, I didn't ask him to ask you to come, but I'm glad you're here. Oh Ty, this is Cameron and Justin, Justin and Cameron, this is Ty," I said, making the appropriate introductions.

Again, Cameron just stood there looking at both Ty and Justin as though they were his competition.

"Hey Sean, let me talk to you for a sec?" Jamaal asked, walking up behind me and putting his hand on my shoulder.

I left Ty, Cameron and Justin standing there while I walked off wit Jamaal over in the corner of the club.

"Look Sean, I just wanted to let you know that there were no hard feelings, a'ight and to make amends, I have arranged a very romantic night for you and Cameron down at the Hyatt Regency Hotel, a few blocks away," Jamaal said, while giving me the hotel key.

"Wait a minute, what about Cameron and the Stock Aide?"

"Let me worry about that, a'ight? Now, just make sure you bring Cameron back to my house by noon time tomorrow."

"Is this some kind of setup? What, once we leave, you gonna have the MP's break down the hotel room and find me with Cameron who happened to have escaped?" I didn't trust Jamaal.

"Now, how can I do that when the guard already knows that I'm the one that signed him out? Now, I told you that I had a nice surprise for you if you were to win. So take the damn key and enjoy yourself," he said walking off.

I stood there trying to think of what Jamaal's motive might have been and the only thing that came to mind was that since I chose Justin, Justin would be upset if after choosing him, I decided to walk off and be with Cameron for the evening. But then I rationalized that Justin and I had plenty of time to be together and my time with Cameron could be my last. I walked back over to where I left Justin, Cameron and Ty and noticed that Ty had taken off somewhere but Cameron and Justin were still there making idle conversation.

"You guys a'ight?" I asked, walking up to them.

"I guess if that's what you wanna call it," Cameron said as a matter of fact.

"Look Justin, let me holla at you for a sec," I replied.

"What's going on?" Justin asked looking dead into my eyes.

"Look, ah, I have something to do tonight, so I'll talk to you tomorrow, a'ight?" I said keeping my eye on Cameron.

"Oh, so that's what you have to do tonight."

"Yeah."

"Sean, I'm normally not a jealous person, but how can you choose me and then leave with someone else?" he asked, placing his hands on his hips.

"Look, I'll make it up to you a'ight? Now, you're supposed to be my BOY, so act like it," I said walking away.

I found Cameron standing over at the bar trying to order a drink. I pulled him away from the bar and lead him downstairs where we could talk and I could change my clothes.

"What are you doing?" Cameron inquired.

"I wanna change my clothes. We're getting outta here to spend some alone time together, is that a'ight with you?" I replied, while stripping in front of him.

"How are we going to do that? Jamaal is upstairs waiting for me to go back with him, isn't he?"

"Naw, you are my gift from him. He got us a hotel room for the night but I just have to make sure I have you back at his place by noon time tomorrow. So, you wanna spend some alone time with me?" I asked smiling and showing my dimples while standing in front of him completely naked.

"Hmmm, now let me think," Cameron said jokingly.

"A'ight, don't think too long," I said, while trying to hurry up and put the clothes on that I came here with.

"Chile, don't get too full of yourself but yes, I would love to spend some alone time with you."

After changing my clothes, Cameron and I stopped at the club office which was adjacent from the dressing room. Fortunately, Ms. Ineedaman was in the office with some white heavy set guy who must have been the manager. I signed a few tax papers as well as a confidential form and got my ten thousand dollar check. Cameron and I then made our way outside the club. The hotel was only a few blocks down the street so we walked and talked the whole way.

"Damn Sean, you have gone from not admitting you're gay to becoming fucking SIR of the year. What am I going to do with you?" Cameron asked, shaking his head from side to side.

"Hmmm, I don't know but hopefully you'd think of something by the time we get to the room," I responded grinning.

"You are so nasty."

"I try."

"You were doing more than that up there on that stage, what's gotten into you?"

"Cam, I really don't know. I felt a little nervous before going on stage and Justin gave me a blue pill and I have been pumped and horny as hell ever since."

Cameron held a concerned expression. "So, you just took the

pill without even asking what it was."

"Look Cam, I don't need a mother right now. I'm horny as fuck and I want to be with you like old times, cool?"

"I've missed you, too," he replied as tears began to well up in his eyes.

I looked at Cameron and began to realize why and how I fell in love with him in the first place. He was honest with his feelings and emotions. He didn't care what anyone thought of him, he always said what he thought and didn't pull any punches. I wanted to wipe away his tears and take him in my arms and kiss him right then and there, but there were too many people walking back and forth. I hadn't reached that point in my new life with showing public affection to another guy.

I looked up and noticed that it began to rain and as the rain fell on my face, Cameron reached up and grabbed my face with his hands. He looked at me with love written all over his face and before I could stop him, he stuck his tongue so far down my throat and pressed his body up against mine, that I didn't care who saw us. As far as I was concerned, Cameron and I were the only ones standing on the corner of 14th and Pennsylvania Avenue.

"I love you," Cameron stated.

"I love you too and more than a brother," I replied. "Come on, there's the hotel right there, let's get out of this rain before we both catch a cold."

✑✦✦✑

I woke up the next morning with Cameron in my arms sleeping peacefully, his back was against my front, spooning as they call it. I looked over at the hotel clock that sat on the night stand and it read, 6:45 a.m. As I laid there, I had so many thoughts coming in and out of my head. My life had changed dramatically in that, I was only twenty five years old and was already a widower. And it was quiet times like this that I would think of Venus and become sad. I truly missed Venus, not only for myself but also for my children. I don't seriously think that Venus and I would have ultimately stayed married but we would have always remained close, if nothing more than for our children's sake. But on the other hand, last night reminded me of why I'd fallen in love with Cameron in the first place.

Cameron was funny; he made me laugh all the time, he was affectionate, the sex was off the hook and I could always be myself around him. I'm not sure what it is I'm looking for but he was the closest thing to whatever it is I wanted in a mate. But unfortunately, he was married and belonged to Chauntel. I began thinking how ironic things were between him and me. When we first met, I was the married one and he was single. Now, I'm single and he's the married one. I went from being straight to being gay and crowned SIR of the year by a homosexual organization. Whereas with Cameron, I really didn't know what his status was. Sure, we fucked like dogs last night and I loved every minute of it but he still belonged to Chauntel and therefore our future together was still up in the air.

Of course we talked last night, but we didn't talk about anything that didn't involve sex. Hopefully Jamaal will keep his promise and Cameron would be released permanently from the Stock Aide as well as have all charges dropped. What made it all worth while is that I know he felt the same about me. But my concern was, should we follow our hearts, regardless as to who got hurt or should we do the right thing?

I then began thinking about my children, and I know that they need me more than anybody, especially Lil Man. As a father, I knew it was important to be there for him as a role model. I also began thinking about the muthafucka who'd sent me that note at Venus' funeral and that text message. Someone was out to get my ass and I had no idea who it was or what I'd done to deserve being threatened and stalked. My cell phone began to vibrate interrupting my thoughts.

"Hello," I said, trying to get out of the bed so I wouldn't disturb Cameron.

"Are you awake?" Justin asked.

"Yeah, what's up?"

"I talked to Jamaal a few minutes ago and he told me you're supposed to bring Cameron back to the house by noon time?"

"Yeah, and? It's only seven in the morning." I said, while looking at the clock again.

"I just wanted to make sure you knew and that you would have enough time to get him back here."

"We'll be there before noon time a'ight?" I stated, while

walking into the bathroom.

"Oh okay, also I need to give you something."

"Give me what?" I questioned, while taking a leak.

"I can't say right now but it's a DVD that I think you may want to look at."

I laughed. "A DVD of what, porn?"

"No, but it is something you need, trust me."

"Well, what is it?" I asked, climbing back in the bed.

"I can't say right now."

"A'ight, whatever, I'll see you before noon," I replied while hanging up the phone.

Cameron woke up. "Who was that?"

"Justin."

"What did he want?"

"You are so jealous, aren't you?" I laughed while holding him in my arms.

"No."

"Yes, you are. You don't fool me."

"Whatever."

"Are you hungry?"

"That depends on what you're talking about," he said, grabbing my dick.

"You didn't get enough last night?"

"No I didn't," Cameron replied, while going under the sheets.

"What are you doing?"

"What do you think?"

Cameron and I made love for two hours straight and it blows my mind that our sex is so intense. I don't know whether it's because our bodies fit like a glove or whether it's because of the love I have for him, then again, maybe it's both. Cameron had dozed back off to sleep and I got up to take a nice hot shower and I started thinking about the myth that people believe in and that's the idea of two men with their crusty and ashy bodies rubbing up against each other and how disgusting it was. I too at one point used to think the same thing.

However, truth of the matter was, most men's bodies aren't like that at all. Now a day's, men have just as many creams and lotions for our bodies to make them smooth, shine and smell good, as women do. Besides, most men who take care of their body are very serious about how they look. Trust and believe, a woman didn't want a man with dry, crusty and ashy skin either.

I finished my shower and woke Cameron up so that he too could take a quick shower while I got dressed. I looked at the clock again and we had less than an hour and a half to make it back on time.

"Hurry up, Cam!" I yelled into the bathroom.

I realized we didn't have enough time to catch a train back to Mike's house so I checked my wallet and I only had twenty two bucks in it.

"Oh fuck," I said to myself. We were gonna have to catch a cab back in order to get there on time and I didn't have enough money.

"Cam, you got any money on you?" I yelled.

"Why don't you stop yelling, I'm standing right here."

I turned around and realized that Cameron was standing behind me drying himself off with a towel.

I turned around. "Oh my bad, so do you have any money?"

"Yeah."

"How much do you have on you?"

"About forty bucks, why?"

"Whew, good, I'm gonna have to borrow that for us to catch a cab in order to get you back on time, a'ight?"

"Oh okay," Cameron said, digging in his pants pocket and giving me the money.

I slapped him on the ass with the towel he left on the floor. "Cool, now hurry up."

In twenty minutes flat, we were in a cab provided by the hotel and heading toward Mike's house. It took us an extra fifteen minutes or so only because I couldn't exactly remember how to get there, considering that it was night time when I arrived on Friday. We exited the cab and thank God, my car was still there.

"Whew, we just made it," I said, hitting Cameron upside the head as we began walking up the long path to Mike's house.

"Sean, stop hitting on me, I'm not Thomas," he replied then snapped his fingers at me.

"Whoa, where's that coming from? I don't see you as Thomas." I stopped halfway up the path.

"Well, good. So, stop hitting on me then," Cameron ordered, while tackling me on the lawn.

"Ah, ugh," Justin said, clearing his throat while standing in the doorway.

I picked myself up off the lawn and pulled Cameron up and we began walking to the doorway.

"I'm glad you made it on time," Justin said sarcastically.

"Watch yo attitude, a'ight," I spat at Justin while Cameron and I walked inside of Mike's house.

"Here, take this before Jamaal sees it," Justin said, handing me a DVD.

I put the DVD in my side pants pocket as Cameron and I took a seat in the living room.

"So, where's Jamaal?" I asked Justin.

"He's downstairs."

"Oh really, doing what?" I asked wit raised eyebrow.

"Well, he met this guy last night at the club before we left and brought him here," Justin said, as a matter of fact.

I looked around the room. "Hmmm, I see."

"Look SIR, please promise me you will look at the tape as soon as possible, ok?" Justin asked, while sitting in the chair across from me.

"Hmmm, SIR. I think I like that. Now, if I can only get you to call me that," I said, looking at Cameron.

"Don't hold your breath," Cameron replied while crossing his legs.

"Where's Mike, Rick and Cat."

"I'm right here," Mike said, coming down the steps in his bathrobe.

"Hey, you." I stood up to give him a brotherly hug and dap.

"So, Mr. Sean, I hope you enjoyed yourself last night," Mike said, while examining Cameron.

"I did. Let me introduce you to someone. Mike, this is Cameron, Cameron this is Mike."

"Nice to meet you, Cameron," Mike said, approaching Cameron with a handshake.

"Likewise," Cameron responded, standing up and shaking Mike's hand.

"Where's Cat and Rick?" I asked again.

"SIR, Rick and Cat are downstairs," Mike responded while taking a seat.

For the next thirty minutes or so, Justin, Mike, Cameron and I sat in the living room waiting for Jamaal to finish doing whatever he was doing downstairs with his new victim. To help pass the time by, they all clowned on me about my performance in the contest last night. Most of it I really didn't remember but what I did remember was that I won and had a ten thousand dollar check in my pocket to prove it, so they could clown all they wanted. Justin did tell me the pill he gave me was an ecstasy pill and that it makes you horny as well as make you do things that you might not ordinarily do.

Chapter 27

After waiting for Jamaal for another hour or so, he finally emerged dressed and ready to go.

"I'm glad to see you were on time Sean," Jamaal stated, as he walked into the living room, interrupting our conversation.

"Yeah, whatever," I said, while getting up.

"I trust you and Private Jenkins had a good evening," Jamaal replied, with a smirk on his face.

Cameron got up from his chair. "As a matter of fact, we did."

"Good. So Justin, why don't you go get your things so Sean can drive you back home," Jamaal ordered.

"Get my things, what do you mean?" Justin asked with a puzzled look on his face.

"Since you belong to Sean now, you need to get your stuff because you won't be coming back here," Jamaal spat.

I didn't know whether Justin was happy about never returning or not, but he gathered his things and within minutes he was walking out of Mike's door with a couple of suitcases in tow. I said my goodbyes to Mike and Cat, although Rick was nowhere in sight but it really didn't matter. I knew that we would never get along and besides, once he saw Cameron again, I didn't wanna have to break up a fight between them, so it was all good.

"Sean, I'll take Private Jenkins back to the Stock Aide. I'll meet tomorrow morning with the Adjunct General and have all the charges dropped, so he should be out by noon," Jamaal stated, while getting in his car.

"Call me on my cell as soon as you get out, a'ight?" I whispered in Cameron's ear then hugged him.

"I will," Cameron responded.

Cameron got in Jamaal's car and Justin and I got into my car and drove off in different directions. Justin was worse than Cameron, he talked the whole time as I drove him back to his house.

"Sean, I'm really happy that you chose me last night," Justin said softly.

"Is that right?" I replied, while driving.

"Can I ask you a question?"

"Sure."

"Why did you choose me?"

"I thought it was the right thing to do and besides I didn't like the fact that Jamaal had hit you last night."

"So, you do care? I'm surprised you didn't choose Cameron."

"I didn't choose Cameron because he's married and I didn't wanna involve him in this kind of lifestyle. Besides, Cameron will always be in my life, regardless."

"You still have the DVD I gave you?"

"Yes, so what's the deal with the DVD anyway?"

"I think you need to look at it."

"So, I gathered you've already watched it?"

"Yes, I have."

"And?"

"I'll watch it with you once we get to my house, how's that?"

"Cool."

Justin continued to run off at the mouth about the DVD as we rode down BWI Parkway but really wasn't telling me what the shit was about. I couldn't imagine why the damn thing was so important that he couldn't wait for me to watch it.

Minutes later, I finally pulled in Justin's driveway. As we exited my car, he damn near ran up to his front door to unlock it. I walked in and took a seat in one of the chairs in his living room.

"Give me the DVD," Justin ordered, with his hands out.

"Here you go," I said, taking it out of my side pocket and handing it to him.

"Would you like something to drink before watching it?"

"Do you think I'll need one?"

"Yeah, you will," Justin replied, walking over to his bar and making me a mix drink.

I pulled out my cell phone to check on whether or not I had any missed calls and there were seven of them. I listened to my messages while Justin handed me my drink. Four of the calls were from my mom wondering where I was and why I hadn't called her in the last couple of days. On my way back to the barracks, I had to remember to call her back and let her know that I was okay. Two calls were from Gabriel wondering if I was still upset with him and the last call was from Ty, checking to see if I was coming back to the room last night. He obviously was planning on having company as usual.

"So, are you ready to watch it?" Justin asked, while putting the DVD in the player.

"As ready as I'm ever gonna be," I replied while deleting my messages.

As soon as Justin pressed the play button, I noticed that the image on the screen was of Thomas' bedroom. No one was in the room, but I could hear voices arguing in the background. The next thing that appeared on the screen was Thomas frantically running into his bedroom looking around for something and then Jamaal appeared looking as though he was angry about something. They both stood in the middle of the room eye balling each other while arguing.

I still couldn't make out what they were arguing about although I tried reading their lips. What happened next was all the evidence I needed to convict Jamaal with Thomas' death. Thomas walked over to his closet and pulled out his gun, Jamaal leaped on Thomas as they both struggled for the gun. Jamaal managed to take Thomas' gun from him and use it on him by shooting Thomas twice in the chest. Thomas then fell on the bed as Jamaal looked around as though he was trying to figure out how to clean up his mess. Jamaal walked out of the room and came back with a towel.

The DVD showed Jamaal wiping off the gun with the towel and placing the gun in Thomas' hand as he laid stretched out on the bed bleeding to death. I sat there shaking my head in disbelief. I knew that Jamaal had killed his own cousin. That was never a doubt in my mind but to see the callous look on Jamaal's face made me sick and angry.

"Where did you get this," I said, turning my attention toward Justin.

"I got it a couple of days ago."

"From who?" I asked, becoming angry.

"Calm down Sean, take a breather and I'll tell you." Justin looked afraid.

"I suggest you hurry up," I replied, as my nostrils began to flare.

"Well, after you left here that other night, I began to think about what you had told me about your dream. That next morning at work, I called Thomas' wife Cindy to ask her some questions. She had informed me that she had learned about Thomas' infidelity but didn't have any proof. So, she had a few cameras installed in the house, one in the basement, one in the living room, one in the bathroom, and the last one in their bedroom. I asked her if she ever retrieved them and she said she hadn't, so I went to their house and got them. There wasn't much of anything on the other tapes, but this one showed what really happened."

"You got this on Friday morning and you already knew about this before I came over to Mike's house that evening?" I asked, angrily getting up from my seat and grabbing Justin up by his collar.

"What's wrong? I thought you would be happy," Justin replied covering up his face.

"What's wrong is that you knew about this before I came over to Mike's house and you let Jamaal put me through all that bullshit and you could've stopped it. Hell, Justin, I called you at work and on your cell phone but you never returned my call." I pushed Justin's ass up against the living room wall.

"Please Sean, don't hit me, don't be upset with me. Yes, I knew Jamaal was planning on having you be a part of the SBI Organization but I didn't know he was going to rape you the way he did. Jamaal is all about himself and after he did what he did to you, I was the one who talked him into putting you into the show. I knew you would have a good chance in winning and therefore you could get from under him and he would also be promoted within the Organization. And I also hoped that if you did win, you would choose me as your BOY and I too could get from under him." Justin began to cry.

"That's no reason to have me go through all that bullshit; we all could've simply gotten out from under him if you had just given it to me." I threw his little ass over on the couch. I went over to the player and pulled out the DVD before heading toward the door.

"Sean!"

I opened the front door. "What?"

"What you've said might be true, but I also wanted to be your BOY. I know that might not mean anything to you but it means a lot to me," he said, sitting on the couch, sniffling.

"Whatever," I replied then slammed the door behind me.

I made it back to my room and fortunately, Ty wasn't there. I was so tired and drained that all I wanted to do was take a hot shower and go to bed. After my shower, I laid in my bed thinking about all that happened to me within the last forty-eight hours. Tears began to roll down my face. I wasn't sure why but what I did know was that it didn't matter whether Jamaal kept his promise about getting Cameron out of the Stock Aide or not, I was going straight to my Commander first thing in the morning with the DVD in hand.

Sometime in the middle of the night, I was awakened with the sounds of moaning and groaning. I looked over at Ty's bed and noticed he was fucking the shit outta some white chick. I couldn't make out who she was but it was no one that I knew.

"Yo, Sean, you want some of this, bruh?" Ty asked as he saw me waking up.

"Naw man, handle yo business," I said, turning over and putting the covers over my head. No sooner than I was about to go back to sleep, I heard Ty arguing with the white chick.

"So, get the fuck out."

"See, that's why you black motherfuckers get on my nerves," I heard the white chick say. I pulled the covers from over my head and noticed that the white chick was putting her clothes on.

"Bitch, get out!" Ty yelled, as he grabbed her by the arm and shoved her out the door.

"What the fuck was that about?" I asked, sitting up on the side of my bed and turning on my nightlight.

"These simple bitches get on my nerves yo," Ty replied, wrapping a towel around his waist. I'm going to go take a shower, I'll be back."

I couldn't help but smile to myself thinking that this was the fourth or fifth chick that Ty had thrown out of our room since he moved in. What was funny was the fact that I'm sure Ty wanted them to fuck him and they wouldn't. I couldn't blame them. I don't know too many honeys out here that would enjoy fucking a dude. I turned my nightlight off and put the covers back over my head to go back to sleep.

Minutes later I heard Ty coming back in the room and climbing back in his bed. He then began tossing and turning as though he couldn't sleep. I grabbed the covers from over my head and turned in his direction to see what he was doing. Now, I don't know about most people but Ty was turning me the fuck on as I watched him fuck himself with his dildo. In my opinion, this was no different than a straight dude watching a female enjoy herself. My dick got hard as a rock. Ty had a nice little muscular body and an ass that would put most women's ass to shame. Of course I wasn't going to say or do anything considering what Ty had done to me a couple of weeks ago.

"Yo, Sean, you awake?" Ty asked, breathing heavy.

"Yeah," I whispered without hesitation.

"You wanna fuck me?"

I know that might sound kinda strange to most heterosexuals as well as some homosexuals but at that moment Ty asking me to fuck him was no stranger than him asking me the time of day. I began to realize one thing about my lifestyle and that was some gay brothas show their friendship through sex and that's all it is, just sex, merely helping another brotha out in the process. In other words, this was just another way in being there in a time of need. There would be no strings attached and the friendship would remain in tact.

"Sean, you heard me?" Ty asked, while moaning softly.

"Yeah, I heard you."

"Come on then, I just wanna be fucked." Ty stopped and I guess thought for a second and continued, "Look Sean, I know what I did the last time was foul, but I'm serious this time, fo real, yo."

"Why me?"

"I want you to be my first," Ty said, then sat up on the side of the bed.

"Why?" I questioned again.

"Because I consider you a friend and to be completely honest, while checking you out at the contest you were in, you really turned me on while you were up there on stage masturbating," he said with a smile.

I thought about his reasons and they were as good as any but to tell you the truth, his reasons really didn't matter because I wanted to fuck him anyway and he knew it. I got up from my bed and began taking off my wife beater and boxers as I held my hard dick in my hand and walked over to Ty's bed. I stood there and watched as Ty laid on his back and began shoving his dildo in and out his ass. I kneeled down in front of him and pulled it out. I then buried my face into Ty's ass and began licking him slowly.

His asshole began to literally open and close on its own with every lick I gave him. We both began to moan with pleasure and I felt myself pre-cumin. I turned Ty on his stomach and lifted his ass in the air to dig my tongue into him a little deeper while also being able to lick and suck on his average but beautifully cut dick.

I thought Ty was about to lose it with all the moaning and groaning he was doing but I too was seriously feeling it. I wanted to feel what he felt like inside. I also knew that based on this experience, this would decide whether he would continue having sex with dudes and consider himself gay or be his first and last experience being with another dude. Ty must've been excited about having me in him because he reached over in his nightstand and pulled out one of his Magnums for me to put on. I placed the condom over my swollen dick and slowly entered Ty from behind.

Not having any experience with taking a real dick, I was surprised that Ty handled it like a champ. He moved his ass back and forth and began to squeeze his ass cheeks around my dick as though he was giving the head of my penis a choke hold. I seriously thought I was gonna lose my mind. It's unbelievable what an ass can do, not to mention how hot and wet it can become. And just like Cameron, Ty didn't need to use any lube. He was so wet, I could see the juices from his ass spill out with each stroke I gave. I was so turned on that I pulled out of him and snatched the condom off as I jerked my dick on his ass. Ty must have not been ready for me to pull out because before I could cum, he backed his ass up on my dick and I watched it disappear back into him, raw.

It didn't take long for me or Ty to cum at that point. The suction of his ass cheeks and the heat from within side of him had me cumin' hard.

"Oh fuck," I said, between moans as I pulled out and nutted on his backside.

"Hmmm," Ty responded, as he jerked himself and simultaneously cumin' along with me.

I got up and wrapped a towel around my waist to go take a quick shower and to get a few more hours of sleep. After my shower,

I came back in the room and Ty seemed to be knocked out. I laid in my bed thinking how good he felt but I also felt bad because he was only nineteen and I was twenty five. Although he was of legal age, I felt as though I took advantage of him and the situation. I hoped that this wouldn't change our friendship.

"Yo Ty, you awake?"

"Hmmm, no," he replied, still half asleep.

"You okay?"

"I'm great, why?"

"I mean, are we ok? You still my BOY, right?"

He laughed. "No, niggah, I ain't yo BOY, but I am your friend."

"Funny. I just wanted to know if we were still cool."

"Yeah, we're still cool. You're not gonna start acting like some little bitch, are you?"

"Fuck you," I said, throwing one of my pillows at him.

I looked over at my clock and it read, 2:38 a.m. No more words were spoken between me and Ty. I fell into a heavy sleep until my alarm clock awakened me at 5:15 a.m., letting me know that it was time for me to start a new day and a new week in Uncle Sam's Army.

Chapter 28

After our six o'clock formation, I made a bee line straight to Commander Randall's office with tape in hand, to bring charges up on Jamaal Watkins for the murder of Dule Thomas.

"Ah, excuse me; is Commander Randall in his office?" I asked the front desk clerk.

"Do you have an appointment?" she asked.

"No, I don't but I have to speak wit him, it's very important."

"What is this in reference to?"

"It's confidential. So, can you call him and see if he has a few minutes to see me?"

"Okay Specialist Mathews, can you just take a seat over there and I'll check," the clerk asked, while pointing to the metal chairs lined up against the wall.

I took a seat in one of the metal chairs and watched as she called in to Commander Randall's office. His office door was close but I could hear his phone ring. The Commander picked up on the third ring and I listened as she informed him I was out front and wanted to meet with him.

"Specialist Mathews, Commander Randall will be with you in a moment," she informed me then hung up the phone.

"Thank you," I replied.

"Specialist Mathews, how are you?" Jamaal asked, walking into the office.

"Hey."

"I just wanted you to know that I'm here to see the Commander and after talking to him, I'm going over to the General Adjutant's office and do what I said I was going to do," Jamaal whispered as he sat down next to me. He held what appeared to be Cameron's files.

"Yeah, okay," I said, as calm as I could. I didn't want to cause a scene, but felt sick to my stomach and angry as hell from the thought of knowing what Jamaal did.

"Okay Specialist Mathews, you wanted to see me," the Commander said, opening his office door.

"Ah, yes Sir," I replied, getting up from my seat.

"Ah, Mathews, why are you here to see the Commander?" Jamaal asked, with a confused look on his face. He quickly stood up and grabbed my arm.

"Get the fuck off me!" I yelled, then snatched my arm from his grasp.

When I walked into the Commander's office and closed the door, I saw the paranoid look on Jamaal's face. Hell, if he knew what I knew, he would get the hell away from here as fast as possible. I couldn't wait to see the expression on his face when they came to lock his ass up.

"So, you wanted to see me, Specialist Mathews?" The Commander asked, as I stood at ease in front of his desk.

"Yes, sir. I have something I think you need to watch," I said, handing him the DVD.

"What's this?" Commander Randall asked.

"That DVD will tell you who killed, Specialist Dule Thomas, Sir."

"Where did you get this from?" Commander Randall asked, suspiciously while looking at the DVD as though he would find the answer.

"I really can't answer that question Sir, but I beg you to look at it. Now if you can, Sir."

Commander Randall got up from his seat and walked over to a cherry wooden hutch that sat along the left side his office and opened it. Inside was a 19 inch T.V. hooked up to a DVD player. He inserted the DVD and came back over to his desk, took a seat and pressed the on button to the T.V. with a remote.

"Have a seat, Specialist Mathews," Commander Randall ordered.

I did what I was told and took a seat in one of his black leather chairs and faced the TV screen and watched the video of Thomas being murdered for the second time. Each time I watched it, it made me sick. I wanted to literally kill Jamaal myself. No sooner than the DVD had stopped, Commander Randall picked up the phone.

"Yes, this is Commander Randall; I'd like to speak with the Adjutant General Please."

While on hold, Commander Randall instructed me to go to work and not talk to a soul about the DVD, and that he would take care of everything. I walked out of his office feeling good and knowing that Jamaal's ass was finally going down! Fortunately, Jamaal was no longer out front as I exited the Commander's office and I was happy that he wasn't. As angry as I was, I was afraid that if he was still there, I would say something or do something that would've messed every thing up.

As soon as I entered my office, the first thing I saw was a large manilla envelope on my desk and being in the military that only meant one thing. I took a seat at my desk and picked the envelope up to inspect it and sure enough, this was a personal letter from Uncle Sam transferring me to only God knows where.

Oh fuck, I thought to myself.

Now, wasn't the time for me to be deploring somewhere, especially somewhere overseas. Everything here at home was finally coming together. Jamaal would be locked up in a matter of hours; Cameron was going to be released from the Stock Aide, I was going to spend more time with Lil Man and I still needed to find out who the fuck was stalking me.

I threw the envelope into my desk drawer without opening it up because I just didn't wanna think about having to go somewhere else and I thought by placing it in there, it would be like out of sight, out of mind and I could get through another day of being in the military because it was truly burning me out. I was tired of being controlled. I had another two years or so before reaching my End Term of Service, and I didn't know if I could hang that long. After all that happened, I wanted to live my new life as a civilian.

Besides, I only joined the military because I was married and had a family. Now that I was a widower and had a ten thousand dollar check in my pocket and waiting for the insurance money from Venus' death, I wanted to get out of the Army, but I didn't want a dishonorable discharge. I wanted to go to school and get a degree. I wanted to do some traveling with Lil Man, and take him to Disney World or maybe to Hawaii where there were palm trees, blue water and warm weather. I wanted a simple nine to five kinda job whereby once my day ended; I could go home and be "gay" or do whatever I wanted to without Uncle Sam breathing down my neck.

After a few hours of shuffling papers around on my desk and thoughts coming in and out of my head, I decided to just get it over with and see where Uncle Sam was sending me. I opened my desk drawer and pulled the envelope out. As I held it in my hands, my heart began to pound a mile a minute.

I started thinking, *what if I was being deployed to Iraq or Iran, where there was a war going on?*

I took a deep breath and ripped the envelope open. The God's must have been on my side when I noticed that on December 1st, I was to report to my new duty station at Fort Shafter which is located in Honolulu, Hawaii.

Without realizing where I was I yelled, "Thank you Jesus!"

As I stood up to do my happy dance, I began to hear a lot of commotion going on out in the main office. I opened my door to see Jamaal's face being crushed as five MP's held him down on the floor, cuffed him then read him his rights. I was surprised to see Jamaal screaming and crying like a little bitch. It made me feel good as I walked and stood over him laughing my ass off. No one else seemed to find it funny as they stared at me in disbelief.

"What did he do, I wonder?" A few of my co-workers said among themselves.

I knew exactly what he did and I was happy that he was finally getting what he deserved, I thought to myself.

I walked back in my office smiling from ear to ear as I heard Jamaal screaming and kicking as the MP's dragged his tired ass out of the office.

As I sat at my desk, I realized I hadn't talked to my mom, so I picked up the phone to give her a call.

"Well, it's about time you decide to call me," my mom spat into the phone.

"I'm sorry Ma. I've been really busy for the past few days. How's Lil Man doing?"

"He's fine, he's been asking for you," my mom said angrily.

"Again, I'm sorry, but I told you that I was staying here on base this weekend so I could help Cameron get out of the Stock Aide and Ma, my plan worked. They locked up Jamaal this morning for Thomas' murder so Cameron will be getting out sometime today," I stated excitedly.

"Well Sean, I'm glad to hear that, but you could've at least called me at some point this past weekend to tell me you were okay. I didn't know what happened, I thought you might've gotten in trouble or something."

"My bad, Ma." I felt guilty.

"Don't my bad me, here talk to your son," my mom replied handing the phone to Khalil.

"Hi Daddy. I miss you. When are you coming home?" he asked in his normal child like manner.

"Awe Lil Man, I miss you, too. I'll be home sooner than I planned."

"Are you coming home today?" he asked excitedly.

"Naw, it won't be today but maybe tomorrow, how's that?"

"Okay Daddy, are you gonna bring me sumf'n when you come home?"

"Sure, what would you like?" I said, laughing into the phone.

"Skittles," he whispered into the phone.

I couldn't help but laugh knowing that he was whispering because my mom didn't like him eating too much candy. She said it made him too hyper.

"Sure, I'll bring you some skittles a'ight, just don't tell, Granny, okay?"

"Okay, here's Granny."

"Yeah," my mom said into the phone.

"Ma, I'll probably be coming home tomorrow and I need to talk to you."

"Why, what's wrong?"

"Nothings wrong. I just need to talk to you, okay?"

"Alright, what time will you be home? Maybe I'll cook something so you can have a home cooked meal. Lord only knows what they be putting in that military food."

"I know, right," I said, laughing into the phone. "I don't know Ma, I guess around five or six in the evening."

"Alright baby, I'll fix something good for dinner tomorrow. Now, let me go before I strangle your son."

"Okay Ma, I'll see you then," I said, hanging up the phone.

Just as I hung up, there was a knock on my door.

"Come in."

"How you like me now?" Cameron asked, standing in front of me and smiling ear to ear as a free man.

I was so happy to see that Cameron had been released from the Stock Aide. Without thinking or closing my door, I grabbed him and kissed him right on the lips.

"Hmmm, maybe I should get locked up more often." I guess he was caught off guard by my boldness.

"Yeah right, very funny," I replied, closing my door and sitting back down at my desk.

Cameron and I sat in my office the entire day, ordering lunch, and talking and laughing about Jamaal's ass being locked up. But the thing that wasn't funny was the fact that I'd received orders to go to Hawaii and Cameron was giving a choice by the Adjunct General to go back to Korea or stay at Fort Meade. And since he'd been falsely accused of a murder he didn't commit. He chose to stay at Fort Meade, thinking that we would be here together again, like old times.

As my day came to an end, Cameron and I walked out of my office heading back to my Commander's office so that I could start processing out. Because I was being deployed, Uncle Sam normally gave soldiers thirty days of leave time to process out and take care of any personal business they may have before leaving. I knew I was gonna spend most of that time with my family and Cameron. So after checking in with my Commander and getting permission to start my separation from Fort Meade, I decided to leave Fort Meade, drive Cameron home to Chauntel, so I could see Lil Man and sleep in my own bed.

Driving down the highway and listening to Cameron talk a mile a minute felt like old times. We laughed about how much had change within the last couple of years. Mainly about how much I'd changed. Cameron got a big kick out of the fact that I seemed to be more involved into the gay lifestyle than he was; after all, I had become SIR of The Year for the SBI Organization. An Organization that Cameron had never even heard of.

"So, where does that leave us?" I asked in a serious tone.

"I don't know Sean." He sounded sad.

"Why don't you try to get assigned to Hawaii, too?"

"And why would they wanna do that? I mean, no one gets assigned to Hawaii and how you did that, I don't know," Cam stated suspiciously.

"What, you think I had sumf'n to do with that?" I asked looking at him.

"Well, did you?"

"Hell, if I had that much clout, I would have you assigned there with me," I said laughing.

"So, why would Uncle Sam re-assign me to Hawaii?"

"I don't know, to possibly make it up to you for having been falsely accused of murder."

"Hmmm, I don't know, Sean but I'll definitely look into it."

"So, in the meantime, what about us?" I asked again.

"If I don't get a chance to be reassigned to Hawaii, there won't be no us," Cameron replied softly.

With that being said, I pulled up to Cameron and Chauntel's apartment and double parked and waited for him to exit.

"Well Cam, I think this is your stop," I said, putting my car in the park position.

"Yeah, I guess it is," Cameron replied sounding sad.

"What's wrong? Chauntel is expecting you home, right?"

"Yeah she is but…," Cameron began to say while getting out of my car.

"But what?" I asked, rolling down the passenger side window.

"Never mind," he said walking up to his apartment.

I sat in my car and watched as Chauntel opened the door for her husband as she jumped up and down smothering him with hugs and kisses. My heart felt like it was breaking, the same way it did when I first took Cam to the airport to go to Korea. *Life can be such a bitch,* I thought to myself.

I put my car in drive and drove all the way home in silence. Half way home, my cell phone rang.

"Who's this," I replied, without looking at the caller ID.

"Hey Sean, where you at," Ty asked.

"I'm on my way home, why?"

"Home, why are you going home?"

"I received my separation papers today."

"Oh damn, fo real, and you weren't even gonna tell me?"

"Naw man, I was gonna tell you. So much has happened today that I just didn't think about it."

"Where are they sending you?"

"Fort Shafter, in Hawaii."

"Get the fuck outta here, are you shittin' me?"

"Nope," I replied laughing.

"You a lucky muthafucka, you know that, right?"

"Stop hating."

"Yo niggah, I don't hate. I'm just sorry yo ass is leaving me."

"Yeah, whatever anyway, I just pulled up in front of my crib, let me holla at you tomorrow."

"Okay cool. Hey Sean?"

"Yeah."

"Ah, since you work over there in the Sidpers Department why don't you finagle some of them papers and take my black ass to Hawaii with you?" he asked laughing into the phone.

"Yeah, right," I said hanging up the phone.

Of course I didn't know whether Ty was joking or whether or he was serious with his request but I didn't have the power to do anything about it anyway. Although, it made me wonder whether or not Ty wanted to be on the sandy beaches of Hawaii or whether that was his way of just wanting to be with me.

Before exiting my car, I realized I didn't have Lil Man's skittles so I climbed back in my car and drove down to the convenient store on the corner and brought him the biggest box they had.

⚬⚬⚬

Instead of knocking on my mother's door, I tiptoed in using my key so that I could surprise both of them. But they both were asleep on the couch with Lil Man in his pajamas lying across my moms lap. The T.V. was on and the movie they were watching was the old classic, *It's a Wonderful Life*. A movie, my mother always made me watch with her during the Christmas season. But as much as I wanted to wake them up and surprise them, I decided to just let them sleep and we all would get an early start in the morning. Especially with all the running around I had to do.

I eased back out and locked the door behind me and went down to my own apartment. As I was trying to open my door, my cell phone went off. I looked at the caller ID and saw that it was Gabriel's number.

"Hey you," I said, walking into my own apartment.

"What's up?"

"Not too much, just walking into my apartment."

"Oh, so you're home?" he asked surprisingly.

"Yeah."

"What are you doing home?"

"It's a long story."

"I'm listening."

I stripped down to my boxers and wife beater while telling him all that had happened at work and the fact that Jamaal was finally arrested for Thomas' murder today. I laid across the couch and talked to Gabriel for at least two hours. After I told him about being reassigned to Hawaii, he became quiet, a little too quiet.

"Gabriel, you there?" I said looking into the phone.

"Yeah, I'm here," he replied softly.

"You a'ight?"

"So, when do you leave?"

"December 1st."

"Wow, I've always thought about going to Hawaii one day."

"Well, now that I will be over there, you can come and pay me a visit," I replied, while fondling myself.

"Yeah, well, something tells me that if I would ever get a chance to go to Hawaii, I wouldn't come back here," He said in a serious tone.

I didn't know how serious he was in wanting to stay in Hawaii, but at least I knew he would come to visit if I offered. I looked at the clock on the wall and noticed that it was almost 11:00 p.m. and I was both horny and hungry at the same time. I knew if I invited myself over to Gabriel's hotel room for a quick freak session, he would be all for it but on the real; I just wanted to sleep and get some rest

Chapter 29

The next morning, I got up at the crack of dawn to start my day. I took a quick shower and threw on a pair of sweats and walked into my kitchen to get something cold to drink. I saw that my mom had gathered my mail and placed it on the dining room table. I began looking through it when I noticed an envelope from The SGLI Insurance Company. I knew immediately that this was the insurance check from Venus' death. I sat down on one of my dining room chairs to read what the letter had to say. As I skimmed through the form letter, a check fell out and dropped on the floor. I leaned down to pick it up and noticed that it was payable to me, in the amount of $57,794.13.

At that moment, I thought I would be happy when I finally got the check but instead, it made me angry because this was telling me that Venus was really gone and according to the government, this was all she was worth. And I don't know why but then I started crying like a baby. All I kept thinking was that I wanted Venus back so she could live her life and be with her children.

After wiping the tears from my eyes and pulling myself together, I began looking through all the other mail and came across an envelope that didn't have a return address on it, but yet it was addressed to me. I open it up and to my disbelief there were several pictures of Venus lying in her coffin as well as pictures of her grave site.

"What the fuck is this?" I asked out loud.

I was so angry that I began shouting obscenities as though the person who sent it was right there. I stood up and began pacing back and forth across my living room floor. My nostrils were flaring and my temples began to pulsate. All I saw was red and wanted to seriously kill who ever the muthafucka was who was obviously trying to torture me. Suddenly my phone rang, breaking me out of my trance.

"What!" I yelled into the phone.

"What's wrong Sean?"

"Ma, you won't believe this shit. Somebody sent me pictures of Venus lying in her coffin and of her grave site. I don't know who it is but once I find out, I'm gonna kill 'em!"

"Well, first of all Sean, you need to calm down. Do you realize what time it is? You gonna wake up the whole block with all that screaming and yelling you're doing. And when did you get home?"

"I came home last night." I tried to calm down as I continued to pace back and forth.

"Oh okay. Well, why don't you come on up and I'll fix us a nice breakfast and we'll talk.

"Okay Ma, I'll see you in a few," I said, hanging up the phone.

❧

Thirty minutes later, I finally pulled myself together, folded the insurance check up and gathered up the sick photos and headed upstairs to my mom's apartment. Before knocking on the door, I stood in the hallway, smelling the pleasant aroma of bacon cooked. It's amazing how a smell could bring back so many memories. I knocked on my moms' door and waited as I heard her yelling at Lil Man about something.

"Hi Ma," I said, immediately hugging her.

"Hey baby," my mom said, then looked at me funny. She noticed that I was holding on to her for dear life.

"Daddy, daddy," Lil Man hollered as he ran up and grabbed me around the leg.

"Hey, son. I missed you so much," I said, releasing my mom and picking him up.

"Daddy," he squealed then leaned over and whispered in my ear, "Do you have my Skittles?"

I couldn't help but laugh. It's amazing how kids could forget to take a bath, pick up after themselves or brush their teeth, but didn't forget about gifts or treats.

"Yeah, I got it and I'll give it to you lata, a'ight?" I replied in a low tone.

"Thank you, Daddy."

"Okay, what's with all the whispering?"

"Nothin' Ma. Just a little somthin' between me and my son. Ain't that right?"

"Yup," he replied with a wide grin.

"Okay son, go in your room and play for a little bit so I can talk to your Granny, a'ight?" I planted a kiss on his forehead before putting him down.

"Okay," he said running off into his room.

"So, what's going on, Sean?" my mom asked walking back into the kitchen.

I sat down on one of my mom's kitchen bar stools and I talked to her about my stalker as she continued to cook. Other than the note that I received at Venus' funeral which she already knew about, I told her about the text that I received the other day as well as showed her the pictures that I had received in the mail.

"Sean, maybe you should go to the police," she suggested while stopping long enough to look at the photos.

"And tell them what?"

"Tell them the same thang you just told me."

"That would just be a waste of time. I don't even have a clue as to who it could be. At first, I thought it might've been Jamaal, but he's in jail now, so it can't be him."

"So, what are you going to do?"

I then began telling her that I might not have to do anything considering that I was leaving in less than a month and being transferred to Hawaii. My mom wasn't too happy that I was leaving, but she was glad that I wasn't being sent to some war zone. We thought it would be best that Khalil stay with her and that once I was settled, and got an apartment; they would come and visit for a few weeks. I also showed my mom the check that I'd gotten from the insurance company.

It was kinda funny because she almost choked at the amount of the check while taking a sip of her coffee. She admitted she had never seen a check that large before. I did keep one secret and that was, I didn't tell her about the other $10,000 dollar check. I didn't want explain how I'd gotten that one. My mom seem to be ok with having a gay son but I didn't think that she was ready for having a gay son who won money in a contest for being gay! Although, the SBI is more than that, I didn't think my mom would see it that way. So I left out the extra money.

Besides, my mom always said, "Don't let your left hand know what your right hand is doing. After talking for over an hour or so and grubbing down on my mom's breakfast, I got lil man together and took him with me to run some errands while giving my mom a well deserved break.

◎◎◈◈◎◎

The first thing I had to do was go to the bank. I opened up a special account for both Venus and Lil Man and put 20 G's in each. I also put 5 G's in my checking account and the rest into my savings. I didn't know how good it would feel having some money in my account as I left out of the bank.

Our next stop was the mall. Now, I could have gone to any of them but there are times I really enjoy being around my own people, so I took Lil Man over to Mondawmin Mall. Mondawmin had just gone through a total renovation and was centered smack dead in the heart of West Baltimore. Most white and middle class black folks don't go there because it was so ghetto. But those who lived in the area went there to cash their monthly checks, buy a new outfit for the club, or buy their lottery tickets and liquor. For those who were just looking for a hook up, there were boosters' outside where you could get anything from drugs, pussy and even a kitchen sink.

I held onto my sons' hand tightly as he looked around in amazement. Call me or uppity, but I never wanted to grow up in an area like this. However, I'm glad I did because it taught me about the streets. I kept Lil Man as far away from this environment as much as I could, but he could care less where we went. He had a ball just spending some quality time with me. We went from store to store and he had me buying him all kinds of shit like it was Christmas. By the time we left there, I'd charged almost $5,000 on my credit card and the majority of that was spent on him, but I didn't care. I would've bought him the world if he asked.

By the time we left and pulled up in front of our apartment building it was dark outside. We were out later than I expected to be and I knew my mom would be pissed for not being back in time to eat dinner, but I figured I would put the blame on Lil Man, besides, that's what kids were for.

We climbed the steps to my mom's apartment and I opened the door with my key. Lil Man and I walked in and found my mom sitting in her lazy boy chair watching T.V.

"It's about time y'all showed up," she spat while turning on the mute button.

"I'm sorry Ma. Lil Man and I just got a little carried away with the time, my bad," I said, putting the bags down on the floor and kissing my mom on the cheek. "Lil Man, go into the bathroom and wash your hands and get ready for dinner, okay?"

"Well, y'all dinner is in the microwave," she replied, while turning off the mute button as she continued to watch whatever she was watching.

"Thanks, Ma. By the way, this is for you," I said, handing her a bag with several of her favorite black author books. I knew that would make up for coming in so late. My mom always enjoyed reading, ever since I could remember. If she wasn't working on putting a big table top puzzle together, she had a book in her hand.

"What's this?"

"Open it and find out," I replied, while going into the kitchen and washing my hands in the kitchen sink.

"Hmmm, you think you slick don't you, trying to butter me up with some books."

Lil Man and I sat at the dining room table and ate my momma's famous fried chicken, buttery mash potatoes, string beans, and cherry Kool-Aid. It was after 9:00 p.m. and Lil Man was so tired and sleepy that he kept falling asleep right there at the table. Not wanting to torture him any longer, I picked him up and made my way to the door.

"Ma, I need to put Lil Man in the bed. Poor thing, he keeps falling asleep at the table."

"Don't worry about the dishes then, baby. I'll take care of it."

"Thanks."

After going downstairs to my apartment, I put Lil Man in his Batman pajamas, then laid with him in the bed and watched the news. I hadn't watched the news in weeks. I wanted to know what was going on in the world, but I must've been tired myself because before

I knew it, I was out like a light.

I woke up the next morning as the sun came shining through my bedroom window. I looked over at my son and saw that he was still asleep. At that moment, I jumped out of the bed and took my morning leak. Standing over the toilet, I heard Lil Man crying. I ran into my bedroom to see what was wrong and he looked as though he was having a bad dream.

"Lil Man, you okay?" I asked waking him up. He lifted himself up and climbed into my arms with tears strolling down his face. "Awe, what's wrong?"

"Mommy. I miss her," he replied, while hugging me real tight.

"I miss Mommy, too," I said, hugging him back.

He continued to cry. "I want Mommy."

"I know son, but Mommy is in a better place. You know she's in Heaven helping God with His choir, right?" I replied, trying to comfort him.

"Yes," he replied softly.

"Hey, I know what, how would you like to hang out with me again, today? Just you and me?" I asked, wiping his tears away.

"Oh boy," he replied with a smile as he jumped off my lap and headed for the bathroom. It's amazing the resilience children have when they're sad one minute and happy the next.

Hmmm, if only grown people could be that way. I thought to myself.

⧟

Within a couple of hours, I dressed Lil Man as well as myself, stopped up to my mom's for some breakfast and out the door as we headed toward Fort Meade, so that I could finish processing out. My first stop was to the Administration Building. After that I had to go to Kimbrough Army Hospital and process out of there as well. Next stop was to clear my M-16 Rifle down at the weapons supply room. Lil Man followed me patiently as I went from one building to the next. Once I was through processing out, I decided to stop by the Stock Aide and pay Jamaal a little visit. I really wanted to know why he'd killed Thomas and this would probably be my last opportunity to find out.

228

I parked and exited my car as I grabbed hold of my sons' hand. We entered the building and fortunately, SFC Roberts was on duty.

"Hey Sean, how are you doing man?" Roberts asked as Lil Man and I approached him. "Who is this you have with you?"

"Hey Roberts, this is my son, Khalil."

"Hey Khalil, how you doing?" Roberts asked. He leaned over his desk to shake his hand. "You look just like your daddy."

"Hi," Lil Man replied.

"Look Roberts, I was wondering if I could go down and pay Jamaal a visit."

"I figured you would eventually stop by here."

"Well, can I?"

"Yeah, sure why not, no one of importance is here today, anyway. He's downstairs in the same cell you and Cameron were in."

"How ironic is that, huh? By the way, can my son stay here with you?"

"Sure."

"Okay Khalil, I'll be right back. Now, behave yourself," I said, picking him up and sitting him on top of Robert's desk.

"Okay Daddy," he replied, as he started playing with the stapler on Robert's desk.

I made my way down the long corridor and down the steps to Jamaal's new home. As I approached his cell, I stood there for a minute and watched him sleeping. He actually looked like he was at peace.

"You can actually sleep in peace, huh?" I asked, waking him up.

"What the fuck you want?" Jamaal questioned.

"I just have one question?"

"Get the fuck outta here and leave me alone!"

"Ironic isn't it?" I asked, smiling.

"What are you talking about?"

I held a huge smirk on my face. "I said the same thing to you not that long ago."

"What the fuck ever," Jamaal stated angrily.

"Look Jamaal, just tell me why you killed Thomas and I'll leave."

"You really wanna know, Sean?" Jamaal asked, jumping up

from his cot and walking toward me.

"Yeah, I do."

"Who do you think made me this way?" Jamaal growled as he looked at me with hate in his eyes.

"What do you mean, made you this way?" I asked, growling back at him.

"You think I wanna be gay? You think I enjoy this type of lifestyle?"

"I don't know but from what I could see, you didn't have it all that bad, SIR."

"Fuck you Sean, you don't know shit. You don't know anything about me."

"Maybe not, so why don't you tell me."

Suddenly, Jamaal's facial expression changed from anger to what appeared to be sad. He dropped his head, turned around and walked back over to his cot. He sat on the edge and began to cry. A small part of me was beginning to feel sorry for him but he still deserved what he got and I still wanted to know why he'd killed his own cousin.

"So, are you gonna tell me?

"Sean, you just don't get it do you?"

"Get what muthafucka, I'm listening." I was becoming frustrated.

"You made a choice about your homosexuality, I wasn't given that chance. Thomas took that from me," Jamaal sounded defeated.

"What are you talking about?"

"Thomas and I grew up together and even though I was a couple of years older than he was, I was very timid, not like I am now. Thomas was the more outgoing one. He hung out with all the hoodlums and wanna be thugs in the neighborhood while I stayed in the house and read books. When I was about sixteen, Thomas was fourteen about to turn fifteen, he raped me. He took away my manhood and he also allowed his boys to rape me as well. This went on for almost a whole damn year and I vowed that one day, I would get him back for that."

"I understand your pain somewhat Jamaal but you didn't have to kill him and what's worst is, then trying to blame it on someone else," I said becoming angry.

"Fuck you Sean. Like I said, you don't know shit and you

don't know anything about me."

"No, I don't and at this point, I don't want to. So, you have fun in your new home, okay?" I began walking away.

"Hey Sean, before you leave, answer this one question for me."

"What's that?" I turned around and walked back up to him.

"Where did you get that DVD from?"

"Wouldn't you like to know," I said walking away. I laughed out loud.

"You think this shit is funny? Well, you haven't heard the last of me Sean Mathews!"

That was the last thing I heard Jamaal say as he began sobbing. I couldn't help but think about what my mom used to say, "Every dog has their day."

I guess she was right.

Chapter 30

Over the past few weeks, I spent most of my time with Lil Man and my mom. I took them to Disney World for a weekend and we had a ball. The thought of having to leave them was becoming painful, so I didn't want to leave their side.

A few days before leaving, I got an urgent call on my cell from Justin asking me to come and see him that evening around 7:00 p.m. I figured that now would be a good time to let him know I would be leaving in a couple of days. Even though I was still a little upset about the whole tape situation, I thought maybe I could get some ass before I left. I took a quick shower, threw on my new low rider jeans, wife beater and my new red & white Jordon's. I kissed Lil Man and my mom, threw on my leather jacket and headed down 295S. I pulled up in front of Justin's house at approximately 6:55 p.m. As I walked up the driveway, he met me at the door.

"I'm glad you could make it, SIR," he replied, with a cheesy grin.

"Nice to see you too, Justin." I gave him a big hug.

As I walked into the house and into the living room, I was surprised to see Mike, Cat and Rick, sitting as though they were having some kinda meeting.

"What's going on?" I asked, standing in the middle of the room. I stared at each one of them.

"Please have a seat," Cat said smiling.

"Okay," I said hesitantly, while taking a seat on the couch next to Mike.

"Would you like something to drink?" Rick asked, being nice to me all of a sudden.

"Naw, I'm cool. What's this all about?"

"Well, we have some good news for you," Justin said, standing in the middle of the room.

"And what would that be?" I asked with raised eyebrows.

"Well, we have talked it over and have decided to appoint you as our SIR. Not just mine, but all of ours. That is if you think you can handle the four of us," Justin replied grinning.

As flattered as I was, I knew I had to be honest with them and let them know that I was leaving. Of course the thought of accepting their appointment and sexing all of them one last time did cross my mind but that would probably make matters worse. And even though this is not how I had planned to do it, they didn't give me a choice. So, I took a deep breath and informed them that I was leaving day after tomorrow to be stationed in Hawaii and as honored as I was, I would have to pass.

Everyone seemed to be disappointed about me leaving and Justin took it the worst. He took me off guard because he began to cry. As he sat down next to me, I held him in my arms and tried to comfort him.

"Take me with you," Justin whispered in my ear.

"I don't think I can do that, but maybe you can come visit me?"

Justin didn't reply, he just laid there in my arms and cried. I'm not sure why he took it so hard, but I believe it was more about the SBI Organization and being picked as my first BOY than anything else. Being part of the Organization, Justin was Jamaal's number three BOY, but with me, he was number one and it gave him some clout. However, now he would be right back were he started. I believe with Justin, it was all about status and maybe somewhere deep down inside, he would miss me a little bit as well. My plans for visiting Justin didn't go as I planned but I was glad to see him as well as Mike, Cat and even Rick before transferring.

I left Justin's house about an hour later and stopped by my old room to say my goodbyes to Ty. I had turned in my key so I had to knock on the door, which felt strange to me.

"Hold up, I'm coming," I heard Ty say as though he was waking up.

Seconds later, Ty finally answered the door with a sheet wrapped around him as they he was just waking up.

"Dayum, were you asleep?" I asked walking inside my old room.

"Hey, Sean, my niggah," Ty said, giving me a brotherly hug.

"Why are you sleep, it's only nine o'clock," I said taking a seat on my old bed.

"Yo, man, we had to take the PT test today and I'm tired as shit," Ty responded, falling back down on his bed.

"Well, look, I'm not gonna stay. I just dropped by to say goodbye, a'ight," I replied, getting up from the bed.

"Awe dayum, just when I beginning to like yo ass, too."

"Well, anyway, you be good, bruh and I'll keep in touch," I replied while walking over to the door.

"Hey, Sean, hold up."

Before I could open the door, Ty unwrapped himself with the sheet and walked over to me butt naked. He put his arms around my neck and kissed me right in the mouth. I found myself becoming aroused because Ty and I had never kissed before and much to my surprise, he was a very good kisser. Not to mention the smoothness of his body as he grinded up against me.

"You wanna fuck Sean, one last time?" he asked, while stepping back so I could view his small yet muscular frame.

He began stroking his dick with one hand and sliding his other hand up and down the crack of his ass.

As much as I thought about our age difference and taking advantage of a situation. How could I pass on such an opportunity? Besides, I was horny as hell, so I thought, "*What the fuck, why not?*"

On November 30th, the day of my departure, I woke up at exactly 5:45 a.m. Lil Man was lying right next to me and had the nerve to be snoring, which caused me to wake up. I'd spent the last couple of day's with him and my mom, doing last minute things like packing my bags, picking up my airline ticket, and mostly, explaining to Lil Man why I had to leave. It broke my heart because after losing his mother, he wasn't happy at all that I wouldn't be around for a while. I guess he kinda felt like he was losing me as well.

As I continued to lay in my bed, I began thinking about all the people in my life that I had met over the last couple of years and have grown to love as well as lust after. Venus was still constantly in my thoughts. I mean, even though I was still living my life, there wasn't a day that had gone by that I didn't think about her. This made me sad from time to time but people keep telling me that it gets better with time. Well, I'm still waiting.

I hadn't seen much of Cameron during my thirty day leave. I guess Chauntel and the baby were keeping him busy. We talked a few times but each time we spoke, it felt like something had changed. Deep down inside, I will always love Cameron and I'm sure he feels the same way about me but for now, we were going in two different directions, literally and figuratively.

As for Justin, he continued to call me, sometimes two or three times a day just to see how I was doing and asked if he could still come with me. He would always laugh when asking, so I'm not sure if he was serious, but I really didn't question him. The more I thought about going to Hawaii, the more anxious I became wanting to check out them Hawaiian honies when I got there and I really didn't need someone like Justin around who seemed to be needy. But, he will always be my BOY.

I called Mike and talked with him a couple of times, we never got a chance to hook up although we both wanted to. Unfortunately, either I was too busy or he was too busy. I was still very curious about being with him in a versatile way so we made plans for him to come visit me in Hawaii, once I was settled.

After the meeting with me about becoming their new SIR, I heard that Cat had found another brotha and had since moved in with him. She truly had a thing for brothas' and to be honest, I couldn't blame her, because so did I. I tried calling her a couple of days ago just to say goodbye, but her number had been changed. Mike informed me that she'd changed her number, but he hadn't seen her since that meeting.

I hadn't seen or heard from Rick but he can kiss my entire ass.

I attended Jamaal's hearing and was happy that justice did

prevail because he got two life sentences, running concurrently. Thomas' mom attended the hearing as well but Thomas' wife, Cindy was a no show. Fortunately, Thomas' mom and I got a chance to talk and she apologized for slapping the shit outta me. But after looking back on the situation, I couldn't blame her. After all, if my mother thought that someone was responsible for my death, she would've done the same thing.

Now, Gabriel on the other hand, was full of surprises. We spent a very romantic evening together at the Ramada Inn located in Towson. After dinner, Preacher man actually got down on one knee and asked me to marry him. Needless to say, I declined. It wasn't like two men could get married anyway and even if we could, I still wouldn't have. Although, we both had been through a lot, like cheating on me with my own wife, I couldn't fault him considering all the dirt I'd done. Gabriel made me feel really special that night and for that, he would always have a place in my heart.

"Sean, are you up?" I heard my mom yelling from upstairs while interrupting my thoughts.

"Yeah!" I said, yelling back to her. I jumped out of bed and ran into the living room and opened the door.

"Okay, well I fixed some breakfast for you and Khalil, so get dressed and y'all come on up."

"Good morning, Granny!" he yelled, while standing behind me and wiping the sleep out of his eyes.

"Good morning sweetie. Go wash your face and brush your teeth and come on up for breakfast, okay?"

"Okay," he replied, while racing to the bathroom.

"Ma, we'll be up in a minute, a'ight?"

"Hurry up. You don't want the food to get cold."

My mom went back into her apartment and I helped my son get ready so he could go up to her house for breakfast, since it was going to take me more than a minute to get ready. After taking Lil Man upstairs to my moms, I rushed back downstairs to do all the things I had to do like shave, shit and shower.

After breakfast my mom drove me to BWI Airport to catch my noon time flight. My mom sat up front while Lil Man and I sat in the back. I sat in the back with him so I could hold him in my arms since it would be some time before I would get a chance to do it again. We pulled up at the airport at 9:15 a.m. I didn't want my mom to park in the garage, because I knew she would start to cry and then Lil Man would start and before you knew it, we all would be standing around crying like babies. So, I had her drop me off right in front of the flight departure area. I got out of the car and grabbed my bags out of the trunk, then gave my mom along with Lil Man a huge hug and a kiss. Seconds later, I stood there and watched as my mom pulled off with my son watching me from the back window.

It took me less than twenty minutes to check in and I had a little over two hours to wait until my flight left. Before going through security, I came across an establishment called Bill Bateman's that kinda reminded me of a Ruby Tuesday's, so I sat down and ordered a double Remy and Coke. A few drinks later, I began thinking about this new world, and how my life was about to change. I didn't know why, but I guess it was the alcohol because I was becoming scared about the unknown world of Hawaii. I was also becoming more emotional and didn't want to go to Hawaii alone. And without giving it a second thought, I opened my cell and called the one person I knew would drop everything and come with me. All I had to do was ask.

"Hey you," I said into the phone.

"Hey yourself," the person replied.

"What are you doing?"

"Nothing, just reading a good book."

"Ah, well I'm sitting here at the airport, about to catch my flight and I was wondering if you would like to come with me?"

"Look Sean, don't fuck with me. Are you serious?"

"Yeah."

"Well, where would I stay?"

"I'll find a hotel for you until we can find an apartment."

"Sean, I don't have that kinda money to fly there or help with an apartment."

"Did I ask you for any money?"

"No."

"Well then, so how long will it take you to get here?"

"Sean, you sure you want to do this?"

"Yeah, I'm sure.

"It will take me at least two hours."

I looked down at my watch. "Baby, we don't have that long. The flight leaves in an hour and a half."

They didn't respond right away and I began thinking that maybe this wasn't such a good idea. Suddenly, I got the response I was waiting for.

"I'll be there as soon as I can. Just don't leave without me, okay?"

"I won't. I'll have your ticket by the time you get here."

"I love you, Mr. Sean Mathews."

"I love you, too," I replied, hanging up the phone.

After drinking my third Remy and Coke and feeling a little tipsy, I stood up to search for the closest bathroom. Minutes later, I stood in front of the urinal doing my business, I suddenly heard a somewhat familiar voice say, "If a man also lie with mankind, as he lieth with a woman, both of them have committed an abomination: they shall surely be put to death; their blood shall be upon them."

I turned around so fast, that I began leaking piss all over myself. Standing before me Chauntel's father, Mr. Lomax. I was so startled, I could barely put my dick back inside my pants.

"Excuse me," I said, with a confused look on my face.

"You think you can cause all the trouble you have and just up and leave like nothing has happened?" he asked with a deranged look on his face.

"What the fuck are you talking about?" At that moment, I realized this was the muthafucka who'd been stalking me.

"Because of you, my daughter's marriage has been made a mockery of. Everyone at my church now knows that my daughter married a homosexua. And all because you felt the need to open your damn mouth!"

"And you felt the need to send me that note at Venus' funeral, text me that message and send me those photos? You know what, fuck you and your daughter!" I approached him and then looked at him eye to eye.

"The Lord giveth and the Lord taketh away," he replied while pulling out what appeared to be a butcher's knife from the inside of his jacket.

I immediately jumped back as he started swinging the knife in my direction. As I went to take the knife from his old-ass and fuck him up, I began to wonder how he was able to carry the weapon inside the airport without being caught. Then it dawned on me that we were still outside of the security check point.

While Mr. Lomax continued to swing the knife at me and recite different passages from the Bible about how much homosexuality was a sin, I launched at him and grabbed his wrist and began banging it against the side of the sink. I hoped like hell the knife would eventually fall. He then tried to punch me in my face with his other fist, but I ducked and grabbed him by his neck. Finally, the knife fell to the floor and from that point on, I whipped his ass as though my life depended on it. Once I had Mr. Lomax down on the bathroom floor, I continued to punch him in his face as blood began gushing out the corners of his mouth. I don't know what came over me. I finally knew who my stalker was and I wanted to kill him. Just before giving him one last punch, I realized he was out cold. I leaned over him just to make sure he was still breathing and even though I wanted to kill his ass, I thought about how I would be locked up along with Jamaal, and that was the last place I wanted to be. I stood up, ran some cold water on my face and proceeded to search for one of the TSA employees so they could lock his ass up.

After giving my report to one of the TSA employees and to the county police officer's, I stood there and watched as they apprehended the knife that was still lying down on the floor. I watched as one of the police officer's escorted Mr. Lomax out in handcuffs. I informed them that I wanted to press charges, but was leaving to catch a plane to my new duty station. I showed them my orders and was informed that I would be contacted in a couple of weeks to return in order to testify. I eventually thanked them for their help and went back to the bar. At this point, I really did need another drink.

Over the next thirty minutes or so, and drinking to the point of becoming drunk along with drowning my sorrow, I heard my name being paged over the speaker system. At that moment, I knew that the person I was waiting for had finally arrived. I couldn't have been happier.

ORDER FORM

MAIL TO:
PO Box 423
Brandywine, MD 20613
301-362-6508

FAX TO:
301-579-9913

Ship to:	
Address:	
City & State:	Zip:
Attention:	

Date:
Phone:
E-mail:

Make all money orders and cashiers checks payable to: Life Changing Books

Qty.	ISBN	Title	Release Date	Price
	0-9741394-0-8	A Life To Remember by Azarel	Aug-03	$ 15.00
	0-9741394-1-6	Double Life by Tyrone Wallace	Nov-04	$ 15.00
	0-9741394-5-9	Nothin Personal by Tyrone Wallace	Jul-06	$ 15.00
	0-9741394-2-4	Bruised by Azarel	Jul-05	$ 15.00
	0-9741394-7-5	Bruised 2: The Ultimate Revenge by Azarel	Oct-06	$ 15.00
	0-9741394-3-2	Secrets of a Housewife by J. Tremble	Feb-06	$ 15.00
	0-9724003-5-4	I Shoulda Seen It Comin by Danette Majette	Jan-06	$ 15.00
	0-9741394-4-0	The Take Over by Tonya Ridley	Apr-06	$ 15.00
	0-9741394-6-7	The Millionaire Mistress by Tiphani	Nov-06	$ 15.00
	1-934230-99-5	More Secrets More Lies by J. Tremble	Feb-07	$ 15.00
	1-934230-98-7	Young Assassin by Mike G.	Mar-07	$ 15.00
	1-934230-95-2	A Private Affair by Mike Warren	May-07	$ 15.00
	1-934230-94-4	All That Glitters by Ericka M. Williams	Jul-07	$ 15.00
	1-934230-93-6	Deep by Danette Majette	Jul-07	$ 15.00
	1-934230-96-0	Flexin & Sexin by K'wan, Anna J. & Others	Jun-07	$ 15.00
	1-934230-92-8	Talk of the Town by Tonya Ridley	Jul-07	$ 15.00
	1-934230-89-8	Still a Mistress by Tiphani	Nov-07	$ 15.00
	1-934230-91-X	Daddy's House by Azarel	Nov-07	$ 15.00
	1-934230-87-1-	Reign of a Hustler by Nissa A. Showell	Jan-08	$ 15.00
	1-934230-86-3	Something He Can Feel by Marissa Montelih	Feb-08	$ 15.00
	1-934230-88-X	Naughty Little Angel by J. Tremble	Feb-08	$ 15.00
	1-934230847	In Those Jeans by Chantel Jolie	Jun-08	$ 15.00
	1-934230855	Marked by Capone	Jul-08	$ 15.00
	1-934230820	Rich Girls by Kendall Banks	Oct-08	$ 15.00
	1-934230839	Expensive Taste by Tiphani	Nov-08	$ 15.00
	1-934230782	Brooklyn Brothel by C. Stecko	Dec-08	$ 15.00
			Total for Books	$
		Shipping Charges (add $4.25 for 1-4 books*)		$
		Total Enclosed (add lines)		$

* Prison Orders- Please allow up to three (3) weeks for delivery.

For credit card orders and orders over 30 books, please contact us at orders@lifechaningbooks.net (Cheaper rates for COD orders)

*Shipping and Handling of 5-10 books is $6.25, please contact us if your order is more than 10 books. (301)362-6508